THE FIRST GIFT

by

K. L. Freeman.

"AND WHEN THEY HAD OPENED THEIR

TREASURES

THEY PRESENTED UNTO HIM GIFTS:

GOLD AND FRANKINCENSE AND MYRRH."

Matthew 2 v 11.

Table of Contents

CHAPTER ONE

Judea, 2 A.D.

It was night. Night in the king's life and night in the king's soul. The fear of evil permeated the palace. The king was very upset and when Herod became upset people usually died.

Herod turned and moved towards the Captain of his guards, Jehua, who subtlety backed away. The stench of the King's disease was nauseating even from a few yards.

He waved his hand towards the Captain dismissively and the candlelight reflected in the many jewels on the rings he wore.

"You have your orders; go and do as instructed."

Jehua bowed and withdrew. He was wise enough not to question what he had been told but silently he cursed the Magi. Damn those Persian astronomers! Why did they have to come now? He was due to go on leave. Their visit had been a strange event. The large retinue, with its rich silks and servants, had looked as out of place as it travelled through the poorer quarters of the city as a white sheep in a pig pen.

Why did they have to mention the word *king*? If they had said prophet, seer, or priest Herod would have lived with that, for there were always fervent Judeans mad enough to say they spoke God's word. But oh no, they had to say *king,* the one word that would set off his paranoia. Oh yes, *king.* Now that was something different; a whole new jar of olives. Jehua had known immediately that Herod would want something definitely drastic to be done about *king,*

So now Jehua had to go and kill babies in a tiny village because the Magi had said a ruler had been born there. That was not the work of a soldier. In fact, it wasn't the work of anyone who had a conscience.

Four hours later, Jehua and his men approached the little hill on which Bethlehem stood It was almost dawn, and the air seemed tinged with something other than rays from the halo of the hidden sun. Like the soft extra glow that creeps through the window the morning after an overnight snowfall, another light seemed to be a herald of this dawn.

As the horses' hooves thundered towards the village, a mile away a young woman crouched in a gully hugging her baby to her chest. She had a secret that meant death if revealed and now she was doing something about that. She was escaping from Bethlehem.

If excitement had a colour, then for her it would have been that colour that spread across the slowly brightening sky. The mother, at sixteen now a woman in the world's eyes, but still a girl in her own, was excited; but it was not her emotion which made the oncoming morning seem special. There was something else; she sensed it. Something in which she also knew she had no part.

As she had been leaving Bethlehem down the road which was a mixture of dirt and small stones, picking her way carefully in the dimness, she had heard a strange sound. It was a low, rumbling sort of noise that seemed to come from in front of her, a long way away. It was quite faint so she had stood very still to listen. At first she could not make out what could be causing such a sound this early in the morning. In Bethlehem she was used to hearing the hustle of oxen and donkeys, or the occasional creaking of carts and wagons above the murmur of people talking in the street. This was not like that at all.

While she listened, the noise had seemed to be coming towards her. She had knelt down and put her ear to the hardened dirt track. It was the sound of horses' hooves, a lot of them and quickly getting nearer, but because of the way the road curved around a small hill she could not yet see the horses, or more importantly, the riders.

As the pounding grew louder she had instinctively left the roadway and had sheltered behind a large rock, taking her child out of the sling on her back and wrapping him closer in her shawl. Martha did not know who was coming but there were many of them and she figured it would be wiser to hide until she knew.

Suddenly, the riders were on her as they swept round the bend. She guessed there were about fifty, and she recognised the insignia and the black leather uniforms even in the dim pre-dawn light. They were King Herod's men, part of his personal bodyguard. She shivered at the thought, knowing their reputation.

The galloping horses made such a loud clatter, she was frightened her baby would cry out, but he seemed undisturbed by the sound. The soldiers came by, unaware of her presence. They would be at Bethlehem almost at dawn, before the little village had really woken up and no one had gone out to the fields. Where she should be now, but for certain recent events. She was curious about the soldiers, and briefly thought about retracing her steps back down the track, but decided against it. Today was the beginning of a new life for her and her child. It would be silly to start by going back to from where she had come. There was nobody left in Bethlehem for her now.

She stopped and looked up at the eastern sky, adjusted the sling on her back containing the baby, and then continued her walk along the track. The special star, or whatever it had been, had disappeared many months ago, so she knew the strange morning glow had nothing to do with that event. She missed the presence of that star though. Nobody had seen anything like that peculiar star before, but at the time Martha thought privately it was a good omen for the birth of her son, Mark.

Jehua and his men reached the outskirts of the village where they paused while he gave the soldiers their final instructions. The men had not been advised of the nature of their task until now. Jehua knew it would not go down too well with them and thought it prudent to only tell them at the last minute. He was right. There was much dissent.

As he ordered the men to stop talking among themselves, Jehua made an imposing and sinister figure with his black beard, his black leather armour and black robes, and sitting astride one of the best black Arab stallions in Judea. He spoke very firmly, raising his voice.

"I know that some of you are not happy about what we are to do. However, you are not paid to think whether something is right or wrong, but to carry out orders. You must have faith in your King and his advisors. You already know that acting on advice from his counsellors and the Sanhedrin, King Herod has decreed that all male children found in Bethlehem under the age of two years are to be executed to maintain the safety of the realm. As this is a secret mission, you probably may not be aware of how this came about, so I will recount what I have been told, not that I really care whether you accept it or not."

Jehua paused, and scrutinised his soldiers, looking for signs of weakness or further opposition. Not many would look him directly in the eye. Then he continued.

"Some weeks ago several travellers from Persia came to the court to pay homage, so they said, to a new king born in Judea. These men are called Magi and claimed to be able to interpret signs in the heavens and stars. At first the King thought they had just come to the wrong kingdom, but then he and the Sanhedrin became suspicious as to the true intent of their visit. Suffice it to say that King Herod has decreed this as herem, or a sacred mission, because the royal line of kingship is threatened. The story is that if a certain child born in Bethlehem grows up, and tries to take over the kingdom, then the fighting could bring about rebellion, the end of our nation and our exile from Jerusalem again. The time is not right for us to take on the Romans, nor will it be for many years hence I imagine. They will not tolerate any troublemaking or civil unrest, and would crush us completely. One of these children is the devil's own, according to the King and his advisors, but we do not know which one."

Now, although Jehua did not know it because he had been away, this was something of a lie. Herod had talked briefly with his close circle of friends and advisors, but he had never consulted the Sanhedrin. This was the official council of authorities who had the power to make judgements in Judean religious and legal disputes.

Jehua's dark brown eyes narrowed, and behind his metal helmet his low brow creased to add emphasis to his next forbidding remark.

"Therefore, you will not need reminding that as this is to be conducted as a holy mission; no booty is to be taken. That means no slaves; no goods or livestock of any kind will be taken. You must obey your orders to the exact degree. However, before you start moaning about the loss of "extras" you would normally get, the King has promised everyone a bonus of three months wages upon successful completion of this task."

There was a rare mist surrounding the area, which cloaked the village, almost concealing it, and gave the whole place a ghostly feeling. That strange light Martha had noticed earlier seemed to fill the air again. It was like Bethlehem was trying to hide from the day just beginning; frozen at a moment in its history, which would prove to be better than the one dawning. Then, as the sun's rays came over the horizon, and as though the mist had been suddenly discovered, it started to retreat leaving the little settlement visible and vulnerable. The Captain saw this act of desertion by the mist and knew this was his moment. He signalled to his men, and so began a ride into history.

Some sheep had strayed across the track and the guards never deviated but rode right at them. Their shepherd waved his arms in protest but was knocked to the ground by Jehua's horse. They were the sheep especially raised on the hills around Bethlehem. Most of them would become Passover lambs to be sacrificed at the yearly festival, in the Temple built by Herod. With their shepherd gone, the sheep dispersed. Like little white ripples on the green and brown canvass, they bolted in confusion, little knowing or even caring what had happened to their guardian. A man who would give his life for them.

And thus it was done. In less than twenty minutes the guards had swept through the little village, ripping children from their mothers' arms; skewering children and adults alike on their lances and swords when resistance was offered.

History would not record the names of the nine children sacrificed to a tyrant's obsession but tiny Bethlehem would remember and associate with this event the prophet Jeremiah's warning, 'Rachel weeping for her children' for many years to come. Herod might forbid his friend and biographer, Nicolas of Damascus, from recording this cull in the annals but the people would remember.

One mother would remember in particular as Jehua thrust his lance through her baby and lifted it up in the air, still impaled on the spear, so in the dim light the image imitated the silhouette of a cross. An image that would trouble another mother over thirty years later. The mother of the son for whom these butchers were hunting now but who had eluded them.

Their work done, the soldiers left the village with screaming and wailing still drumming in their ears. As they rode back to Jerusalem the mood of the men was sombre and it began to rain. Jehua removed his helmet and let the rain soak through his hair. He hoped it would cleanse not only his head but his mind of this memory. Yet he knew it wouldn't. It was something they would all have to live with forever.

Of course none of this was known to Martha's son, Mark, who was still sleeping in the sling on his mother's back as she had continued her journey. He would not learn about all what had happened until he grew older, and when one day he would have to escape from Jehua again. So he slept on without knowing about the evil deed, just like he would be completely unaware of all the love and care given to him as a baby by his mother.

As Martha travelled further away from her former home, each step was not quite as springy as when she began. This was not just because of the weight of Mark on her back, but also because she was gradually realising that she had left so hurriedly that she had given no real thought of where she would go, or what she would do. Her plan was to follow the road north as she believed her friend Mary had done, and search each little town along the way until she found her again or somewhere she could find work washing clothes, or something similar.

Martha knew this would not be easy, for without a husband it was perilous in these times for any woman to travel alone or be accepted in a community. She had already made up her mind that she would continue to pretend she was a widow. That had worked well in Bethlehem until an old acquaintance had arrived and thrown her into a panic about being found out. If people knew that her child was illegitimate and the son of a Roman, she would surely be stoned to death.

Sometimes she felt that she was too young to cope with all this. She had not set out to be a mother, it had been unforeseen. How was she expected to know how to nurture a child, when she still felt like a child herself?

It was half an hour or so after sunrise and without warning heavy rain had started. The downpour became torrential. Martha looked down at the brown mantle covering her, stretching down to her feet and almost covering her sandals. It was becoming soaked, and so was virtually the entire tunic underneath. She saw a tree in a ditch, which she had not noticed before, and decided to rest until the rain ceased. The nature of the sky told her that this was only a showery interlude.

The young woman and her baby had only just reached the tree when, for the second time that morning, she heard riders approaching. This time however, the sound was behind her and she was already out of sight, sheltering from the rain under the small bushy thorn tree. She crouched down again and watched as they rode by. It was the same soldiers as before. On this occasion the hooves did not make such a thundering sound because the earth had been softened by the rain, and she did not have much warning of their approach. She thought what a good thing it was that she had seen this tree when she did.

Jehua's men were unaware of her presence as their heads were bowed low. In fact that was the only part of them she could see from the ditch, but she knew it was the same men as before even though they did not ride so proudly. When they had gone, the rain stopped as suddenly as it had started and Mark pulled at her shawl to end her daydream. The sky was clearing and she considered this as a sign that she should go on. She got up, pushed the sling containing Mark around her back again, and stepped out from behind the tree.

Then she stared at it. For a second she had the strange feeling that the thorn tree had been put there especially for her. It had two main branches that stretched out either side of the trunk, like limbs. She found herself smiling at how silly she was being.

Martha started to walk the track again in the strangely anxious feel of the brightening light. She felt that something else, something magnificent, but also tragic had dawned. As she walked around the next bend, curving towards the orange glow in the distance she murmured to her son.

"You know, Mark, I have a funny feeling. Something, or someone, is at work here. It is just like someone is watching us."

In the distance behind her, silhouetted on the ridge of small hill, were the outlines of two horses with strange harnesses and apparel. Their two riders watched her for a few seconds and then nodded to each other. They began to follow.

CHAPTER TWO

Two days later Martha was exhausted from sleeping rough and hunger pains gnawed at her stomach. What little food she had started out with had been used, mostly given to Mark. She had scrounged water from some other travellers, and once had used an unattended well, but now she was becoming desperate.

Fortunately there were no gangs of robbers in this area. That was one thing to the credit of the joint work of Jehua's men and the Romans, who had cleaned out such dangers some months ago. Several merchants and traders in Jerusalem had complained about instability in the markets because of the threat of thieves on the local roads. As money never just talks, but always shouts loudest, the problem had been remedied. The cry for the distribution of bread to the city's widows and poor to be increased, however, seemed to have so small a voice, it was but a whisper blown away on the breeze.

Although Jerusalem was normally only a morning's walk from Bethlehem, Martha had tried to keep away from the city. She had thought her friend Mary had travelled northwards with her husband Joseph and their new baby when leaving Bethlehem but now her instinct told her that they must have gone south. She knew Mary would not go to the big city so Martha had wandered further and further north until she realised she was heading in the wrong direction. She was running out of time to get work, money and proper nourishment for her and Mark.

As she would soon be too weak to travel, she reluctantly turned towards Jerusalem. She only had a few small coins left. Stumbling along the stoney terrain, on the road from Bethlehem to Jerusalem once more, she saw an inn that she knew of by reputation, but had never visited. She approached the isolated dwelling, about as big as a medium sized family house. It had dirty white walls, two storeys, and some cracked brick stairs outside on one wall leading to a flat roof. Near this house was a large open patch of land surrounded by an ageing timber fence, comprised of two rails of wood slung horizontally between wooden posts at regular intervals. It would not keep out many smaller wild animals, like mountain lions or jackals, but was effective at stabling donkeys or horses of any visitors. For this convenience they were charged extra. If they wanted any other form of convenience, toilet facilities, there was a hole in the ground just away from the back of the house, complete with a foul sponge on a stick in a bucket of sour wine. The sponge was for wiping yourself, and the sour wine was either to mask the smell, act as a detergent, or both, according to the conditions. The wine was certainly not something you would consider drinking even if you were completely dehydrated. The sponge implemented in this way, was an invention of the ever resourceful Roman soldiers.

Martha noticed that the inn was unusually quiet, without any sign of rowdiness that could normally be heard. When she arrived outside, she took a deep breath for courage, and then tentatively pushed open the ill fitting door. It had no real hinges, but was fixed by protrusions at the top and bottom, to holes in the lintel and the stone floor respectively. The grating of the wood in the stone hole drew the eyes of the occupants of the smoke filled room. The noise had rendered the rest of the room silent. Nobody spoke.

Martha felt embarrassed, and without a child with her would not have dared enter such a place. Even her child was no real proof that she was not the harlot she thought everyone would assume she was, because she was without a man. After a pause, a big scruffy man behind a low rickety table barked out a question to her.

"Is your husband outside in the corral?"

"I am a widow," she lied. "This is my son. We would like something to eat and drink please. I have money."

Martha showed a silver denarius in her palm. The innkeeper looked at it and then back to her, in a slow calculating way. She knew what he was thinking. Perhaps there was a bit of profit here for him. A denarius was a workman's wage for a day and worth sixteen bronze assess, which was the next denomination down.

"Alright. You can sit over there in the corner. It is a bit away from the smoke so it won't upset your baby so much."

He tried to make a gruff sort of a smile at his small show of kindness, but his bearded mouth became a little twisted so that he looked somewhat demented and frightening. Wiping his hands on an apron made from a smoothed animal hide, he outlined to Martha what there was to eat, as she pulled off the sling from her back and began to squat on the floor. There were only a few tables and the inn keeper seemed to have sole use of one. The other three had some men sitting at them. None of them were going to offer their seats or want her to sit with them. It wasn't done.

"We have not got a lot at the moment,' he continued. 'Some soldiers were through here the other day and ate almost all our store of meat and wine. You can have a stew of salted mutton, with lentils and some onions thrown in. The barley bread is not too fresh but it is eatable. Hardly any weevils in it. Soldiers ate all the wheat bread. They always want the best, but try to pay the least."

He threw up his hands and looked upwards.

"Not much wine either except that which has turned to acid vinegar. I could dilute that with some water, if you like. It'll quench your thirst."

Martha had heard better menus. She thought back to when her family had been alive. She had eaten the finest food available then. How she missed her father, as well as his money.

"The stew will be fine, thank you, with just some water to drink. Although, if you have some goat's milk I could dip the bread in it for Mark."

"Well, there's no goat's milk, only sheep milk until tomorrow morning."

"That will have to do then. Thank you."

The man turned and walked to the huge central fire that caused all the smoke. Hanging high over the fire was a skin, blackened from the smoke which was being used to shrink it so it could be used to store wine. Wrapping a piece of hide around his hands, he lifted off a large earthenware pot from an iron grate holding it above the fire, and inspected the contents. With his face turned from Martha, he sniffed the stew, made a grimace, and replaced the pot back over the fire.

"It will be hot enough soon," he shouted to her. "I'll put some more charcoal on."

Martha smiled, and looked around the room, or what she could see of it through the smoke and gloom. The wooden shutters across the holes, that served for windows, were partially closed. With the fire going, it could not be to keep the heat of the sun out, which was the normal use. There was more heat inside than outside. Martha thought the shutters might be closed because of soldiers passing by occasionally. Despite the fire, she shivered, with nervousness and anxiety. Judeans usually liked eating outside, except in winter, but

14

all the men here were inside. Something had happened to make them nervous. She could sense it.

She risked a glance at a group of men near her, pretending to cuddle Mark, hoping it would not draw attention to her. There were four of them and occasionally one would dip a piece of meat or bread into a bowl of something in the middle of the group. She wondered why they had finished work so early as there were still a few hours to sunset. Obviously they did not come from Bethlehem, as she had never seen them before. In a small place like that, strangers were conspicuous. She tried hard to listen to their talk.

Suddenly one of them with a head cloth covering most of his face, continued the conversation they must have been having as Martha arrived.

"Of course they were Herod's men. Nobody believes that nonsense about rebels in false uniforms do they?"

The other three shook their heads.

"But why?" continued the first man. "Herod must have some reason, mad as he is! It makes no sense to me. This is what we get for having a client king. The Romans protect him and he does whatever he wants and licks their arses."

"What, all of them?" quipped another. "No wonder he drinks so much. His tongue must be dry as a potsherd."

There were reluctant smiles from the group.

"Makes no sense to me either," said another. "But what would make good sense is to keep your voice down when insulting the king. Jehua has spies everywhere."

He looked around him as he spoke.

Sage advice thought Martha as she listened, and decided to remember that. She would trust nobody with what she knew.

For a while the men observed caution and lowered their voices. Martha rocked Mark to and fro as he was becoming restless with hunger. She then noticed two other men at the table furthest from her. There was something different about these two and they looked foreign. One wore a turban, that denoted he was not from Judea. Yet somehow it did not fit in with the rest of his apparel. His cloak was wrapped around him and covered a lot of his face. If he was hot, then it did not seem to bother him. Martha thought he must be used to an even hotter climate.

15

His companion, even though sitting, was clearly a massive man, similarly attired, but had a head cloth wrapped around his face. It was almost as though he was trying to hide sight of any of his skin. From the little she could see, it seemed he was younger than the other. Martha considered whether they had some form of leprosy, but their general bearing denied this. She realised these strangers had seen her looking at them, so she quickly turned her head.

Suddenly, the voices of the first group of men nearer her became more raised again. They seemed to be having some kind of religious debate. This was not uncommon at that time. Three of them were trying to console and calm another one who had an extremely long and wispy black beard.

"God! You talk of God! What God? Where was He two days ago when my sister's child was killed? Off in his smart temple in Jerusalem? He certainly was not in Bethlehem where he was needed," said the long bearded one.

"Don't shout like that about such things, Jude. Do you not fear Him? Have you no faith? Your time in Syria was too long." said an older man.

"I used to believe everything the priests told us, but what with the Romans taxing us to death, and now this latest atrocity, I wonder whether God has given up on us all again, like when we were all taken captive to live in exile hundreds of years ago. If *He* cares, why doesn't *He* show it?" Jude said resentfully.

There were murmurs of assent from a couple of the others.

The older man sat unperturbed, and spoke again calmly.

"You know what the rabbi told us all," he continued. "He said that this had been the work of men, not God, and if God were to remove our freewill many other things would change as well. We would become simple creatures with no minds of our own, no more than captive pets. We have to be able to follow our own choices, and God has to accept that choice, no matter how much He might dislike it, for He is bound by His own rules. If you jump off the Temple tower, you will break your bones. That is a simple law of nature. God is not suddenly going to change His universal laws for you unless there is a wider reason."

Jude frowned, so the older man continued. "Jude, listen to me. I know you are upset, but I have had the benefit of studying under the best teachers. I have learned that when you look around, you can

only see the present, and also what is left of the past because of the ruins of buildings, or whatever. You can never see anything of the future. It is like travelling on a camel sat the wrong way round, with your back always turned to its head. You only see what comes past you, never what is coming. But read the prophets. Prophecy helps to turn your head forward, to the future. We get a glimpse that there is a wider plan."

"Hmm, maybe," conceded Jude. "But it's not much help to us here and now is it. What part of a higher plan is killing innocent people in Bethlehem?"

"Ah, yes. I know, Jude. I know. All you can do is hope, and try to make good choices. Faith and choice, or free will if you like, are intertwined. They are knotted together like your beard, Jude. Some people make bad choices, that is all. Sometimes we all get affected by those choices."

Jude smiled, and pulled his fingers through his long beard, as if to untangle it.

"I guess I am just not as devout as you, Rueben," sighed Jude.

"Nonsense! You go to the synagogue every Sabbath, and the Temple for the feast days. Why do you go if you have no faith?"

"I don't know. It is habit really, and our culture isn't it? I would stand out like a scarecrow in a melon field if I didn't go, wouldn't I?"

There was a silence for a moment. The innkeeper brought Martha her stew and she paid him with the silver coin. He gave her some bronze coins as change and she counted them out on the ground. He had charged her too much but she was too tired and scared to make a fuss.

Martha began to have an uneasy feeling that the soldiers she had seen the other day were connected with what the men were talking about.

The men looked at her casually, then Jude spoke. He appeared agitated again.

"Look, there is a woman with a baby. How can anyone strike down a powerless child? You heard what happened didn't you? How the leader of the soldiers rode up to my sister, Rebecca? You know her, Saul's wife."

17

The others shook their heads. They wanted to hear Jude's version of events.

"I heard this from Saul himself. Rebecca was sitting by the road. Saul had drunk too much wine the night before and was trying to sleep. So because he had complained about their son's crying she had taken little Benjamin outside. Rebecca was holding the baby and trying to feed him when the leader, they reckon it was Jehua, reined in his stallion abruptly at her side. The black horse snorted as though to say, 'You had better listen to this. My master is important.' Jehua asked her what she called her son, all without dismounting and smiling broadly. His manner and bearing encouraged her to answer. So she tells him the name, you know, a bit puzzled, but not suspecting anything. Then he says to place him on the ground by her side, because he wants to look at him."

Jude's voice became croaky, so he took a gulp of wine from his cup. The others waited for him to continue.

"Rebecca's instinct told her something was wrong but she couldn't figure out what. She could not discern why soldiers would be interested in her child, and there was Jehua all smiling disarmingly to persuade her, like innocence on horseback. Well anyway, the smile had its effect and she placed the small bundle of rags, with Benjamin in them, by her side. I wonder what Jehua saw, if it was him? Whether he thought about the little human in those rags? I expect he didn't see anything but the rags. He probably wanted to think of his target as an object, not a living human with thoughts and feelings, and a family."

Jude started to get emotional. Martha could hardly bear to listen. She had tried not to imagine what happened to the children, or their parents, but despite that, she could not pull herself away from listening.

Rueben put a hand on Jude's shoulder and said, "Don't torture yourself, my friend, leave it there if you want."

"No, I am fine. I want to tell it. You will see why I feel like I do and why I said those things just now. Rebecca saw her son on the ground lift up his arms and stretch them out to her, annoyed at the separation. She did not see Jehua raise his lance, or it come down through the air so swiftly with its point of destruction aimed at the little heart. There was hardly any cry from the child, but in one terrible moment Saul heard his wife's shriek of anguish as it broke through the second's silence following the horrific act."

"Sons of Beliah! May they rot in Sheol for this!" exclaimed the man on Jude's right.

"Listen, that is not the worst of it. The force of the blow had pinned the baby to the ground and in a grotesque movement, as Jehua tried to free his spear, my poor sister's son was lifted up in the air, impaled on the wood. She said that the vertical spear and the horizontal child formed a chilling silhouette against the sky, like a sword, or a cross, and that it was an image that would never leave her."

Jude held his head in his hands, while the others murmured consoling words. Martha sat horrified, realising what would have happened to Mark, and maybe herself, if she had delayed her departure from Bethlehem.

"What happened after that? Did the men try to fight?" asked the man on Jude's right.

Rueben gave him a look that signified it was a tactless question.

"What could they do?" laughed Jude bitterly. "They had no weapons, only a few knives and axes. Nobody was expecting an attack by our own soldiers. Saul tried to pull the captain off his horse, but he hit him with the butt of his lance. Then the murderer shook off the baby from the point as Rebecca screamed at him. She fell to the ground clutching at the little body. Simultaneously there were screams from all around as the other soldiers had worked their way through the homes. They were all around the village. There was no escape. It was a massacre."

Silence shrouded the room, heavier than the smoke.

"Twelve killed, I heard, including adults," added the tactless one after a while.

No one responded. All four looked down at their drinks.

Martha felt uncomfortable. She finished her food as quickly as possible. As she was giving Mark a piece of bread dipped in milk, she heard one of the men talking again.

"Strange that it was only children under two years old they killed, wasn't it? Why not all the children?"

The innkeeper had brought more strong drink to the men, and they seemed to be getting drunk. Apparently there was wine for men, but not women. Suddenly Jude got unsteadily to his feet, turned and shouted at her.

"Hey you, woman. Keep that child away from soldiers. Seems they prefer to attack children now, instead of Romans."

"Yes, I will," replied Martha to humour him.

He stumbled towards her.

"Do you go to Bethlehem? You look familiar. I thought I saw someone like you when I last went to my sister."

His speech was starting to slur.

Unobserved by the others, the larger of the two strangers in the corner, started to get to his feet. However, his older friend put a restraining hand on his arm inviting him to wait a little before intervening.

"Sit down, Jude. Leave her alone," said Rueben.

Jude turned away from her and the stranger in the corner relaxed and sat down again.

Martha kept silent and finished her meal. However, her mind was now made up. She could not risk staying here any longer. She had to get to Jerusalem, where she could merge into the crowds. But what would she find there? She felt like crying with frustration and the sheer weariness of all the uncertainty that surrounded her. Instead, she just nodded to the men and went to the door.

When she got outside she felt a little better. She wandered around the other side of the inn, and noticed that there were two horses in the corral. They had unusual harnesses. Somehow, she knew they must belong to the two mysterious foreign men she had seen inside.

Martha paused for a moment to look at the horses. Usually only traders used horses, and then more for carrying goods, rather than riding. But there were no signs of baskets anywhere, nor had there been any inside the inn. Not many people around here were wealthy enough to use horses for any ordinary journey. Some had donkeys.

Then she turned her mind back to her own problems, and began trudging along the track again. It would be dark before she reached Jerusalem. The city gates might even be locked for the night. She knew it was risky, but had no choice.

Half a mile later, she passed the tomb of Rachel, the wife of Isaac, the great patriarch of Israel. She stopped momentarily and turned around. She had the sensation that someone was watching her again, or following her. However, she could not see anybody, despite scanning the bleak and stoney landscape.

Plod… plod… plod. As she walked she tried to think positively, but then she gave in to the tears building in her eyes. Martha still could not shake off the feeling of eyes surveying her. Almost despairingly, as she looked down at Mark in her arms, she spoke aloud about all the recent things that had happened to them.

"What am I going to do? What will happen next?" she wept. "And why do I feel that we've escaped from a lion, only to meet a bear?"

She slogged further over the dust and stones, without looking back anymore. Had she done so, Martha would have seen the outline of the two horses once again appear briefly on the skyline behind her.

CHAPTER THREE.

Jerusalem, Eleven Years Later.

Mark was frightened. Well, it was more concern than fear, because he was normally a brave young man. Probably braver than anyone else who was twelve years old. But he had seen a giant, his skin covered in strange markings, and with a weird hair style, who clearly came from another land. This man seemed to watch Mark as he left from the Temple school this morning, and then tried to pretend that he was not following the boy. However, he was so tall that everybody noticed him. He was at least seven inches taller than anyone else in Jerusalem, and had broad powerful shoulders with legs that seemed to take one stride to every three that Mark could manage in his ill fitting sandals.

He ran home to tell his mother, hoping that his smaller height would allow him to weave in and out of the masses of people and he would lose the giant. He could not understand why this man should be interested in him. His mother would know. Adults seemed to know everything, or pretended they did.

Panting heavily, he skidded to a halt, throwing up dust from the dirt track. He had stopped just outside the wall of the courtyard of the house that he now called home. It was a rich person's home, or someone who liked people to think they were rich. Unfortunately, it did not belong to his mother. Martha and Mark were now household slaves to Haaman, the metal trader, and his wife Esherah. Mark looked all around. There was no sign of the strange man.

A lot had happened in Judea, and to Martha and her son, since she had watched Herod's soldiers on that historic morning. Currently, King Herod, the not so great in many people's eyes, had been dead nearly ten years, and Judea had been under direct Roman rule for three years. The country was now governed by a Roman Prefect under the watchful eye of Quirinius, the governor of Syria.

Owing to the massacre at Bethlehem, Mark's mother knew she had to be careful about revealing anything about his birth, for he had been born very close to that village. So far as she knew, only two children had survived Herod's orders; her own son, and Mary and

Joseph's. Even now she was not sure that Mark would be safe from whoever had wanted the children killed, for Herod had succeeded in stopping any written account of the atrocity, and blaming it on rebels. But many people knew the truth. Martha did not understand any of it, but she reasoned that until she knew otherwise it would be best to be cautious.

She had not seen her two friends since that time in Bethlehem and had not heard anything about them. She often wondered whether Mary had known of the impending massacre, and that was why she had left. Looking back at it now, Martha realised that Mary had given her a sort of cryptic warning, although she had not realised it at the time.

Coincidentally, she had been thinking about all this when Mark came rushing into the courtyard where she was working, talking about someone following him. His mother immediately wondered whether this had anything to do with his escape from the massacre almost twelve years ago. It was the first thing that came into her mind as she had just been thinking about the incident.

However, once Mark started to talk about a giant from another land, she changed her mind. Clearly her son was up to his usual trick of making up fantasies to relieve the drudgery of his life. He had no toys, or friends to play with whenever he wanted. As a slave, the parents of most children treated him as an outcast. The only children he mixed with were the small group of boys at the school in the Temple buildings run by the rabbis, or other teachers of the Law for five mornings a week. All Judean boys attended such schools up to age twelve. Mark went to the Temple because he lived in Jerusalem. Other boys went to their local synagogue school if they lived in other towns. Girls were not allowed in such places, so any instruction they received came from their mothers.

"I haven't got the time to listen to your made up adventures," said Martha. "I have all these pickled olives to press for oil, and if I do not finish it soon Esherah will be after me. You know how she seems to have turned against me lately. They are having another business banquet tonight and she wants enough oil available so the lamps do not go out, like last time. Then I have to clean out the new oven over there before the next batch of loaves go in for baking. Tell me your tale later."

She continued turning the wooden handle of the olive press which was made from finest basalt. The sound of grinding stone started again, with an occasional high pitched grating that played on the nerves.

"But mother, it is true. I did see a man, and he was the tallest and biggest person I have ever seen, with painted symbols all over him, and he watched me all the time. Come and see if he is still there. Please," he entreated.

Martha stopped turning the olive press handle and looked at him. The glare from the late morning sun off the white wall of the house made her squint. Slowly the two vertical circular stones came to a halt in the groove on the small round stone table on which they travelled, and became silent. Although he had a love of all things adventurous, and making up stories about heroes, Mark very rarely told lies and his mother knew this.

"Maybe you did see someone, but I cannot just leave what I am doing can I? We are not free to come and go when we want are we? Sometimes I think you forget that we have to obey our master and mistress at all times or face punishment… or starve."

Mark sighed in disappointment and looked down at the cobbled ground that made up the courtyard. Why did they have to be slaves? Why didn't he have a father to provide for them like most people? All he knew about his father was that he had died just before he was born. Well, that was what his mother had said. She had thought it best. There were good reasons. In reality his father was not dead at all, but Mark did not even know his true identity as his mother had never told him.

Seeing his forlorn look, his mother ruffled his fairish brown hair and smiled. They both hated the life they led, but what choice did they have? She rubbed her wrists. The metal shackles that had been placed originally upon her wrists when she had first sold herself into slavery had left marks, which irritated her skin from time to time. She no longer wore shackles because Haaman trusted her and she had been with him some years.

However, those first years as a slave had left more than physical marks as her first owners had not been as considerate as Haaman. Martha had soon found that a woman alone with a child had little chance of survival without the support of a family, and she had lost her family a long time ago.

24

In Bethlehem, just after Mark had been born, she had been lucky to make a rough living by washing clothes, when the widow who used to do it had died. As Martha had posed as a widow also, nobody had thought it strange that she should undertake such work. But once she had left that little community, the world had offered her nothing, except for slavery or prostitution, and she could not contemplate the latter.

Now the law at that time stated that no Judean could be enslaved against their will in their own country, and there were more laws which governed how Judean slaves were treated. Slaves of other nationalities, or in other countries, had a far worse time, but because Hebrews followed the teachings of their God, Yahweh, Judean slaves had certain rights and privileges. For this reason many very poor people in desperate situations, like Martha, voluntarily sold themselves into slavery to obtain food, clothing and shelter. So that was what she had done.

Mark would later come to learn that it was the best she could do for him, and no doubt many others would have done the same in her circumstances. His mother loathed it when some richer people looked down on her because she was a slave. Her family had been well off once, but wealth can disappear as easily as it appears. She also despised a world in which people judged you by your wealth and image, and not for the kind of person you were. Martha considered that the world's priorities were wrong.

Mark felt his mother lift his chin to look at her. She looked into his blue eyes. "Cheer up," she said. "I cannot come now, but tomorrow I have to go to the market, and we shall look for your giant then. If he is as tall as you say, he will be easy to spot."

Martha smiled, but inwardly she wondered who was taking an interest in her son. There were always strange people around in Jerusalem, particularly at festival times. The Passover festival was in a few days, and the city always became packed with many travellers wanting to make sacrifice at the Temple. This was also a time when slave traders from countries far away would mingle with the crowds in the hope of stealing a child or two that became separated from its parents. She hoped it was no one like that whom Mark had seen.

"Martha!" yelled a deep voice.

"That is the master. Get on with your chores now. I will talk to you later, Mark."

The house had rooms surrounding and leading off from the very spacious internal courtyard, colonnaded on three sides, and two goats were nibbling what remaining weeds were left in the dry ground between the cobbles. Mark watched his mother walk through the nearest doorway towards Haaman's voice.

She went through a small hallway into a room with walls covered in plaster with ornate designs embossed and carved into them. She wondered whether Esherah was getting tired of these. Haaman couldn't be bothered with furnishings and domestic routine. He left such tasks to his wife, who did have a flair for design, but lately he seemed reluctant to spend money on changing the décor. Perhaps he was going to move again. It was no small matter decorating. The plaster carvings couldn't just be gone over or taken down. The whole wall had to be re-plastered and fresh motifs scraped, or brushed into it. It was a costly business and therefore only embarked on if you were keeping the same residence for some years.

While waiting for Martha, Haaman put down a papyrus document he was reading and stared out through his window at the midday sky over Jerusalem. He pulled at his black beard and twiddled the hair around in his fingers, which was his habit when he was anxious about what to do. It was a time for decisions. It was a time for action. In short, it was that time he always knew he would face. Should he go back to his native Syria, or not? Should he continue renting some slaves, or buy the ones he had and take them with him? If so, which ones? He had been putting off these decisions for weeks.

"Stop fiddling with your beard, you know it drives me mad," chided his wife Esherah softly. "You haven't eaten yet today. Perhaps some fresh bread from my new oven and a little cheese will calm you."

She was very pleased with the oven. It had pride of place in the courtyard and although not the biggest, was large enough for their needs. More importantly, it signified to her neighbours that her husband was a man of some wealth. That was important to her. She was a profoundly shallow person who loved things superficial and glamorous, and the triumph of froth over substance. Not many had their own oven, let alone one made from good pottery, which could bake twenty flat loaves at a time or ten raised ones. Esherah had

26

often thought that it was a miracle how she had managed before with that mud brick oven, the amount of guests Haaman invited.

Martha entered the room.

"Get me some cheese and a piece of new bread if it's ready," said Haaman as she approached him.

"Yes, Master."

Martha kept her head bowed. This was not just out of subservience but also because she didn't want to make eye contact with Esherah, who was sitting to the right and seemed to have recently taken a dislike to her. Unknown to Martha, this was partly because of her attractiveness. Esherah also suspected her of trying to win her husband's affections. That was a contest Martha had no need to enter. Haaman had only rented her as a slave because he was attracted to her. The woman glared at the servant as she left the room. She was suspicious of the fact that despite years of slavery there was still a spark of independence and fire about Martha.

Esherah wanted slaves to know their place; way beneath their owners. Slaves or poor people that thought independently, and did not have a lowly spirit, were dangerous. She thought that one day they might start thinking they were equal to other people, and then what would become of the world?

"Oh, and some olives too," yelled Haaman after Martha.

She turned and came back.

"Sorry, Master, but there are no more olives left. I've just crushed the last of them to make some oil for the lamps."

"Damnation! Well go and get some more then," said Haaman irritably. "But bring me the bread and cheese first. I'll be glad when the autumn is here and we can get some fresh olives again. These pickled ones are too salty and don't have the same firmness."

He turned to Esherah and carried on grumbling. "I wish we could get cheese made from cow's milk too. Why is Judea is plagued with goats and hardly any cows? One day I am going to try and do something about that. Either that, or move back to a more civilized country. "

His wife said nothing, but he continued to glare at her.

"Why are you wearing that that new silk wrap I gave you last week?"

Esherah paused from her sewing and looked up at him slowly. She liked sewing, she found it soothing.

"Don't you like it?"

She smiled innocently.

"Yes it's fine but I didn't give you a valuable silk to just wear about the house and no one to see it."

"I wore it for you. I like to look nice for you even when none of your business friends are around."

Esherah had hit the nail firmly on the thumb, as it were. She knew her husband only gave her things to show his friends how wealthy he was becoming, not out of affection for her. In one brief reply she had let him know this without being provocative. He frowned, groping for a suitable response.

"Why are you so irritable?" Esherah continued.

Haaman sat down and put his head in his hands. His large fingers went through his matted long black hair, and the four gold and silver rings he wore on each dark skinned hand glinted as they caught the sunlight from the open lattice shuttered hole in the wall which served as a window. The imprinted mark between his thumb and his right wrist was also visible. This had been made by the Romans and showed he was a licensed metal trader, dealing mostly in copper and gold.

"I don't know. I've got so many decisions to make."

He picked up the document in front of him again.

" Look at this! Thirty silver drachmas a year for Martha and her son. I'm in the wrong business. I should be a slave trader not a metal trader. And because I rent them, it's money thrown away, " he moaned. "Thirty pieces of silver."

"Yes, but you did get her cheaper because of the boy being so young; and you were wise," said Esherah.

"Wise?" puzzled Haaman as he lifted his face towards her.

Esherah knew her husband's weak spot… flattery.

"Yes," she continued. "Not to buy out-right. How would you know at that time how they would turn out? True, they have become good slaves, but more because of your treatment of them than their own qualities. I thought then it was a shrewd move on your part and I still do. They might have had a disease."

Haaman's face muscles relaxed a little. His countenance had always been an index of his mind and Esherah had long ago learned to thumb through it quickly. Of course, she knew the real reason he had rented was because he couldn't afford the full cost of buying another slave at that time, and had wanted to keep up with his friend Shamah who had been spending copiously. She knew this, but Haaman didn't know she knew. He had wanted Martha as a serving slave, not a producing one, so it would look better when he invited his business friends round.

"Umm, well I suppose it wasn't too bad a decision," Haaman pretended to concede. Suddenly he stopped pacing around.

"I have made up my mind. I will see Agothos later this day and settle the issue. Both Martha and the boy seem fit and well and should last me years. I will buy them outright, as long as the discount is good."

As Martha was returning with the bread and cheese, she saw Mark listening outside the room.

"What are you doing here?" she hissed. "Go and do your own work or we will both be in trouble."

Just as she said this they heard the shouting from Haaman and both held back to listen. He had been a reasonable master to them, certainly better than the early ones to whom they had been rented. Mark hoped they would have been permanently bought slaves before now. Everybody knew that owners treated their own slaves better than hired ones. They had invested their capital and would at least care enough about the slave's welfare to protect their money. Rental customers were not so concerned, and the life of a rented slave was usually grim; working seven days a week and frequently at night too, although the law forbade this for Judeans.

Mark had also worried that at some time he and his mother would be split up. With a real owner-master his mother might get the chance to obtain the odd small gift of money to save and form what the Romans called a peculium, to one day buy her freedom. This was not possible for rented slaves. Only fully owned slaves were allowed to have money or property even though they were still legally dependent on another person. So hearing Haaman saying he was going to buy her and Mark was good news. Martha smiled at her son and waved him away.

"I am going," whispered Mark, "but do not forget that I still want to go and look for the giant."

Martha entered the room. She brought the food towards her master and he gestured towards the small stone table where the contract lay. Suddenly realising it was there, and that she might see it, he swept it up in his left hand and placed it into the limestone jar he had grabbed with his right. He replaced the lid firmly so that the papyrus would not be exposed to moisture and start to rot.

"Shall I go and get the olives now, Sir?"

"Yes." Then, noting the hesitation in her voice, he added, "Why not?"

"Well, the mistress did want me to clean the new oven."

"That is not as important as my olives. You can do that later."

Esherah frowned her disapproval but said nothing.

"Is there anything else you want, sir?"

Haaman indicated there was not by shaking his head slowly. The long rivulets of his black braided hair swayed hypnotically before the young woman's face.

"Just tell him to put it on my account. I'll be calling on Benjamin Ben-Ada soon so if he asks, tell him to stop fretting over the money, you know how he is. You'd think he would have got used to me the years we've done business wouldn't you? I always get the better of the haggling and bartering anyway"

Martha smiled agreement and Haaman's heart lurched. He did find her attractive, even in her well worn greyish-white mantle, which stretched down to her feet, virtually covering the entire faded brown tunic she wore underneath. Even though the head-dress covered her long black hair. If only she would be more cooperative with her favours. He disliked forcing her but he had needs and she was one of them. Yes, he had used her but she had never submitted gracefully. That irritated and frustrated him as did the furtive couplings.

If only Esherah would turn a blind eye now and then. If only his wife was not such a good organiser and hostess he might think of getting another who was more manageable. A year ago he had thought about taking another wife, but in view of his experience with Esherah and her jealousy, decided that two wives would probably cause him more grief than joy.

"Oh, can I take Mark with me Master? He needs to learn more about the market now he is getting older."

Martha really thought it would give her a chance to see if that man Mark had seen was still around.

Haaman smiled at her. "Yes, that is a good point."

"And don't be too long. I still want that oven cleaned and new bread baked," snarled Esherah.

Haaman let out a sigh, and Martha went out through the doorway.

Mark was in the courtyard talking to Lois, the master's daughter. He had started to notice lately that girls were more than just an annoyance. Although they could not wrestle or throw stones very well, which at one time had been important, they now seemed to possess something that attracted him. Not all of them, but certainly the ones he found pretty; and Lois was pretty.

She was not much younger than him and despite Esherah's wishes was very friendly to Mark. He was tall and growing out of the brown walnut stained tunic and grey mantle he wore. With his strong features and blue eyes, which were unusual for most males in that area, he would soon be considered a handsome young man. His mother looked at him with pride and knew she would have to tell him the truth about himself soon, but for now she was going to enjoy the stroll to the market.

Martha called to Mark and explained that he was to accompany her on her errand. He was pleased, and half hoped they would see the giant again. He had a feeling that something new was about to happen in his life, and he craved excitement.

They walked past the wall of the courtyard and down the track, bordered by some of Jerusalem's more affluent homes. They passed the well. It was not a real well, for Jerusalem had very few natural water holes. However, the practical Romans had created several smaller wooden aqueducts from the main one, to feed various holes in the ground lined with stone, and this was one.

The more expensive houses were always ones near this sort of well, as it saved a lot of time in carrying earthenware jars back and forth over long distances. However, everybody had very large water containers in their homes, which they filled from water gathered by the smaller jars. When full, these massive stone jars could not be easily lifted even by two men. Not that men carried water. Such work was left to women, except when it was part of a business like water selling. In this climate, travellers would pay good money for a drink of even cloudy, tepid water. Jerusalem thrived on the tourist economy, and at Passover especially, the whole of the capital seemed to throb to the rhythm of coins changing hands, or being flung into Temple receptacles as offerings.

Mark saw such a water seller near the well now, and recognised him as the man he saw frequently on his visits to school. Normally he saw him nearer the Temple, and he wondered why he was this far away. He liked the water seller as he took time to speak to Mark and often made him laugh, but today he was not laughing at all. In fact he looked a little frightened, and clearly he was having trouble trying to draw up the leather bucket and pour water into earthenware jars that were packed onto his open cart. Angry men and women were remonstrating with him.

As Martha and Mark drew nearer they could hear raised voices arguing and threats being issued. It was easy to learn what all the commotion was about, for the residents were not pleased that they had to wait while Elias filled all his jars.

"I am hurrying as fast as I can, and if you give me a hand I will do it quicker," he said.

"That is not the point. You should use the pool down near the city wall. This is the third time you have been back here," retorted a resident. "This is for local house owners in this area only."

"Look, I am not breaking any laws. I have a licence from the trading council that allows me to draw water and sell it. There is plenty of water left for you."

"Yes, when we can get to it. You do not have a licence to aggravate us though. If we let you do it, everyone will be coming here, and we will not get any peace. Why should we have to wait? We are not poor people. This is a higher class neighbourhood. What are you hoping? That if we get tired enough, you can sell our own water back to us? Huh! We are not pilgrims or visitors."

"You can take advantage of them if you like, but not at our expense," chipped in another. "Go back and use the pool of Siloam, or one of the others."

"I cannot get near it. You know what it is like at Passover. There are hundreds more people around the pool than normal, so I thought you would not mind me coming here until the festival finishes next week. I did let some people go before me at this well, but if I kept doing that I would never fill my own jars."

"Well, we *do* mind. Move your ox and cart."

While the exchanges raged, Elias' ox had stood impassively, almost immobile. Now it turned its head towards him, almost as if it queried what his next move was. It shook the yoke, the heavy wooden harness fitting over its shoulders, as though wanting to be free of the burden.

Mark whispered to his mother that he thought they were all treating Elias unfairly as he had not been selling water for long and he was still getting to know the business. She replied that she saw both sides of the argument, but tempers were always a bit short when large crowds gathered, and mob mentality was never very clever. Mark moved to get closer. He wanted to do something to help Elias, but Martha put her hand on his shoulder.

"Let us move on," she said. "There is nothing we can do here."

Just as she said that a man caught hold of the ox yoke and tried to turn it to make the cart move. Elias intervened to stop him.

"Don't do that," he shouted. "You will have the cart over."

Having become hot and tired of all the fuss, he pushed the man away angrily. It was a mistake. The crowd surged around him to take hold of him, and the ox stated to panic. Suddenly it shook its head and started a slow, lolloping run. The jars swayed precariously on the cart, and at the same instant Mark took action. He shook off his mother's hand from his shoulder and ran in front of the startled animal, hoping to grab the harness and save the precious water. He had acted on instinct, without thought that even though he was tall for his age, he was not strong enough to stop an ox that did not want to stop.

For a few seconds he was pulled along by the animal as he held grimly onto the yoke and also the leather harness over the head of the ox. The boy's sandaled feet dangled and bounced on the dirt road, and the jars also bounced on the wooden planks in a kind of orchestrated dance, while water sloshed through the lids and over the rims.

Fearing serious injury, Martha shrieked aloud for someone to help her son, and her cry was answered by an unusual and amazing stranger. Like a big dark shadow a figure seemed to appear from nowhere, and flashed by her. It was the giant Mark had seen earlier.

CHAPTER FOUR.

Quickly covering the ground with powerful strides from his mammoth thighs, the stranger gripped the ox's horns with his massive hands, twisted its head, and forced the creature to slow down. As its mouth came up near his lowered face, the giant turned his own head away to avoid the animal's foul breath.

The sinews and huge muscles of the giant man gleamed with perspiration. Peering up through the harness, and with his legs still dangling below, Mark could see the dark skin on the stranger's knuckles turn very pale as the fingers clamped themselves around the horns. However, Mark still grasped the harness, which had saved him from being trampled or run over by the heavy cart. He was not going to let go of it before he was certain the ox had calmed down.

Once the beast became still, the man glanced at Mark.. Holding a horn in one hand, and Mark with the other, he looked the boy up and down, silently examining him for any sign of injury.

Martha came running to them talking swiftly. She seemed to alternate between scolding Mark, and thanking the stranger for his intervention. Mark, like his rescuer, remained silent. He was trying to take in the image before him. He had never seen anyone like this enormous man, and could not begin to discern to which race or tribe he belonged.

The boy stood with wide eyes and mouth slightly open, as though dazed, looking up at the giant who he had earlier feared. He felt no fear now. Nobody who wished him harm would have tried to save him. Mark looked at the man's impassive face. It gave the impression of deepest Asian descent, far beyond Armenia and the Caucasus mountains, but his four strands of braided hair and body art were more Babylonian. He wore only an open, sleeveless, white strip of cloth over his shoulders and back, and Mark noted that the brown skin on the whole upper torso was a mass of coloured circles and swirls that could be of mystic significance. Unlike Judeans, but in keeping with nearly all Romans at this time, his face was clean shaven. So was the head apart from the four plaits rising from the middle of his otherwise bald dome. The strands were of equal length, dropping to the shoulders, and arranged in the shape of a cross. Each pair of diagonals was dyed a different colour, yellow and black.

He was an unusual and awesome sight; a man in his late twenties, and clearly at the peak of his physical development. As the other people started to gather around them, he broke his silence. Looking concerned, he said to Mark, "You are fine. I must go."

He said this in a slow and slightly halting manner, like someone who was uncertain of the language, and then turned away.

Mark came to life.

"Wait! Don't go. Who are you? Why have you been following me?"

The stranger turned and frowned. "You saw me?"

"Yes, earlier today."

"You have sharp eyes, little one. I am Hiro. We will meet again when the time is right, and my master wishes it."

He started to walk away, taking long rapid strides.

Mark jogged alongside, trying to keep up.

"Who is your master, and how will I know the time is right?"

Hiro laughed, and the many gold earrings all up the sides of his ears shook in time to the movement of his head. "You are persistent aren't you? I can say no more. You will know when we all know. Do not try to follow me."

With that last instruction, Hiro stopped and glared down ferociously.

The change of demeanour was so sudden and startling that Mark immediately did as commanded. Then he heard his mother calling as she came near again. He turned to her. Within seconds Hiro had disappeared through the crowd. The people near the well had forgotten all about their argument, and were now discussing the action they had witnessed.

"Mark, come here. Do not run off.. You are far too impetuous." She hugged him with relief from the tension she had felt. "I suppose that was the giant you told me about?"

"Yes, but he would not tell me why he followed me, only that his name is Hiro. I do not understand any of it."

"Well, at least he cannot mean you any harm, I suppose. Although he is a strange one and no mistake."

Martha did wonder whether a slave trader might have an interest in preserving children he later wanted to sell, but dismissed it straight away. In any event she would not alarm her son by voicing such a theory.

"You will just have to wait until you see him again. At the moment we must get down to the market as quick as we can, or Esherah will be after me again."

"Yes. We might see where he went. He will stand out in any crowd."

"Maybe, but with Jerusalem packed with many times the normal population with all these pilgrims, you are talking about well over half a million people to look at!" laughed his mother. "I have a feeling that if he does not want you to find him, then you won't."

They walked down the track, bordered by some of Jerusalem's more affluent homes. To change the subject, Martha talked about their situation and the possibility of Haaman buying them outright. She told Mark that although they were slaves, they could be a lot worse off.. Mark disagreed, but she said she still considered that God had been kind to her in a way. They were slaves yes, but in a good household and with regular food and clothing. All responsibility for providing these items and the resulting worry had been removed from them. Martha argued that her decision to be a slave had been the best one in the circumstances, both for her and Mark. She always tried to see the positive side of every situation and it was largely this that enabled her to survive where others would not.

Martha's outlook was flavoured with the philosophy that being bitter and sorry for yourself never made things any better.

"Those things were only objects for making the hole you are in deeper, if you let them," she said to her son. "Whereas if you step on them you can use them to get higher and claw your way out. When a bad time comes, some people become bitter or cynical, and some give up in despair. However, I follow the wise, and trust in God. One day we will be free, I just know it. For now though, we are certainly better off than Lazarus over there."

Lazarus, was only a few years older than her and was a professional beggar. He seemed a good man, just unfortunate to have been born with a crippled and useless left hand. When his family had all died through disease, begging was the only means of supporting himself. This was quite normal and acceptable, as society had no other way of dealing with disadvantaged persons, and the government, such as it was, did not care what happened to them. It never appeared to spend any of the tax revenue on citizens in need. However, the law made it clear that beggars should not be too aggressive in their work or make themselves nuisances. It was sufficient that they stay mostly in the background and restrict themselves to crying out for alms. Passers by then could make their own decision to give, based on choice rather than pressure.

Occasionally Levites, or other people aspiring to the priesthood, would help out if there was a surplus of offerings or tithes. This happened a lot at festivals, but much depended on the greed of the priests rather than their generosity. All Judeans were urged by the Temple authorities to tithe, that is, to give a tenth of their income to the Temple for God's work. However, in the last hundred years or so the people thought they were too sophisticated to rigidly stick to the old ways, and many did not comply with the religious laws. They either cheated on the amount given, or pretended they had given more than they had.

Seeing Mark and Martha, Lazarus waved.

"What are you going to buy now?" he queried as they drew closer.

"Oh, just something for the master," she said evasively. She knew that if she said food Lazarus would keep on at her for some on the way back.

The beggar persisted. "Is it food?".

Martha stopped and looked at him crouched in his rags in the shadow of a wall. She had made possibly a mistake some months ago in giving him just a few olives and later a little grain, and since then Lazarus had sought to take advantage of her kind nature.

"This has got to stop, Lazarus," she said as sternly as she could but with a twinkle in her brown eyes that betrayed her. "I nearly got into trouble last time with the mistress because I gave you something. It's not my food to give, is it? You know I like to help when I can, but will you take my punishment if I'm caught?"

"I don't know of anybody who would take another's punishment. Only a fool would do that and I'm no fool," smiled the man, and winked at Mark.

"Or someone who loved you greatly," said Martha softly. Then she laughed. "I'm no fool either, which is why you'll have to accept that I'll only give you something when it's possible, and as long as you don't keep on when you see me. Agreed?"

37

"That's fair. You will still talk to me though?"

"Yes, if I've got the time. Anyway, fortune should favour you this week. Jerusalem is absolutely packed with strangers and travellers."

"True enough. It's the best time of year for beggars…Passover. Even better than Yom Kippur which always seems more serious somehow. This festival has an air about it. Spring is here and people are more light hearted. There is something else too. Not just excitement, but something I can't quite put my hand on. I think it could be…"

"Tension?" said Martha.

"Yes, there is that, but there is something else."

"Hope?" volunteered Mark.

"Yes that's right. It's hope. You have the feeling, don't you, that something, anything, could happen. In some years it has, of course. Not that it has ever done us much good in recent memory. We're still ruled by Romans and administered to by rogues. Every time we are occupied by an enemy it always feeds the nation's hope that a real leader, the Messiah, will break the bonds of our captivity and bring us peace."

"Messiah?" queried Mark.

"Yes. The chosen, or anointed one…a warrior priest. You know, the one prophesied about in the scriptures. What do they teach you in the rabbi's school these days?"

Lazarus looked directly at Martha and shrugged.

"All that happens is every few years some messianic, religious fanatic, small time leader surfaces. Claiming to set us free of tyranny, he ends up increasing it from the resulting backlash. It seems to me that until we embrace our real Messiah, Israel will always be a slave to someone or something."

Mark nodded slowly. The body may be impaired, but the brain certainly is not, he thought.

"There is clearly more to you than the eye takes in, Lazarus," said Martha. "Thinking too much can get you into trouble."

"Thinking, no. Talking, possibly," he replied, and winked at Mark again.

"Look, I must get going. Take care," said Martha.

As they walked away Mark smiled at his mother.

"What are you smiling at young man?"

38

"Nothing." Then after a short pause, he added, "You like him don't you?"

"Yes, he is alright, I suppose. Why?"

"Well, it is just that you act differently when we see him."

"No I do not. Don't be so mischievous."

Her son smiled back at her again.

"Look, I am twelve and nearly as tall as you. Next year I will be officially a man. I know things."

"Oh, do you?"

Despite herself she could not prevent a laugh from parting her lips. Then she confessed, "Yes, you are right. I do like him, but do not read too much into that. I feel sorry for him too. He has not had an easy life, and I know that he resents being thought of as a man in disgrace, and cannot worship in the Temple because of his disability. I do not agree with our elders who teach that he is in sin because he is crippled in an arm."

"Nor do *I*," said Mark with emphasis.

"Yes. Lazarus is more than a beggar. He has a fine mind and a good sense of humour."

Mark turned his face to her again and cocked his head on one side impishly at her reply. She knew that Mark wanted a father figure to take them out of slavery.

"Do not start that again, young man. What sort of a couple would we make, a beggar and a slave? This topic of conversation is closed."

Although she tried to sound severe, it did not work. So Martha pulled her head-dress round to cover more of her face to hide her embarrassment, as revealed by the blush of her sallow skinned cheeks. They continued their walk from the upper part of Jerusalem, where Haaman's house was situated, into the lower part of the city where the markets were allowed two times a week. Being a bright Spring day, only a day before the start of the month of Nisan, it seemed everybody in the teeming city was going somewhere.

They could see the carts bringing some of the new barley harvest into town. Oxen and donkeys struggling to make their way towards the east side where a little of the barley would be used as a thank-offering in the Temple. Martha felt sorry for the Priests, who would be so busy tomorrow sacrificing many thousands of lambs at the altar for the Passover ceremony, and worried whether she would be able to take her son to see the events.

Mark could see part of the Temple up on the hump of Mount Zion, and pointed to it excitedly. It was shimmering like a golden island in an ocean of humanity. The best wonder of the age, in an age of wonderment.

Despite all that had happened to her, Mark's mother was still true to her faith. Her slave contract entitled her to time off for Pesach or Passover as it was commonly called, even though she and Mark could never celebrate it properly, and there was always a wrangle with Haaman to achieve this. Perhaps it would be different this year, but he hadn't said anything about it yet, and she had not been able to mention it to him because he had been so pre-occupied and out of the house a lot.

Mark had never made sacrifice before, but he was now of an age when he would soon be required, like all Judean males, to "attend the Lord" at least three times a year. At twelve years old, it was customary for fathers to start preparing their sons for the rituals when they became 'bar-mitzvah', meaning 'son of the law'.

With his father absent Mark was technically now the head of the family and should make the expected sacrifices. That was all right in theory, but where was he to get the finance for a pair of birds, let alone a lamb? Even the lowest offering of the poor, a small portion of fine flour, was really beyond him and his mother.

Martha knew other servants stole small amounts from their households to keep the Temple laws, but that did not appeal to her. As she once said to a slave friend, "Breaking one law to keep another and maintain appearances, is surely a hypocrisy the Lord himself must frown on?"

Still, Martha liked to go and watch the crowds, and feel the excitement and colour of the pageant. There wasn't much else to relieve the drudgery and boredom of her life, or the lives of many others come to that.

The row of whitish coloured dwellings on each side of the road came to an end, and they turned into the market area she wanted. There were seven different ones. The booths and stalls sold everything, from basic necessities like sandals and cloth, meat, fruit and vegetables, to luxury goods. The latter were supplied by goldsmiths, jewellers; and silk, linen and perfume merchants. Hammered silver came from Tarshish, and gold from Ophraz.

There were also carpenters who specialised in comfortable furniture, and chests made from fine wood, beautifully carved or inlaid with bone or ivory. All these tended to keep their stalls away from the smells of rotting meat or vegetables, and food being cooked. They did not want their richer customers mixing with the more plebeian types as the Romans called them. Shopping for luxury goods was something to be made pleasant; an enjoyment, and where negotiating the selling price was a painless experience. This couldn't be done in the pushing throng of common crowds. Here it was profits, and not the prophets, that called to the various merchants' Guilds.

Yet, there was certainly money to be made from basic commodities. A trader called Tamarah had started buying olive groves a few years ago, and now had almost a monopoly in supplying their oil to Egypt, and nearly everywhere else for that matter. He was reputedly the richest man in Jerusalem, although many gave that accolade to Joseph who came from the region of Arimathea, meaning "Heights". He had a thriving metal trading business and Haaman had recently started to feel the effects of Joseph's competition. He was about the same age as Haaman, but unlike him was a very respected man of noble nature, who also knew the wisdom of diversifying his interests.

Joseph had begun to make roads into other trading areas, and by co-investing into a small shipyard he would eventually have his own fleet to trade further and quicker. Many said he was someone who would make his mark on more than just documents in the world, but some thought he lacked ambition or ruthlessness to be the supreme businessman. Money hadn't yet made itself a god in his life.

Martha and Mark made their way through the crowds towards Benjamin Ben-Ada. He was visible above others by standing on a chest.

"Probably where his takings go," mused the boy.

Despite the cacophony of noise from shouting traders and customers he could hear him arguing loudly with his eldest son. As they pushed towards the people milling round Benjamin, Mark caught the smell of camel breath and spices from the Orient. An

Eastern caravan had seemingly not long arrived nearby, and as if to emphasize the point, a camel spat in his ear as he passed.

"Yes, I know you're here," Mark said crossly to the animal, "you don't have to make a special announcement for me!"

He moved on a few steps, wiping the side of his face, but wanted to linger over the stalls from the caravan.

"Come on Mark, we have not got time now to examine all the stalls."

As she said this, his mother cast a quick glance over the merchandise and the way the stalls were arranged. "It seems these merchants are new to Jerusalem, or care little about the authorities," she continued. "They have paid no attention to the niceties of the market traditions. No doubt angry or jealous locals will call in the market inspectors soon."

The tables were piled high with bric-a-brac, silks, precious stones, bracelets, hides; small jars of perfumes made from Arabian myrrh, and gold brooches and trinkets. She could see one of the men scooping out a measure of fragrant frankincense that someone would no doubt offer to be burnt on the Temple altar. Just the very smells evoked visions of faraway places. The odour of the traders themselves however, gave evidence they had not washed since finishing their arduous journey.

As one came past him Mark screwed up his nose.

"Pooh," he said out loud without realising it. " You lot are going to need more than the ritual cleansing before Passover if you go to the Temple."

A distinguished looking Persian heard, and turned his splendidly blue turbaned head towards them. Martha thought she had seen that wrinkled, mahogany face a long time ago. Even though dusty, his robes were colourful and obviously of good quality.

"We are not of the House of Israel, but Zarathustrans," he grunted through his greying full beard. "We have no need to abide by your ceremonial laws. Even though we do share your belief in just one god, it is not the one of Abraham. In any event, young man, do such laws prohibit you from being polite to strangers who haven't had time to bathe?"

"No, of course not. I am sorry if I appeared rude. You speak excellent Aramaic," he added ingratiatingly.

Neither said anything for a few seconds, and then to end the discomfort that silence can bring, and choosing not to pursue the point, the Persian smiled kindly and spoke.

"My gratitude. I have a relative who comes from the Galilee area. It's a pity my camel hasn't an equal grasp of your language, or he could have got your attention another way."

The humour broke the barrier between them, and Mark laughed out loud and not just out of politeness.

"Camels cannot speak," said Mark.

"Who says so?" responded the Persian with a twinkle in his eyes.

"I do. I haven't heard one talking."

"Well, maybe that is because you have never trained one properly."

Mark looked dubious, and was obviously still not convinced.

"Or maybe," continued the man, " camels do not think you are worth talking to!"

As he said this, the Persian's face creased even more in a wide smile, and Mark realised that he was being teased.

All three of them laughed, but Martha was also threading through every memory she had in her mind. She was sure she had seen this man before, but when, and where?

"Here," said the man to Mark. "If you want to smell something pleasant, smell this."

Holding the camel reins with his right hand, he reached out with his left hand and picked a small piece of something from a container on the nearby stall. Mark took it and looked at the hard white opaque substance. He gave it a sniff. It was very aromatic, and reminded him of something similar to one of the perfumes Esherah wore occasionally.

"What is it," said the boy.

"It is the hardened gum resin from a special tree in Arabia. Frankincense most people call it. If you go to the Temple tomorrow you will smell it being burnt. Keep it."

"But he could not keep it," intervened Martha. "It is very expensive stuff. Even I know that."

The Persian looked at her kindly and smiled a warm, compassionate smile, as though he knew she had fallen on hard times.

"It is true that a larger quantity would be expensive, but that little piece could have fallen on the ground and nobody would miss it."

"The owner might," said Mark.

"I am the owner, my son. All the stalls you see here in this section belong to my caravan."

"Amazing," said Mark. "Thank you very much. I will keep it, not burn it, and the smell will remind me of you and Arabia. One day I want to travel to other countries, like you do."

The man looked at Mark with a strange sort of smile.

"I expect you will. I expect you will."

Mark was just going to mention that it was unlikely, because he was a slave, when his mother asked, "From where have you come? Arabia?"

The merchant turned at looked at her intensely, almost as if he was taunting her to recognise him.

"I am originally from Persepolis in Persia. But if you mean the caravan then yes, Arabia, from the southern part. We travelled the old route. Up and across through part of North Arabia to Petra in the Nabatean kingdom. Have you ever seen Petra?"

"No. I haven't done much travelling."

"Oh, you should see it; the rose red city. Such splendid dwellings and tombs cut directly into the red rock of the valley. Anyhow, there we turned north to Hebron and came on to Jerusalem. We could have taken the road west to Gaza at Petra, but reckoned that a greater profit could be made here at your festival. There was a time, some years ago, we took a different route."

The Persian's eyes stared vacantly, as though he was looking through time, remembering something of importance and considering the consequences.

"But things happened, change came, and we never used it again. Anyway, no matter what route you use you have to keep paying out. Water for the camels, then for fodder, then for stabling, then for customs dues at the various frontiers. By the time you get to the coast it has cost five or six hundred denarii for each camel. And then people complain of high prices. Hah, they do not know the half of it!"

"Then you deserve a good profit after a long journey like that. Erm… I really am sorry about what Mark said earlier. I suppose the camel threw him off balance and made him irritable. I hope you find the rest of your stay more pleasing, and profitable."

The man bent his head in a small courteous bow.

"May you both also find whatever freedom you desire, and a light to guide your destiny."

So saying he touched his chest and then his forehead lightly with his fingers as a salutation, then turned back to his colleagues and pulled the camel after him.

"What an interesting man," said Martha. " I wonder what he meant by that reference to freedom. He cannot know that we are slaves, unless he noticed the marks on my wrists. But that wouldn't necessarily mean I was one now. It's probably just a quaint Persian expression. They do have an almost poetic manner in expressing themselves. Or it might have meant that he wished we eventually be free of Roman rule."

"I liked him," replied Mark. "He had something about him, as though he knew lots of things. He is rich too. Did you notice his gown? I have never seen such quality, even on Haaman."

Martha considered the matter some more, but just couldn't place what had seemed familiar about his face. There was an aura of mystery around him, and he had dignity. This man seemed to echo a tenuous link with her past, in what now felt like another lifetime, but the memory seemed shrouded or suppressed from her.

Still mulling this over she found herself in front of Benjamin's booth.

"Now stay by my side, Mark, and do not say anything unless I tell you."

There were many people mingling in front of her, trying to see what goods were on display on the trestles, and also in the timber carts. Some listened to the dialogue between vendor and buyers to gauge an idea of what each item might cost, and whether they could afford it. No one ever published prices. Owing to the risk of theft and the amount of trading, many of Benjamin's family were helping to serve, and stop nimble hands from sampling the food without paying.

Martha eventually obtained her olives, persuaded the dealer that her master would indeed be calling on him shortly to pay the account, and then she led Mark away. They walked back up the track to the house. Martha had mixed emotions when she saw that Lazarus

45

was not still there, even if the number of olives was safe from reduction by him not taking a few. Mark was sorry that they had not seen the giant Hiro again. He looked at his mother and knew that her thoughts had turned back to the mysterious Persian. She was clearly still wondering where she had seen him before. Some distance behind them, Hiro, the giant, followed unseen.

CHAPTER FIVE.

Haaman's Gift.

The house that Mark and his mother had come to think of as home came into view. With its two-storey look and spacious courtyard full of the latest appliances it was certainly one of the better dwellings in the area. It was difficult to know how rich Haaman was. He displayed all the material objects of a wealthy man, had several servants and slaves and gave fine dinner parties. Oh yes, he had all the trappings, but Martha suspected this was more to do with image, than real wealth. His credit was good because of it, and that is why he was allowed to have things a long time before paying for them.

"You took your time, didn't you?" grumbled Esherah as Martha entered the courtyard.

"The market was very busy."

"Was everything in order at Benjamin's?"

"Yes, of course."

"Well, draw some water from the jar over there and make sure it is clean enough for your master to drink. Then prepare his food. Do not use that other jar we were using yesterday for the water, as Lois found a mouse in it. Someone left the lid off and it must have fallen in and drowned. You can clean it out later after you have cleaned the oven."

"I didn't leave the lid off mistress," volunteered his mother, as Mark glowered at Esherah.

"I did not say you did, did I? Just get on with your work."

With that curt reply Esherah walked into the house and went upstairs.

Martha shrugged at Mark and started to draw water into a cooking pot and carried it to the earthenware stove in the back room. The embers of the last fire were still hot and she quickly made it blaze again with a few pieces of thorn wood and dried goat's dung. She needed to boil some water to make the cleaning of the oven a little easier. As she did this Haaman approached them.

"I am just going to get your food, master. I expect you would like a bit more bread and cheese with the olives, if you are still hungry?"

Martha said this in anticipation of him asking her.

Haaman nodded to show his agreement and also his understanding of what she was doing. "I see you got some good olives," he said as he lifted the lid off the small earthenware pot. Then he turned to the water jars. "This water alright to drink?"

Mark answered, as his mother was attending to the fire. "Yes, sir but only from that jar there."

He pointed to the tall stone jar mentioned by Esherah.

"Ah, the mouse problem."

He smiled to himself as he watched Martha. "I heard your mistress shouting about that earlier."

"It wasn't mother or me," said Mark defensively.

Haaman said nothing, but just raised his eyebrows as if to warn Mark that he should be careful how he spoke to his superiors. Then his face relaxed and he asked Martha tentatively, "Everything all right with Benjamin?"

"Yes, sir. I told him you would be calling about the account shortly like you said." There was a slightly puzzled look on Martha's face and Haaman noticed it.

"Why are you looking so pensive? You're sure he didn't say anything else?"

"No, nothing master. It's just that the mistress asked me the same thing a few minutes ago. Almost like she expected some trouble from the dealer."

"Can't think why, he knows I always pay him every new moon. Just coincidence I expect."

It could be that she thought, but it was now almost two weeks past the last new moon. It was a full moon that had bathed the rooftops last night. While she started to cut up some bread for the cheese and olives, she rallied her courage and said, "Master, may I speak with you a little while please?"

"Yes. What about? Haaman looked at her quizzically.

"Well, it is the feast of the Passover tomorrow and I would like to take Mark to the Temple as he is of age even though we have nothing to sacrifice. I know you normally let me have some days off at this time, but you haven't said anything about it recently and I didn't want to be a nuisance as you have been so busy."

"I had not forgotten Martha. In fact I had already made arrangements in my mind for the others to cover for you and Mark," he lied.

Haaman did not want to lose face to a servant, and a slave at that. Yet there was something about this woman. He thought that it was a wonder that no one had married her after the death of her first husband (at least, that is what she had told him). What a waste as just a slave, but she never talked about her past.

"No," he continued, "you are not a nuisance. You may have your days off, you are entitled to four this month for your festival, aren't you?"

Haaman came very near her and leaned on the wall so his shoulder and armpit were close to her face. Martha suppressed a frown from his aroma which was a nauseous combination of diluted spikenard scent and body odour.

"Yes sir. If it pleases you, and as you say you have cover, we would like tomorrow and the next three days after."

To Martha's surprise, all he said was, "Agreed."

She had expected some show of annoyance, not immediate acceptance.

Then, coming even closer to her he bent low and so Mark would not hear, he whispered, "I shall expect you to repay the favour later. Maybe tonight, or when you return. You understand?"

Martha thought his approval had been too ready to be without condition. She sighed. It was important that Mark attended the Temple this Passover and for his sake she knew she had to sacrifice her self esteem. After all it would not be the first time.

She nodded.

Haaman started to prowl around the stove area, picking up utensils and pots and casually inspecting them. Martha wondered if he was concerned about the cost of replacing any worn ones, or was he thinking about something else? Suddenly he turned and came towards her again.

"This Passover thing you Hebrews think so special. What is so important about sacrificing a lamb at this certain time?"

"It commemorates our escape out of Egypt a long time ago, when the Lord delivered us from the Pharaoh."

49

"Yes, I know all that, but why a lamb? Why not an ox or a bird?"

Martha paused, drew in a breath, and let it out. "Well," she began, "Moses our prophet instructed all the Israelites to prepare for the escape by baking only unleavened bread, you know, without yeast, and to kill a lamb and roast it so no bones were broken. The blood of the lamb was smeared on the posts of their dwellings so that the Angel of Death would know the Israelites were there, and *pass over* them, not killing the first born male. You understand? The blood of the lamb saved them from death."

Mark was bursting to interrupt. He waved his arm to attract attention. Haaman looked at him and raised his eyebrows again, this time to show it was in order for the boy to speak.

"I know about this. The rabbi told us about it this yesterday morning. There is also a connection before that, with God providing a ram for Abraham instead of him sacrificing his first-born son Isaac. Abraham was obeying God, and was going to kill his son, but an angel stopped him and pointed out a ram caught by its horns in a hawthorn bush. Poor thing. All the thorns must have been sticking in its head. That's a grisly crown to have isn't it? Imagine how painful that must be. Then it was killed instead of Isaac. You see it is the sacrifice and obedience that is important, our rabbi says. Abraham was prepared to obey God, no matter what it cost him. The Temple is supposedly built on the hill where Abraham sacrificed the ram. "

"Ah, I do see," Haaman nodded. "Very clever. So the lambs sacrificed at Passover have more than one significance."

He thought for a while, then he said, "I don't know. Three years in this town and I still don't understand your religion. Who could make up something so complicated? It seems my gods haven't anything as intellectual to offer in this respect."

"Maybe that is because it is not made up!" exclaimed Mark. He did not want to sound rude, but the solution seemed obvious to him.

His mother intervened quickly in case Haaman had taken offence.

"Mark means perhaps your gods haven't interacted with the lives of your people. Have any of your gods answered prayers?"

"I don't know. Not for me certainly, but then I am not that religious a person. Has your God answered yours?"

Martha smiled. "Why, because I am a slave?".

50

"Umm," he smiled back.

"That's hard to know. I haven't led a blameless life, so perhaps my situation is because of my sin."

"You Hebrews. Always on about sins. However, if that is true, then why aren't I a slave as well, instead of being your master? I expect I've done my fair share of what you would call sinning."

Martha screwed up her face.

"I don't know. I am no authority on this sort of thing. You would do better to ask a rabbi, one of our teachers of Torah."

"Torah? That is your law isn't it?"

"Sort of. *The Torah* is to do with the books of Moses and other prophets, but *Torah* itself is more to do with instruction, teaching, our culture, our way of life. All I can say to answer your question is that the potter makes what he will, and a jar cannot complain it is not a vase. Everyone does wrong, but some things stand out like a lamp in a dark room, highlighting the way to judgement. Other sins are not so conspicuous, but cannot be concealed forever."

"Like you can conceal sores or ulcers under your tunic, where their putrid canker and rottenness can fester away without anyone else knowing. But sometimes you have to stand naked?"

"Er, yes exactly," said Martha somewhat taken aback by the graphic vehemence. "Whether we do good or bad is, I believe, all revealed on the final judgement scales. Who is there on Earth that can judge a man's motives, or his heart? One insignificant act of kindness, of no account to the world, may become the gold ingot that sends the scales thumping down on the side of righteousness, and saves someone generally considered worthless. Who can tell? Anyway, the threat of judgement is a great aid to living a good life now, and having a decent society. However, there is one thing I do feel. Our God has a purpose for everyone who believes in Him, even slaves, and sometimes I do get the feeling that he's still guiding me."

Haaman laughed.

"More a blessing for me than you, if he guided you here! So what is the significance of the bread without yeast in it?"

Again Mark jiggled about to show he wanted to demonstrate his knowledge.

"I know. I know," he said.

"Go on then, Master Know-Everything," laughed his mother.

"I had to learn this by heart. The Israelites had to leave in a hurry. They couldn't wait around for yeast to rise. Yeast also symbolises sin, or evil, and they were meant to leave all that behind. That is why we have the Feast of Unleavened Bread at the same time, which commemorates the first seven days of the Exodus from Egypt. They used to be two separate celebrations, but because of practical difficulties they have been combined. We also eat bitter herbs with the lamb to remind us of the bitterness of captivity."

"Very apt in your case," said Haaman tactlessly.

He saw Martha look down at the ground and he realised she might have thought he was being unkind. Normally, this would not concern him, but because he liked this young Judean woman and wanted to have her in a good humour later that evening he felt obliged to lift her mood a little.

"This lamb… I suppose people get rid of the weak or flawed ones first? Good way of performing your ritual without spending too much money if you ask me."

Martha gasped, " Oh no! You can't do that. It has to be an unblemished lamb, a perfect one, the best. If not, it wouldn't be any sacrifice would it? Sacrifice involves giving up something you value."

"Er yes, I see what you mean," said Haaman feeling a little foolish.

He worried that she might think he was mean and was also concerned that there might be some hint of doubt about his financial status lately. Did Benjamin the trader really say nothing to her? He knew servants talked to other servants and he could not have that sort of image portrayed about himself. It was bad for business. He frowned as he pondered.

Seeing the frown Martha added, "I'm sorry master, I did not mean to correct you. I always thought you knew about our religious festivals from your friends."

"No, I never talk about such things with them. Business and religion don't mix easily. I suppose I am a bit superstitious though."

"Surely that's almost the same thing as believing in a religion isn't it?" Martha said tentatively. She did not often get the chance to say what she thought, and was taking full advantage now. "If you obey a superstitious command or impulse, you are as good as saying that some god or power is going to punish you if you do not perform that ritual. You might just as well worship the real God."

"I suppose you are right. I'd never thought about it like that. You are pretty clever for a slave, even if you are a bit lacking in manners."

Then, like an overwhelming, compelling thought, an idea came into his mind. He wanted to do something for this woman and her son. Maybe it would put him in good stead with this God of theirs. If not, at least it might make her be more compliant with what he had in mind later. He liked his women to be a little submissive but not having to make them feel they went with him out of duty or force.

Suddenly he found himself saying to Martha, "Look, as it is Mark's first time to offer to sacrifice, I'll pay for the lamb you need. Only a small one, mind you. I am not going to make this a regular occurrence but, well I don't know, perhaps if there is anything in this belief of yours, it won't do me any harm to be on the right side of your God. I could do with that at the moment."

Martha looked at him totally astonished.

"Thank you master. I don't know what to say. I…"

Her words trailed off. Mark could not believe what he was hearing.

"Don't say anything, not to the other servants, and especially not to my wife. She may misconstrue the position and I don't want a lecture from her about wasting money on slaves. Here, take this, it should be enough."

He pulled a few copper coins and two silver denarii, inscribed with the head of the Emperor Augustus, out of the small leather pouch on the girdle of his mantle. He held out the denarii to her. She took the small Roman coins, murmuring more thanks, and put them in between the sole of her foot and the good sandal without a hole. She had nowhere else to hide them. As she had never received any money for herself as slave, there had never been a need for a pouch in which to put it. If Haaman asked her to purchase anything, it was always put on his account.

"Now, let me eat my cheese and olives," said Haaman, embarrassed at her gratitude and his sudden generous impulse.

He walked away puzzling and thinking to himself.

'Why in the whole realm of reason did I do that? She must be a devil that has possessed me. Still, it is only a small amount of money

53

and hopefully her gratitude will pay a dividend with her affection. Yes, that would be nice, very nice.'

He stopped and smiled.

Haaman's gift was the first one that Mark or his mother had received in his lifetime. Now they could go to the Temple properly tomorrow, which unbeknown to them or Haaman, was exactly what they were meant to do.

But behind the other partially open door to that room, Esherah had heard all the conversation and started to formulate her own plans.

CHAPTER SIX.

Mark's History Revealed.

Later that same afternoon, Mark was helping his mother in the courtyard, preparing the dough for a new batch of loaves and fig cakes. Martha seemed preoccupied and Mark was doing most of the work.

"Mother," asked Mark as though a serious question was coming. "Am I helping you do this, or are you helping me?"

"Eh, what do you mean?"

Martha's thoughts were interrupted. She looked at the twinkling eyes of her son and realised that he was making fun of her. "I'm sorry Mark, I was under a different tree for a little while there wasn't I?"

"What were you thinking about?"

She sighed.

"Nothing really. Just life and the funny twists and turns it has. It's a bit like a river; born as a sparkling small stream out of the bowels of a hill or a mountain; plunging downwards from the minute it is born, racing towards the place where it becomes wider and slower, meandering through the plain with its once bright water dulled by debris acquired through the journey. Then picking up speed as it races towards the waterfall, it bumps through the torment of the rapids, gradually slowing again but ever pushing on to its home the sea, where at last it finds peace in fellowship with all the water since time began."

Mark looked at her thoughtfully.

"You really think our lives are like that? Mmm, I suppose some women do get fatter and slower as they age, and brains become dulled."

He raised his eyebrows and squinted out of the corner of his eye as if to indicate humour to his mother. Just as she was about to protest he added, "Only joking! What brought all that on anyway?"

"Seeing you earlier, talking and playing with Lois, I suppose. You like her, don't you?"

Mark shifted his body from one side to the other as a sign of his reluctance to answer a question that he sensed was like a soldier's shove with the shield before the real thrust of the sword appeared.

"She's all right… yeah. Look don't start all that smiling at me like mothers do when they think they *know* something."

Seeing his embarrassment was all the answer she needed, rendering further probing obsolete. "Fair enough. You've grown so tall now and with those good looks I expect all the girls are attracted to you, not just Lois," she teased.

Red faced, Mark turned and made as if to go until his mother held his arm and hugged him.

"Shush, shush," she cooed. I have another reason for mentioning you're growing up. Tomorrow is Pesach, and we must go to the Temple and give thanks. Then we have another three days off to join in the celebrations. Isn't that great?"

"Yes!" shouted the boy.

"And that is not everything. As Haaman has generously given us the money to buy our own lamb for sacrifice, we can eat our first Passover lamb together. Later, we will give him some, although how we are going to roast it without Esherah realising the money came from her husband might be a problem. I will sort something out. Perhaps I can use the oven belonging to one of my slave friends in another household. If not, we will donate it to the Priests to give to the poor, although the Lord knows there are not many poorer than us."

She laughed.

"But who will sacrifice it, mother? You can't. I thought only men are allowed into the Court of the Israelites, and can present the lambs to the priests?"

"Why, you are going to do it, of course. You are now old enough to do this as a man in your own right. You know that surely from what the rabbi teaches you?"

Mark looked troubled. "Yes, I do know that, but I was hoping I would not have to actually do it."

"Don't worry," she consoled, "I'll go with you as far as I'm allowed, and then I'll get some kindly soul to show you the ritual. You'll be fine, I promise."

The boy seemed reassured by that, but was still thoughtful.

"What's the matter now?" Martha put her arm around his shoulder. " Big boy like you still scared of going to the Temple? God will understand that it is your first time. Everybody has to have a first time, you know."

"No, it's not that. I was thinking about my father and what it felt like for him, and how old he was when he first did the ritual."

Once again that day Martha breathed deeply before speaking. If she lied now, it might result in an irretrievable breakdown of trust between her and Mark. It was time to tell him the truth about the past.

"Your father never performed the sacrifice," she began.

"Never?"

"Yes, never. Well as far as I know. He wouldn't have to. He isn't Judean."

She let the words sink in and be absorbed. This next bit would be hard to admit.

"Whoa, wait a moment, Mamala. You've just said two strange things. First, my father isn't Judean, and secondly you refer to him as though he's still alive. What tribe is he, and if he is alive why isn't he here taking care of us so we wouldn't have to be slaves?"

"He is a Roman. A centurion when I last saw him, and still alive probably, not that it makes any difference. We will never see him again."

Mark walked restlessly around the large flat stone on which the dough lay, hardly able to understand what he was hearing. "What… what happened… just who am I? You must tell me the whole story," he cried.

"All right, but come and sit on this mat with me and calm down. I have one condition to which you must agree or I will tell you no more."

"What is it?"

"You must never, if you value your life, repeat what I tell you to anyone. Well, at least until you are much older and big enough to take care of yourself. That is very, very important. Do you agree? "

"I have no choice."

Martha repeated, "Do you agree?"

"Yes."

"Swear to me before God."

"Yes, yes I swear before God," Mark said exasperatedly. "Get on with it, please."

Martha cupped her chin and lips with her left hand, and rubbed the skin of her cheek as though evoking a distant memory. Her thumb and first finger closed either side of her nose, pinching it slightly. She stared at her son in his tunic. She suddenly noticed it had not been dyed well, which is why Haaman had probably bought it. It would have been cheaper.

"It all began with the plague that ravaged my home town of Reena. My parents died as a result of that, and being an only child in my teens I just wandered around. What I told you about your grand-parents being dead is true. A lot of my parent's friends had died as well, and as I was crying in the road the day after my mother died, Marcus, your father, found me. He was so handsome in his centurion's uniform, and authoritative, that it seemed natural to allow him to arrange for the burial and other things that needed attending to. Neighbours were kind and basically good people but they had troubles enough of their own with the rampant disease. There were a lot of orphans. In fact, no family was spared a death. It was chaotic, with the survivors trying to scratch out an existence if they were poor. My father was reasonably well off but he died without ever telling us where his gold or money was hidden. He was always scared of thieves taking everything. Perversely, it was that master thief Death that stole his life, but left his treasure."

She paused as though saddened by the thought, and then continued.

"Our house had been burnt down as a result of the plague precautions. It wasn't intentional, but they started to burn some things, mostly to get rid of the pervading smell of rotting flesh and garbage. People couldn't cope with the ceremonial burial laws. There was filth everywhere. Unfortunately, things got out of control and with most people too sick to help others, the fires spread where they weren't supposed to. Some people did try to form a human chain from the well, passing stone jars of water along, but it was hopeless. Our house caught alight from the one next to it. Only the stone foundations and parts of the walls remained."

"Is the town still there?"

"Oh yes, but it's not the place it was apparently. Funnily enough I heard one of the traders talking about it the other week. It seems

58

the spirit of the place has died and people are superstitious about living there because of what happened."

"Go on... please," he added, after a look from his mother.

"Well, your father, Marcus Facilis, was one of two centurions sent there with their men from a nearby garrison to stop people travelling in and out of the town, and thereby contain the disease. It was one of his jobs to keep an eye on the outbreak and do some diplomatic work with the locals, and try to keep the merchants and traders happy."

"That must have been a tough job, knowing how much we hate the Romans," said Mark ruefully. He then realised the implication of what he had said, and looked up startled.

"Yes, precisely," murmured his mother. "That's why you must remember your promise, amongst other reasons."

"What other reasons?"

"We will come to that. Let me continue, someone might come in soon. What was I saying? Ah, yes. It was an almost impossible task. I mean, nobody really likes their conquerors do they, but I had never seen real hate before until after the soldiers killed one of the traders for trying to get out of town. Well, that's what they said. He had only been visiting Reena and wanted to return to his family in Jerusalem. He might have eventually died from disease anyway, but Flavius' men, that's the other centurion, thought he was trying to start up his own secret supply of goods and food to the town. They were not going to allow that. Only the soldiers had the say as to who brought supplies in; and only after they had received a suitable bribe. There was talk that he was going to expose their crooked dealings, so that's probably why they killed him and made up the escaping story later. They cut him up into quarters and placed each one around the town as a deterrent to others who might not obey their mighty commands," said Martha bitterly.

Mark made no comment. He had already seen enough cruelty in his short life not to be surprised at more. "Did the people hate my father after this?"

"Obviously the townspeople were full of hatred after the incident, but it really didn't have anything to do with your father. The town was under military law, so there was nothing they could do."

59

"Why were the Romans bothered about your small town? They normally couldn't care less if we lived or died. Was it something to do with the census around then?"

"Well, there was that to it. That was the official reason. Although we all know how long it took to complete it don't we, almost ten years. Even then it was mostly due to Quirinius that it got completed at all. That's why it's known as his census. Your father used to say that being three and a half months' journey from Rome by land had its good and bad points. Any message has a six month return period, so if Herod didn't want to do something Rome ordered, his administrators just kept questioning and could get a year or two's breathing space, bearing in mind no ships sail in the winter. Most people reckon that's what the first Roman Prefect did, because of the trouble getting our people to do anything. It is quicker by sea, but risky because of the fact that any sudden storm could easily overturn the sort of boats they use. Marcus said that anything important usually went by land for this reason."

"What was the point of it anyway?"

" Tax purposes mainly. Romans love administration. They had this weird notion of finding out where everybody was born, so they had a common reference base and knew how much each area should pay in tax. They knew everybody would not be able to go to Jerusalem as it would have brought the whole city to a standstill, so they arranged twelve focal points according to the twelve tribes of Israel. Bethlehem was one, and people descended from Judah could go there to register. This was especially appropriate for those who were of the line of King David, for that was his town."

She paused, thinking about her friend Mary and something she had once told her.

Mark waited as his mother seemed to wrestle with a puzzle in her mind. Then, losing patience, he tapped her shoulder to encourage her to continue.

"Anyway things kept happening to hold up the census, just like this plague in Reena. So at that time they didn't want people from Reena going all over the country, mingling with others travelling to register, and in so doing spread the plague. But I heard from Marcus that Herod had beseeched a visiting dignitary from Rome to order the town's quarantine because he'd didn't want it spreading to nearby Jerusalem where he was. I personally don't think it was the plague. I still think it had something to do with the wells having bad water. People would have a fever and be sick. They'd get thirsty and when given more water, it seemed to make them worse."

"So why didn't you get it then?"

"I don't know. Not everybody was affected. I'm not a healer, I don't understand these things."

Mark was clearly troubled by these revelations and seemed to be thinking deeply.

"I don't understand how you could get friendly with a Roman," he said flatly. "I mean, it's almost unheard of… mixing with an uncircumcised and unclean gentile."

His mother looked at him with an anguished expression.

"I know what everybody thinks about Romans, but Marcus was different and tried not to treat us like pigs. When he heard about my situation he wanted to help. Perhaps he saw a good public relations opportunity."

Mark grunted. " Hmm. More like he saw someone to take advantage of. Were you pretty then, mother?"

"It's not for me to say…" She broke off. "Hey, what do you mean *was* I pretty?"

The boy laughed and she realised he was teasing her again. Mark was not certain how to handle this information, and so he felt he needed to resort to humour occasionally to prevent what might be a cavern of silence enveloping both of them.

"Leaving that aside, at first Marcus kept his distance, but when the disease seemed on the wane, we became really friendly," continued his mother. "Look, I am not trying to justify what happened. I just wanted you to appreciate what it was like for me, and also to finally get this off my chest. It's been awful living a lie so long, evading the topic as you've been growing."

She looked straight at Mark.

"I realise what people would say, even now, about me seeing a Roman, let alone have his child, and I was so lonely and vulnerable. My parents had meant everything to me and most of our relatives were dead, or had moved elsewhere. Marcus was kind and took care of me. He was young for a centurion too, only about twenty-five. Normally you'd expect twelve years service in the army to get that rank, but the first-rate soldiers make it sooner. He was good with words, and just as good with the sword by all accounts. You are going to have his strong physique."

"What is my father's full name?"

"Marcus Favonius Facilis. You have taken his first name, although it is in the Judean form of Mark. I thought it was safer that way. One day, when you are a lot older, you can revert to Marcus, if you want."

Martha put her hand through her son's tousled hair and stroked it back off his forehead.

"Your fairish hair comes from his mother's side of the family. She was a Celt, and which is probably why Marcus is tall, like you will be. It's funny really, for natural Romans have always had a fear of Celts because of their superior stature."

Mark moved his head backwards away from her hand, as though irritated, and stood up. He went to pick up the dough and thwacked it down on the stone with some force.

"Try to understand. I was young and made a mistake."

"One you could pay for with your life if certain people hear about it," muttered the boy.

"I know. That is why I have had to lie for so long. I have always told you the truth except for this. I thought it was best for us if I pretended your father was dead."

The woman paused. She seemed preoccupied as though thinking of the consequences should she be found out.

Mark waited a few seconds before encouraging her to go on.

"What happened when you realised you were having me?"

"Unbelief at first. I'd never...... your father was the first man I had known. Then I became really scared. I thought Marcus would just ignore me and that the villagers would stone me when they found out. As it turned out, after the initial shock he did everything to help me, but made it clear marriage was unthinkable. So, before it showed too much he arranged for me to go to a place he knew in the hill country. Not too far from Bethlehem."

"What did you live in?"

"A tent, like my forefathers! An ex-army one that Marcus smuggled out. The weather was mild and he came to see me every now and then with provisions."

Mark looked at his mother. Although he was angry, he could sense how frightening it must have been for her and how isolated she must have felt. His anger was not directed at her, but at the confusion he now felt in his head. What was he, a Judean or Roman? Was he Mark, or Marcus? What did he do now? He whacked the dough down again.

"How did you manage to give birth on your own?"

"I didn't have to. Praise the Lord for Rebecca, an old friend of my parents. Your father managed to persuade her to come to me near the time and she helped. She had five children of her own! I don't know whether she did it out of love, or because Marcus could put pressure on her. Either way, she did, and she kept her mouth shut. I never saw Marcus again after the birth. He was a career soldier and was posted somewhere else. I never knew where; Rome I believe, but it might have been Antioch. He mentioned he could go there if the trouble in Galatia came to a head. After that I went to Bethlehem and pretended I was a widow whose husband had died in the plague. Nobody knew me. Not many people ever travel out of their home town or village much, do they?"

"Bethlehem?" Marcus shouted. "That's another lie you told me. You said I was born in Jerusalem just before my father died. Hold on a while, if I was born near Bethlehem it must have been around the same time that massacre occurred. I heard the Rabbi talk of it once to a Pharisee. They say King Herod was behind it don't they, although it was officially denied?"

"Shush! Don't shout. Yes you are right and that is the other reason I referred to earlier. We left there that same morning it happened. You must never talk of it. You cannot be certain that the Secret Police or Sanhedrin guards are not still looking for survivors. I know it's unlikely but you don't know what this government might get up to if they think someone escaped that purging. If it was important then to kill innocent babies, it's probably still important now."

"Why? I'm sorry, I don't understand. Why would they be interested in us?"

"Not us, Mark, but you."

"Me?" Mark stopped playing with the dough and tilted his head on one side.

"Yes, you. They wanted to kill all male children under a certain age born in Bethlehem. I heard about it later."

"But I wasn't born actually in Bethlehem."

"It was as near as you could get. There is no other town nearer and as far as anyone would be concerned, Bethlehem was your birthplace."

"But I still don't understand. Why did they kill the children? This whole story is too much to take in," whined the child.

"You haven't heard all of it yet either," chuckled his mother. "Just before you were born a huge light appeared in the sky; like a star or something. Herod got the idea that it meant a new king was going to be born so he wanted to eliminate any competition.. Anyway, this was the rumour that went around, and it spread everywhere."

"So as I'm the only boy to survive, I'm going to be a king?"

Mark looked at her incredulously.

"Judging by what has happened so far, I would not have thought so. Although, you are special. I have always believed you have a special destiny. It is something to do with being born under that star, a sort of omen I reckon. But you weren't the only survivor. Another boy, Jesus, the son of Joseph and Mary, escaped before us. I was friendly with them. Mary seemed to empathise with my situation."

"What has happened to him?"

"I've no idea. I have never seen them since."

Martha suddenly moved away from Mark as she saw Esherah and her son Pheras coming into the courtyard from the house. She whispered to Mark, "Get on with some work. We will talk again later."

Pheras was playing with a piece of wood, trying to see how long he could keep a stone in the air by hitting it each time it came down. He glared at Mark. He had a jealous streak like his mother, and did not like Mark because even though Mark was a year younger than him, he was physically superior and better looking.

As he approached Mark he deliberately hit the stone at him, feigning it was an accident. The slave boy grimaced a little as the stone struck his head, but was not going to admit, or show that it hurt, in front of Pheras. He felt a rage starting within him, fuelled by the disclosures of his parentage. He moved towards the other boy, but Martha saw the anger in her son's eyes and stepped in between them.

"Mark, get me some more water please. The dough is beginning to dry out a little." She looked at him forcefully and he turned and walked away towards the house.

"Yeah, get on with your work slave," Pheras called after him contemptuously.

Esherah and Martha exchanged glances. The latter picked up the dough and started to shape it. She too felt a burning in her chest but had been in servitude long enough to smother it. She also knew that Esherah would like to find some way of cancelling the holiday she and Mark were due. Martha was cleverer than that.

Esherah sniffed and walked out of the courtyard into the road calling Pheras as she went. Whilst she could punish a slave for any assault on her son, she did not want to have her son subjected to the indignity of a beating by a Hebrew slave boy. For that is surely what would happen if the two boys fought. It would dishonour her husband, and neither he, nor anybody, would forgive that in the prevailing culture. She was far too full of herself to swallow even a mouthful of her pride. Her husband may now intend to own Mark and his mother, but it would not mean they would have an easier life. On the contrary, Esherah was determined to make both of them realise exactly where their place was in the scheme of things, and soon.

CHAPTER SEVEN.

The Temple and a Reunion.

That night, as Mark lay on the thin wool-filled mattress, spread out on the raised part of the floor, he thought about the day's events. There was still a chill in the night air, and he tried to snuggle further under the goats' hair quilt. In the heat of summer he would often take his bed and sleep up on the flat roof, provided Haaman or Esherah were not there.

Under that vast canopy of inestimable stars he would fantasise about better times, and wonder just what all those twinkling diamonds were about. What was there behind all the darkness? Was the white light of heaven somewhere beyond it? It seemed to him that the night sky was like a huge black silk sheet, that someone had pierced thousands and thousands of times with a needle. Shining through those holes came the white light of heaven, forming patterns. Looking upwards like that would make him look outwards from himself. There was the realisation that his small world was not the only thing in life. It made him forget his problems. There had to be something else. All this just couldn't be here by accident, could it?

Sleep was difficult because of the turmoil he felt. But it was not just turmoil. There was a sense of excitement too. This morning he had awoken as just a slave boy. Tonight, he found he was the son of a Roman centurion, and despite all the teaching from his Judean upbringing, he felt a sense of pride. He could not help it. The Romans ruled the world, and now he might be able to claim Roman citizenship. Yet he was also a loyal son of Abraham, like all true Judeans. Tomorrow he was due to sacrifice in the Temple, and would become almost a man. But was the God of Abraham, the God of the Romans as well? They were gentiles, and not the Chosen people. They had different gods. Where did that leave him? Everything was just too confusing.

Then there was all that business with Hiro, the giant. Was that something to do with his mysterious father? Hiro had talked about having a 'master'.

Although Mark would soon be seen by most people as an adult, he doubted whether his mother truly saw him as that. He thought she still saw signs of the child in him. In his heart he really knew that she might be right. He felt like he was half child, half adult. The unsettling condition of adolescence was upon him, where he was old enough for some things, but not old enough to do all the things he wanted. He never gave a thought to how difficult this might also be for his mother. How difficult it might be for her to let him go into adulthood when the time came. Like everyone else, he would only learn this when he had children of his own.

Mark decided to think about the next four days off instead. He let the feeling spread over him, and luxuriated in that for a while. Often the anticipation of a holiday was better than the actual event. He hoped that would not be the case this time. Not only did he have four days off, but also his mother had mentioned that Haaman had returned from Agothos proclaiming that she and Mark were now Haaman's property. He wondered how much Haaman had paid for them. How much were their lives worth in his scheme of things? How much were they worth to anybody?

Somewhere in the darkness a goat coughed, and other domestic beasts grunted. An insomniac griffon-vulture, straying from its normal wilderness, hunting for scraps, seemed to shriek out a reply to the goat. The streets were often full of bits and pieces thrown out by housewives at this time of year. They would make sure that no yeast particles would remain in the house before Passover. Yeast was associated with evil, and no part could remain in the home during the Holy festival. So every Spring they cleaned it out.

Mark heard the watchman call to someone in the street. Probably it was a beggar, but it might be a traveller, caught without lodging because all the inns were full for Passover. Owing to the influx of pilgrims the air was laden with other noises not normally present.

A jackal that had crept stealthily into town raised his song to the full moon. He was not the only scavenger that found festivals to his liking. There would be many at the Temple tomorrow, but with two legs instead of four. The jackal's wailing was met with an oath from the watchman, and a stone thrown as the only reward for his song.

Gradually the stir and shouts of the people faded away leaving only the indistinct sounds of animals and insects twitching, or rummaging. Mark never realised that he had drifted off into a peaceful sleep. In the same way he had no realisation that the coming four days were to change his life forever.

………………………………………

"What a mass of people," said Mark the next day, as he pushed his way through the excited crowds heading towards the Temple.

His mother struggled valiantly to keep with him. There was no need of any stranger to ask the way. The crowd would carry them there, and the Temple itself was shining from the burnished gold plating that covered its walls on the upper building. It was so bright in fact that no one could look at it comfortably because of the way the sun's rays reflected off the golden parts and the white marble.

The pair gradually made their passage up the hill until they came to the Temple mount. This was the vast artificial platform which Herod had constructed so the second Temple, built almost half a millennium ago with the help of the Persian king Cyrus the Great, could be gradually reduced, and this new one absorb and spread over the older parts.

It was a massive area with the northern and southern walls around three hundred yards long each, and the east and west walls both over four hundred and eighty five yards long. In total it was almost one hundred and fifty thousand square yards.

The old sacred building had crested the hill to the north of the City of David, so Herod had to order the land around it to be raised to facilitate his new design. He wanted plenty of space to outdo Solomon, if you could outdo a legend.

The trouble was that Herod had never been truly accepted as a proper king. Although most rulers had a bodyguard, Herod had needed one more than most. He had been hated more by his own subjects than by foreign enemies, chiefly because of his cruelty but also because he was never really a Judean. His father was Idumean and his mother Nabatean, a part of the country far south of Judea.

Herod had been clever though. He had set out on a building scheme that he thought would make his people like him. He built many great things, and when he started to rebuild the Temple, he thought it would be a lasting reminder of his accomplishments. Yet, as is often the case, it was for an act of destruction, not restoration, for which his name would be immortal. The murders at Bethlehem were still widely known about, despite Herod's attempts to cover up the facts and dismiss it as the work of traitors.

Throughout Herod's life his family had constantly squabbled and he had never really managed to stop it. This had been mostly his own fault as he had had nine wives. Jehua, once the captain of his Royal Bodyguard, had often thought how quiet his own life would have been if Herod had not been so sensuous a man. He seemed to love with the same intensity he hated. If ever there was an argument against multiple marriage, it surely could be found in the chaos that had been Herod's private life.

No one alive at this time had any idea of what the very first Temple, Solomon's, had looked like before its destruction about six hundred years earlier, but its grandeur was legendary. It was also the main reason why the magnificent cedars of Lebanon, which were once abundant in the snowy mountain ranges north of Israel, were diminishing. So many were cut down then for Temple construction, and succeeding centuries of such violation, for the needs of war and building, had modified once great forests into isolated clumps.

A wall along the slopes of the Kidron valley supported the Temple platform. When an eagle in flight looked down on the complex, it would appear that there was a large rectangular open area bordered by colonnaded walls, called the Court of the Gentiles, and the Antonia fortress at the northwest corner of it. Towards the centre of the open area was another rectangular structure, the Temple itself. On the west side a viaduct led directly to the entrance to the Temple from the upper city. The two southern entrances were reached by separate flights of steps, and between these steps was the ritual bath-house, which was where Martha and Mark were heading.

It had taken one and a half years to build the sanctuary itself, but even now, thirty-two years later, building and repair work was still going on in the outer courtyards. Owing to the fact it was built on hallowed ground, a whole army of priests had been specially trained to do most of the construction, as only they could set foot in certain parts. Cynics had often made comment that the length of time to complete the work was directly proportional to the length of time the priests wanted to remain employed. Upon completion, the ordinary Temple duties would not require so many workers.

There was an hour to mid-day. Martha had already regretted not setting out earlier in the morning, but had to wait until Mark had attended his class at the rabbi's academy. It was the best schooling for boys to be found in the Mediterranean, second only to Rome itself.

As he had now reached twelve years old, today had been Mark's last day, but his heart had not been in it. He was no longer certain of his nationality. He felt a fraud, unclean, and no longer part of this community. He turned to his mother and signalled her to pull over to shelter underneath one of the outer west walls, near the viaduct. Some thirty-five feet above them pilgrims thronged along its stone road towards the west entrance of the Temple.

"We need to get round to the south entrances, for the baths," gasped Martha. She had to raise her voice above the general din of the crowd.

"Mother, I don't think I can go any further."

"Nonsense! My son is a weakling? You shouldn't be out of breath yet."

Then she saw the look on his face and reacted with a mother's natural concern. "You aren't unwell are you?"

"No, it's not that. I'm fine. Well, except for my head. I don't think I can do this…this sacrificing thing. Uh, before you say anything listen to what I have to say. What you told me yesterday has changed everything. I'm no longer a true Judean am I? I've been brought up to believe in the God of Abraham, to be a child of the House of Israel."

He lowered his voice and hissed.

"But I'm not. I'm only half a son of Abraham, and what's worse is that the other half is the product of our, er, their worst enemies, the Romans. I'm no more than what the Elders would call a…a gentile. Therefore, I shouldn't go past the Court of the Gentiles, let alone make sacrifice. The punishment for that is death, and you were worried that someone might kill me if they found out I was born near Bethlehem twelve years ago. Huh!"

He snorted in disgust.

"But they won't find out will they? Only I know and I'm not going to reveal it. Are you? As far as anybody in the world knows you are entitled to make sacrifice."

"Yes, but it's not right is it? Aren't you worried that God will punish us? He knows everything, or so I've been taught."

"Of course He does."

Martha put her arm around her son's shoulders and brushed away her forming tears with the other hand, which held the coins to purchase the lamb.

"Oh, Mark, Mark. What have I done to you? I never meant for this confusion to happen. I did what I thought was best, as all mothers do. When you were a child it was safer, and perhaps easier, to conceal the truth from you. But when you look at it, not that much has changed. Yahweh is still the only God. He is still your God, whatever your race or colour. You also bear the circumcision scars, marking His covenant with you. Only if you truly no longer believe in Him would it be wrong to make the sacrifice. As for the Pharisees, let them worry about their own problems. You have observed all the required laws from birth. No one can challenge you. We are not going to lie to each other anymore, but there is nothing to be gained by proclaiming your half Roman ancestry now. Who knows, one day it may be to your advantage to claim that as well?"

The boy blew out his cheeks as a relief from emotion.

"I suppose so," he said grudgingly. "Let's get it over with then."

The two forced their path towards the south and went up the large steps to the baths. They immersed themselves in the ritual bath, the mikveh, which was no more than a glorified quick dip in the purified rain water. They walked down a few steps through water about head height, and up the opposite steps. A ritual, though, which would be echoed and adapted in seventeen years time on the banks of the river Jordan, by a camel haired, locust eating, hermit called John.

They went from the baths to the triple gate. This led into a gloomy passageway, which teemed with hundreds of people making their way beneath the Stoa, or meeting hall, to the Temple platform. The stench assaulted their nostrils. Mark was used to the everyday body odour of crowds of people, but never before had he experienced anything like this. His mother had always gone to the sacrificial services alone, just to watch.

It wasn't just the closeness of everybody, at least many of them had performed some form of bathing that day. It was the smell of blood and incense, and filth from animals that surprised him. It swept down from the Temple itself, and mingled with the sticky air in the tunnel and the fumes from spluttering olive oil lamps on the walls. A mixture of sweetness and decay. The smell of blood and incense always permeated the altar part of the Temple further in, but today the priests had to do the daily sacrifices earlier and accommodate the slaughter of two young bulls, a ram, a goat, and seven lambs, in addition to the regular offerings. This same number would be killed each day of the Passover festival; but this afternoon, this one special sacred afternoon, the real killing began with all the Passover lambs as well, offered up by the people. So it was not surprising that the smell of blood was in the air more than usual.

Although quite wide, the passageway was stifling and packed with people, many of them carrying sheep, or trying to pull them along, and birds flapping and squawking in cages. It was chaotic, with the bleating of the lambs adding to the general hubbub of Greek, Aramaic, and Hebrew languages all aurally intertwined. For a moment he felt nauseous, and the warm claustrophobic air and heat of bodies added to his discomfort. He had to get out of this passageway, but he wasn't certain it would be any better out on the main Temple platform. At least it would be more open; there would be more air. Mark made a concentrated effort to get ahead, not worrying he might leave his mother behind. Being slightly smaller, he managed to push his way along by ducking under arms, and gradually weaving his path through to the front.

It was a struggle to stay upright, and Martha was lifted up and swept along without her feet having to touch the ground at all. She began to feel herself slipping down and realised she would disappear under the feet of the horde, but was unable to prevent this herself.

"Mark, help me," she shouted despairingly.

She could not see him, but suddenly felt a hand grip her arm with such strength that it could not be Mark.

"Don't be afraid Martha, I've got you," said a slow deep voice at her side. She turned her head as much as possible and felt a strange exhilaration as she looked on a face she had not seen for almost eleven years. Smiling down at her, with that broad strong visage, and greying beard, was Joseph the carpenter, Mary's husband.

"Joseph! Thank you. I thought I was falling under everybody. Is Mary here?"

"She is just ahead. Don't try and speak now. Let us get out on to the courtyard."

Joseph led her firmly through the rest of the way until they emerged into the sun again. They saw Mark waiting at one side of the passage, and Mary and her children on the other.

"Mark! Come here. There are people I want you to meet."

As he shuffled over to her she caught hold of him and excitedly pulled him by the hand.

"All right, all right. What is the rush?" he said irritably.

"Remember I told you about the friends I made in Bethlehem? Well, here they are. This is Joseph, and here comes Mary and her family. Joseph helped me in the approach when I was falling. I would have been crushed but for him."

"I held her arm, that is all," said Joseph modestly.

He extended his hand to Mark, who clasped it and noted the steely grip of someone spending a lifetime in heavy manual labour. Joseph was not that tall, but had thick, wide shoulders to complement his stocky build. Clearly his trade was flourishing because his clothes were of good quality. His mantle was of a light purple colour. Not the deep purple that nobles wore, but dyed in some lighter extract of the expensive purple dye that came from Thyatira further west along the Mediterranean coast in Asia Minor.

Mark could also tell Joseph came from around Galilee by the lack of a join in his tunic and mantle. It was the way they wove their cloth in that area. A white cloth covered his head and fell around his shoulders. These were obviously his best clothes, worn especially for the Temple visit.

By contrast Mary looked less resplendent. Both her head-cloth and over mantle were a light brown colour, but were still of good quality. She was of a light build, and at some seven inches shorter than her husband, was about the same height as Martha. It was also evident that there was a large gap between the ages of the couple. As she came nearer, five boys and two girls came with her. Mary held out her arms to her friend.

"Martha! How wonderful to see you again. We often wondered what happened to you both, after the…well you know," she lowered her voice, " the Bethlehem business." The two women hugged.

"Oh, we made our way out of there before the killing started. That is something I must talk to you about, but later, perhaps. And you...where did you go? Are these all your children? You look so well, and affluent. Oh, there are too many questions."

"We went to Egypt, but it's a long story and you are right, we must catch up on all our news later. We cannot stand here talking while this crowd pushes us around. Maybe you can celebrate the Seder meal with us tonight? Where are you staying?"

"Oh, we live here now, in a big house in the Upper City on the west side. It's not ours. We work there as..."

Martha paused. For the first time in years she was ashamed of her position in society. It had been ages since she had been in the company of people who knew her in her other life. Her previous, and what she considered, her real life. It was too much for her. The anguish and hurts of so many years suddenly rose from the dark depths where they had been suppressed, and burst out of her in deep sobs.

"Martha, Martha. Don't be so distressed. I can see the marks on your wrists. I know how hard it must have been for you. Remember our talks in Bethlehem? This is I, Mary, and you are still you, aren't you? You can be just who you are with us."

Her words cut straight through any sham and showing off, that often besets reunions of friends. Mary spoke from her soul with a love, compassion and perception few people could equal. She held Martha close until her sobbing stopped. Martha looked over her friend's shoulder and saw who she thought must be Mary's eldest child, looking at her intently.

He had Mary's same light brown hair, falling in waves down to his neck and shoulders. He was not stocky like Joseph; in fact he had nothing of his build or looks, but seemed to have more of his mother's colouring and bone structure. For all that, it was apparent that he had been working in the family business due to the air of quiet strength surrounding him and his upright stature.

But it was his eyes that held her. Unusually blue, like Mark's, and out of keeping with the native colouring, they had a softness that conveyed understanding. She felt he saw her whole life; that all her secrets were laid bare and irrelevant in those twin pools of azure. Mary's son held her gaze, and very quickly she felt calmer.

Somehow all those hurts and wrongs didn't matter anymore. She felt something which she had long forgotten; peace.

"I'm all right now. Thanks Mary. I don't know why I did that. It's not me is it? You know, put a brave face on everything."

"Perhaps it needed to be done, and this was the right moment," replied her friend wisely.

Joseph moved to change the mood. "So, this is your son...er,"

"Mark," interrupted Martha. Then looking at Mary she added, "Or Marcus if you prefer."

It was the first time she had used the Roman form of her son's name in public. Something about Mary and Joseph made her want to be honest with them.

"Yes, of course, Mark. I have never been good with names," continued Joseph. "He has grown into a fine young man."

He nodded his head approvingly. "This is our eldest, Jesus." Then he pointed to each child in turn. "James, Joseph junior, Simon and Judas, and my little flowers Rebecca and Sarah."

Mark immediately felt warmth for this man. He had not referred to him as a boy. His instincts told him that this was a family it would be good to know.

Martha smiled at them and then said, "Look, it must be providence that we met because I was going to have to find someone to take Mark to the priests for the sacrifice. He's head of the family now."

James and Simon looked up quizzically, but their mother gave them a frown to keep them silent. She knew part of Martha's secret.

"Will you take him Joseph?"

"Of course. Where is your lamb?"

"We haven't bought it yet. It was our next thing to do before we found you."

"Come on then, let's attend to that."

Joseph started to move off, and then he paused.

"Wait! What are we all thinking! With Martha and Mark there are now eleven of us. That means we have more than enough for the prescribed number by festival law. We were going to share our lamb with Matthew and his wife, but they won't mind joining another group from our travelling band from Nazareth. You must share with us."

"Yes, of course. Say you will join us, Martha," entreated Mary.

75

Martha looked over at Mark, and he nodded.

"If you are sure you want us, then that would be wonderful. I have never had anyone to share with since I lost my own family, and I forgot that the priests like ten or more people to share an animal to cut down their work. Here, I have some money to pay my share for the lamb."

Joseph frowned, and his voice was stern. "Please, Martha, you would not insult your friends who invite you to dinner, would you?"

"No. I didn't want you to think…"

"You are our guest," interrupted Joseph. "Clearly you are a gracious giver. You now have to learn to be a gracious receiver. It is settled. Let us go and obtain the lamb."

Mark felt much better now Joseph was here. He was entirely at ease with him and was no longer worried about the ritual. He thought this must be what it is like to have a father.

The party made their way across the Court of the Gentiles, with its portico walls bearing Roman soldiers along the top, to the western side where those who were in the know pre-ordered their animals the day before. It was only a little more expensive, but well worth the trouble saved in not having to negotiate the entrances with the unhappy creature.

Many inexperienced pilgrims tended to buy their animals in the city outside the Temple courts; out of panic and thinking they were being prudent. The realisation that the "special" price obtained outside was in fact an inflated one, would never come upon them unless idle talk with other pilgrims revealed it. If they hadn't encountered it before, this was their first experience of ritual commercial preying, and not the ritual praying they thought they would experience.

As Joseph tucked the newly collected lamb under his arm he muttered all these thoughts to Mark. "You will learn many things today, my young friend, but there is one thing you should always remember. Even though you are near holy ground, and in a holy place, there are still some people who would rather prey on you, than with you. Also, I do not think it is right that so many sheep are allowed to be sold in this part of the Temple. They should have the sheep pens and stalls outside. A few years ago, some trader brought three thousand sheep in to sell. Since then, everyone thinks it is alright to do just what they like. Madness."

Mark smiled his approval of the wisdom and noted that Jesus, who had also had taken in the words, was staring fiercely not only at all the animal and bird sellers, but particularly at the moneychangers lining the colonnaded portico of the courtyard. Their purpose was to provide the requisite necessities for travellers and exiles in exchanging all other currencies into Tyrian shekels which was the only money that could be paid into the Temple for offerings.

Joseph followed Mark's gaze and said, "Jesus has never approved of all this commerce in the Temple precincts. He feels that the Father's house, as he calls it, is not the place for the swindling and deception that goes on. I suppose he has a point. Strangers are nearly always cheated on the exchange rate."

"He seems to know far more than I do, even though we are the same age," said Mark without rancour.

"Yes. But do not be cast down about it. There will not be many who can match his wisdom. If we don't keep an eye on him, he will be over there in the colonnades, or in the Court of the Women debating scripture with his elders. He loves it, and he asks such searching questions that older people tend to get annoyed with him because he exposes the weakness in their arguments and they can find no answers. I often marvel at the things he comes out with, and I'm meant to be a teacher in our synagogue back in Nazareth!"

The old carpenter chuckled to himself. He looked at the others chatting intensely, then he slapped Mark on the shoulder and raised his voice.

"Come on all of you! Time is getting on; we must force our way to the front of this crowd to be sure of getting in the first batch of sacrificers. Otherwise we will be relegated to standing around waiting for them to finish."

They made progress as swiftly as possible northwards across the courtyard until they came to a low wall. There were notices on it in Greek and Latin proclaiming that anybody who was not one of the twelve tribes of Israel, and was found beyond this point would be executed. Mark felt a shiver flow over him, and stopped where he was. What was he to do?

77

CHAPTER EIGHT.

The Sacrifice and The Gold.

Mark turned and looked at his mother, who whispered, "Don't worry. It will be all right."

Mary sensed the concern and, with a knowing glance at Martha, she took Mark by the arm. Her perceptive gift made her able to deduce the anxiety in Mark, and the reason for it, especially as she knew about Mark's father.

Mary gently nudged him through one of the openings in the low wall towards a short flight of steps leading up to a massive stone wall. Behind this were the inner courts and the magnificent Temple itself. Mary's action had somehow lessened Mark's apprehension.

Joseph's party had a choice of nine entrances to take to go beyond the wall. Each entrance was guarded by a door decorated in silver and gold, and each door had an armed guard either side of its opening. These were the temple guards, who held a javelin at an angle of forty-five degrees with its blunt end on the ground, and carried a sword and dagger on their belt. There were many other guards scattered around the courtyards. As well as their weaponry and leather armour, they carried a shield and a special horn to summon assistance by a sequence of blasts.

On festival days these guards would be backed up by Roman soldiers, but even they were not officially allowed beyond the Court of the Gentiles. The Romans were never far away though. Past experience had taught them to prepare for trouble at these times, and the Temple authorities were glad of the extra policing.

The soldiers resided in the Fortress of Antonia, which towered over the northwest part of the outer walls. They were only minutes away from any part of the Temple area and from the top of the fortress walls could survey everything below. Mark had noticed earlier the glint of sunlight from the helmets of the soldiers' on duty and their spears as they lined the tops of the porticoes He could distinguish the two centurions by their red plumes, set sideways on the crest of their helmets. There were also some men with bows and their quivers full of arrows. He thought of his father, and wondered how many times he must have stood there, if ever.

He resolved that one day he was going to try and wear that uniform if it meant him being freed from ownership by someone. He would gladly exchange that for the different enslavement a soldier's life offered, and it seemed Romans did not care who fought in their armies as long as they obeyed orders.

Such is the power of birthright and inheritance. Legacy changes viewpoints overnight and without shame, and that is what had happened to Mark now he knew he had Roman blood. The fact that sons of Israel were excused conscription into the Roman army, because they could not bear arms on the Sabbath for religious reasons, was an irrelevance to him at this moment.

Joseph decided that today, with everybody pushing from the west it would be best for them to try one of the three eastern doors to gain entrance to the Court of the Women. His theory paid off and the little group found themselves ahead of some of the other people who had been around them, and they were now clearly in the vanguard of the people who would be the first to sacrifice.

"Now listen, Mark," said Joseph. "Here is where the women and children must remain. Normally I would go alone to the altar rail, as the representative of the rest of my family and our group, but today you will come with me so you can learn. If anyone challenges us, leave all the talking to me. The women will be all right here. It's like a giant social event where they can catch up on the gossip. Listen to the noise."

Mark did, and could hear the cries of recognition as travellers met up again after being separated crossing the outer court, or friends who had been not been seen for some time greeted and laughed with each other. There were also people who thought themselves preachers, or prophets, and spouted forth to any they thought might listen. On other days scribes and would-be scholars would stand or sit around expounding views on religion and where the world was going wrong. Some even spoke openly about their hopes for the promised Messiah who would lead them out of the tyranny of the Romans. Whether they would have spoken quite so loudly had the Roman guards been in this courtyard was another thing.

Joseph continued his teaching for Mark's benefit. "You'll notice the walled enclosures in each corner. That one's for storage and wood inspection. You can't have wood with worms in it used for the altar fire. That one is where the lepers go to be inspected by the priests when they think themselves cured."

Turning to the opposite wall he continued, "Over there is stored the oil and wine used in the services. And that one is for the Nazirites. You know who they are don't you?"

"They are the ones who are a bit strange aren't they? They think they are special…consecrated. They don't drink wine, cut their hair, or go anywhere near a dead body?"

"Yes. That's right. Clearly you have listened to something the rabbi taught you. Now scattered round you will see thirteen chests shaped like rams'- horns. Just like the same shape as the shofar that sounds from the place of trumpeting on the outer southeast wall calling us to prayer. Coins are thrown into the mouths of the horns, and then they fall into the chests below. These offerings help with the costs of all the Temple sacrifices. The money collected from these is transferred to the main treasury chambers built into the inner forecourt of the Temple. There are also many underground chambers. From the main treasury, the money is divided up into separate chambers according to the use of the money. So, the Chamber of Secrets holds the money that is given secretly to the poor, and the Shekel Chamber stores all the Temple tax imposed on all adult Judean men, and so on."

Mark looked around quizzically. "Where are all the guards? There are only a few in this courtyard. Anyone could steal the chests."

"There are other Levite guards in the main Chambers which you cannot see yet, and there are the Romans watching from the Antonia, and along the tops of the colonnades. But anyway, who would dare to steal Temple gold? The very sacredness of this place guarantees its safety. What strange thoughts you have. I don't know. It must be an age thing. You and Jesus both say the most peculiar things. Let us go."

Mary and Martha stood to one side with the children while the man with the lamb, and the boy soon to be a man, pressed forward with the throng. They headed to the western side of the enclosure and towards the fifteen curved steps leading to the majestic bronze Nicanor Gate.

At this gate Joseph and Mark, and a crowd of other men, waited for it to be opened by the priests, who had by now finished the morning's rituals. This would lead to the Court of the Israelites into which no woman was allowed. While they waited to go into this third court, Mark smelt the blood and incense aroma grow stronger, but he was getting used to it now.

He also heard a new sound. Not strident or raucous like the others, but more lilting and harmonic. It was the unaccompanied singing by priests of some psalms of David the King, who some said was the greatest, despite his faults. The antiphonal chanting seemed to grow louder, but it was probably as a result of people stopping talking to listen and therefore making less noise. It wafted above the general clamour, curled around the hall, and just as though it had everyone's attention, settled upon the crowd like a blanket, muffling everything underneath.

Then suddenly, in contrast, a piercing, shrill blast came from a shofar. The magnificent gate opened which would allow a third of the massed assembly through to commence the sacrifices. Joseph motioned to Mark to get moving, but the push of others behind him had already made him aware of that need. The carpenter carried the lamb clasped to his chest to prevent movement and Mark observed that he also pulled a cloth bag towards the front of him too, as though to make sure it was protected from any unauthorised hands trying to open it. He deduced there must be something valuable in it, and that perhaps it was gold or money for another offering.

They both jostled their way through the entrance and approached the very low wall ahead in the relatively narrow corridor compared to the previous spacious courts. When the court was full the shofar trumpeted again and the big gate was shut with some difficulty against the pressure of the men still trying to get in. This procedure would happen at least three times that afternoon, but Mark was glad they were in the first batch.

Behind the wall existed the fourth and final court, that of the Priests. This was the sacred ground where only they could walk, and barefoot at that. Most people believed that around here, probably beneath the inner sanctuary, was the actual rock upon which Abraham had been prepared to sacrifice his beloved son Isaac.

On the ground before the altar were metal rings and wooden posts, set into the stone floor so larger animals for sacrifice could be tethered, and handled more easily. Mark, however, could not take his eyes away from the sight of the huge stone altar, with its four horns at each corner and a blazing fire in the middle. This fire was never allowed to go out. On other days whole animals, or parts of them according to the type of sacrifice, were burnt. This day the lambs would be taken away to be eaten by the many Passover groups. As priests moved around he could see only parts of the altar, but it was evident it bore splatterings of blood from recent animals who had given their lives to the cause.

Yet beyond this, was something far more imposing. The majestic façade of the Temple rose into the sky, shining with gold and white marble. At the centre a large opening revealed the entrance to the sanctuary itself. Though the doors were open, a beautifully embroidered curtain half concealed them and what lay after.

Annas, the High Priest stood in front of the curtain, and had Mark been permitted further, he would have seen the menorah or the seven pronged lamp stand, the table of shew bread, and the altar of incense behind. Even further beyond them was another curtain which hid a bare undecorated room, the Holy of Holies. Only the High Priest could enter there once a year to burn incense, on the Day of Atonement. Many years ago, before its mysterious disappearance, the Ark of the Covenant had been housed there.

Mark knew this from his rabbi's teaching, and shuddered with awe at the mystery and realisation of how close he was to something in which the creator of the universe resided. He wondered whether God was always there, or whether it was only on special days like today. He wished he had paid more attention to those lessons now.

Some of the men were chanting prayers and the atmosphere had changed to a more reverent one. They were here at last. There was no longer any need to exert pressure to get forward. This was as close as most of them accepted they would ever get to Yahweh in their lifetime. All the straining and stress of getting here was over. It was almost like the peace of death must be, after a lifetime's striving. The fuss and preparation, the petty irritations and disputes between fellow worshippers, had melted into insignificance before the perceived presence of God. He was only a child's stone throw away.

The predominant sound now was of the lambs bleating. These, like the scapegoat which on the Day of Atonement became the unwilling sufferer for men's sins, would soon be thrust into the part of innocent victims, so others could go and acquire guilt again.

Mark considered all these aspects quietly to himself. Yet he wanted to burst out with questions. "Why wasn't there a once and for all solution? Why did they have to make the same sacrifices each year to appease God for the things they did wrong, and also remember the past actions of the Lord? What principle made an innocent animal suffer involuntary for the sins of men? Shouldn't the High Priest willingly sacrifice himself for guilty humans? Now that would make sense. But who would do that? Surely no one would ever take the job if they had to sacrifice themselves?"

He wished he could ask Joseph's opinion now but he knew this was not the right time. Joseph needed to concentrate on his own thoughts and the task ahead. Maybe he would try and discuss this later tonight at the Passover meal. He could see Annas coming forward to the altar and giving some instruction to a group of priests. How resplendent he looked in his blue head-dress and blue robe fringed with golden bells that he wore over the normal priestly white tunic. Over his shoulders and covering his chest and back was another garment, an ephod. This was like a vest and embroidered with bands of gold, purple, scarlet and blue and pulled together at the waist with a similar coloured sash. In the middle of his chest, a gold purse hung down, inset with twelve gemstones representing the twelve tribes of Israel. Like the other priests, he was barefoot.

"It is the moment," said Joseph. "Stay close to me and say nothing. The priests are ready."

As he spoke, one priest clashed two small copper cymbals together and a section of Levites started to sing again, but this time two harps and five flutes accompanied them. Joseph and Mark followed in line to the stone wall in front of them, no higher than a man's knees. There was a row of priests holding bowls made of silver or gold to collect the blood of the slaughtered beasts. Behind this line was yet another row of priests and this multi-tiered system was repeated up to the altar. It acted as a chain of bowls to convey the blood from the front to the altar behind. Eventually it was

Joseph's turn but a question from the priest brought to life what Mark had feared.

"What are you doing here on your own and without a sacrifice?"

He almost spat the words, and was clearly irritated that anything should detract from the loftiness and grandeur his duties gave him.

"He is with me," interceded Joseph. " He is one of our group, but needs to learn the ritual. There is no father, and he is now the head of his family as he is of age."

The priest looked at this man who was strong and confident; who spoke firmly and made no apology for this apparent deviation. Joseph met his gaze and said nothing. Experience had taught him that needless explanation weakened your own authority, and as in all matters of negotiation, whoever broke the silence usually obtained the worst of the deal. It was especially important in confronting officialdom.

The priest looked away at the milling throng of men behind Joseph. There was so much to get through this day and he really did not want to trouble Annas with something he might be rebuked for not knowing.

"I see. I did not realise he was with you. Make your offering."

He handed Joseph a small, but very sharp knife. Joseph placed his left hand on the sheep's head as though it was a blessing. Then Mark saw the head pulled back so the soft flesh of the throat was revealed. The priest positioned a bowl underneath, and with one swift decisive cut, Joseph opened up the carotid artery in the neck. There was no sound from this lamb, although others made shrill bleating noises, as though beseeching clemency before the metal tore their throats.

"You must hold the animal firmly while its blood drains into the bowl," said Joseph to Mark in a matter of fact manner.

Citizens of this age were no strangers to killing animals for food. Whatever the reason, the result was always the same; death for one party, and blood all over the hands of the other. Killing is forever a messy business.

"When you hold the lamb you will feel it grow weaker as its blood flows away. Blood is the very life force, the essence, of everything. You must hold its head until it is gone, and realise that it

84

is a reminder of your sins. When we sacrifice to the Lord, we are remembering that this animal is a symbol of the punishment that should be ours. It may have done nothing wrong, and be a perfect specimen, but true sacrifice involves cost. It is what the Lord as a just and Holy God requires, and teaches us to remember we are far from perfect, and need His mercy to escape from the wrath that rightfully should descend on us. God cannot abide where sin exists. Blessed be His name."

"But it doesn't work for long, does it?" Mark hissed, unable to contain his thoughts any longer. "We have to do this every year. This lamb is not a once and for all sacrifice for our sins. Even the scapegoat led out into the wilderness, to die from a hill outside the city walls on the Day of Atonement, doesn't do that. The same sacrifices repeated every year do not seem to make us any more perfect in God's eyes do they?"

Joseph turned sharply to the boy, looked at him quizzically, started to reply, and then thought better of it.

The priest turned and gave the bowl of blood to the priest behind him, who in exchange gave him an empty bowl. The blood was passed up this way to the priest near the altar who splashed blood on the four horns, each corner of the holy stone, and returned the empty bowl back down the line. This action symbolised the daubing of blood on the door lintels in Egypt when the Israelites were escaping the Pharaoh. And so the sequence went on, lamb after lamb, man after man. No amount of incense could remove the smell of all the red essence.

The lamb was hung on a wooden peg to bleed, then skinned, and its fat offered on the altar. The Levites had begun chanting again. Snatches of their song filled Mark's mind:

> *"In my distress I called to the Lord;*
> *He answered me and set me free.*
> *The Lord is with me, I will not be afraid; what can anyone do to me?*
> *I praise you, Lord, because you heard me,*
> *Because you have given me victory.*
> *The stone that the builders rejected as worthless*
> *Turned out to be the most important of all.*
> *Save us, Lord, save us!*

85

Give us success, O Lord!"

"Set me free indeed, Lord, even though I am worthless," said Mark quietly, but not so quietly that Joseph did not hear him. He felt moved by the boy's spontaneous plea, and an idea began to form to help him be free of slavery. But first he would need to discuss this with Mary and Jesus.

While the post sacrifice events were taking place, Mark pondered the wisdom of it all. Since his true history had been revealed, he had felt somewhat a bit removed from everything he had been taught since a small child. These no longer seemed his people. The Hebrews were an exclusive clan; proud of their elitism that came from the belief they worshipped the one and only true God. What he had told his mother was true. He did still believe, but did God still count him as one of His chosen people?

He had watched as Joseph showed him how to make the sacrifice, but he could not shake off the feeling that he would never actually do that himself. And yet he was equally certain that God was looking over him, and that it was necessary for him to have been here today. But if it wasn't to learn the ritual, what on earth was it? There was definitely a presence in this building, and he sensed God truly was there, and not just in the Holy of Holies, but mingling with the assembled pilgrims, Temple officials, and even the moneychangers and sellers, just like an ordinary human and as Joseph's own son would be doing now.

But if that were so, would anybody recognise him? Even Mark knew God was not like a man. The occasion must have mixed up his head. What was he thinking? He would talk to Joseph tonight.

How quickly he had come to like and trust him and Mary. Perhaps he could make a friend of one of their sons? The oldest had something about him that he could not quite explain. But no doubt they would soon go back to Nazareth, leaving him and his mother in bondage, and to the monotonous drudgery of their lives.

His reverie was interrupted by Joseph who had removed the lamb from the wooden peg after most of its blood had drained. Mark noted the wood had been stained so often that the colour had changed to a deep, dark red. It seemed slightly absurd to him that anything having its blood shed and hung on a piece of wood could be pleasing to the creator of the world. Now if a priest was to let

86

himself be voluntarily hung on the wood, surely that would be the ultimate expression of faith and sacrifice? But that did not happen. Mark knew that people were far too civilized and knowledgeable to let that happen; and how could God ever ask that of just an ordinary person?

"We must get out of here as soon as possible and take the lamb back to where we are staying. I don't want to be carrying this around any longer than I can help it," said Joseph.

He had taken a piece of cloth out of the bag he kept so close to him, and wrapped it round the dead animal so no blood stained his clothing. He knelt down and tied the two ends together so it formed a sort of sling that he put over his shoulder. Then he re-fastened the bag. As he did so, Mark saw something made of gold was also in there.

Without thinking he might be rude he exclaimed, "Gold! Is that real gold for another offering?"

Joseph looked up, startled. "Don't talk so loud. I do not want everybody to know I am carrying something valuable. Yes, it is gold. It is something extremely rare and costly, but it is not for an offering today. It belongs to Jesus and we brought it with us because he wanted us to. We thought he might give it as a thank-offering sometime during the festival week, but he wasn't sure what he was going to do with it. He just thought it might be needed. We have learned to trust his instincts."

Mark's curiosity would not be stifled.

"How did Jesus get such an expensive item at his age?"

"You have the persistence of a mule haven't you? It was a gift to him. I will tell you later. There are too many people milling round and we are in the way. We must return to the family."

Joseph showed the conversation had ended by straightening up and walking back towards the Nicanor Gate. They had to wait while the remaining men finished their business at the altar. Then came the sound of the shofar, and the gate swung open to the Court of the Women. They pushed their way through the next band of men trying to get in, and walked towards where Martha and Mary were sitting on the ground next to a wall, with the children near them. All except Jesus, that was.

"Why don't people wait until you are out of the way before they try to get past you?" complained Joseph as he met the group again.

"Nobody has any patience when they want to be selfish," replied Mary. "They are too frightened someone may get their place."

"And do to them what they are doing to others, you mean?" laughed Martha.

"Very true," nodded Joseph. "So, have you caught up on all the news? Got everything sorted out for the meal this evening?"

"Fairly much so. But there are a few things we couldn't really talk about here. You understand?" said his wife.

"Yes! I understand. It's because we children are here," quipped James.

"Quiet, you," said Mary. "It wasn't only that. There are some things best not spoken of before the whole world. You would not find them particularly interesting anyway, because they happened before you were born."

In saying this his mother gave James a playful clip round the head, and smiled to show she was not really angry. Just as they prepared to move they heard the sound of a horn blown three times. It was not a priest's instrument, but a guard's.

"There is trouble somewhere," said Joseph. "Stay close to me, all of you. Where is Jesus?"

"I gave him permission to go and see the activity around the portico in the Gentiles' Court. I told him to meet us outside the baths before the tenth hour if we didn't see him before. He will be fine. A mother knows these things. You know how he is," shrugged Mary.

Her husband bent and placed the cloth with the lamb on the ground.

"Yes, but something really bad must be happening. Look! The Romans are coming as well. I must find Jesus. Stay here. I am going to find him."

"I'll come also. You may need me as a messenger," said Mark quickly. He was not really concerned about being a messenger; but more interested in seeing what was happening and getting a share of the excitement.

Joseph hesitated, looked at Martha, who in turn saw the imploring eyes of her son. She nodded.

"Right. James, do what your mother tells you, and look after your brothers and sisters. Don't lose that lamb. All of you stay here with the crowd in this court. There are more guards coming. You will be safe."

With that brief set of instructions, Joseph turned and made his path through the packed courtyard with Mark in close pursuit.

"Why is father so concerned about Jesus?" James asked his mother. "It is like he always expects someone will try and harm him."

"Well, it's not that he loves him anymore than the rest of you. Your brother is different than other people, and when you grow older you will realise that more than you do now perhaps. Let's just say that because Jesus is the way he is, your father feels he has more of a responsibility to make sure no harm comes to him."

"I don't really understand that. He always seems so perfect. I can't see why anyone would harm him," replied James a little jealously.

"You will see. You will see one day," soothed Mary and stroked his cheek with the bent knuckle of her forefinger.

As she did this she caught sight of Martha looking at her oddly, as if her words had created some new thoughts in her. This was perfectly correct, since Martha was recalling her conversation with Mark yesterday afternoon.

"All the same," Mary continued, "I wonder what all the fuss is about. I hope it's not another riot. There seems to be one every major festival these days. It never does any good. Only stirs the Romans up to retaliate and make some innocent soul suffer."

More blasts of horns could be heard. The women looked at each other now in joint concern. People were starting to panic. Martha's little group moved closer to the wall, and wondered what would happen next.

Meanwhile, in the tunnels below the Temple, a desperate group of men were conducting an audacious and dangerous raid.

CHAPTER NINE.

The Men With The Plans.

(An hour earlier.)

In the special tunnel under the Temple buildings, Judas the Tanner, now leader of the "Judean Brethren", a newly formed breakaway group of the Zealot variety, crouched and signalled to the twenty men with him to gather round. This was the tunnel which led from the priests' select bathing pool to their own Court. It was the only means a priest had of entering the Temple from bathing, without becoming ritually unclean again. Normally it was used exclusively by the holy men, but today it had been utilised for more unholy purposes. This renegade rabble were fully aware that on this special day all the priests would be busy with the mass blood-letting above, and that once the ceremony had started this passage would be deserted and provide the perfect entry to the Temple vaults, with no one to see the weapons they carried.

Judas drew his small curved dagger and scratched a diagram on the stone floor.

"This is where we are now, and here is the entrance we want. In there is enough money to provide an army with arms and everything needed to make Judea our own again. Think of the mercenaries we could buy to aid us. But where does it go? Most of it to the Levites, the Sanhedrin and worst of all, to the cursed Roman swine in taxes. You all know what we have to do and the risk each is taking. You do not need me to remind you why we have to do this, but in case there are some who feel like turning back, leaving their brothers to fight for them, I will speak again to convince them such action is that of the coward and traitor."

He looked around at his men.

"We are the only true patriots left it appears. Everyone else has bowed the knee to the Romans. Do you think God wants that? Our land, given by Him to our forefathers is now turned into a Roman annexe with false gods and idols creeping in like some silent, subtle plague over God's holy earth. No! He does not want that. We are pledged to push them back to the pit they came from. This is a holy and just mission, which does not defile God's Temple anymore than it has been already by the submission of the people above. God will bless us for this."

He stopped his rhetoric and looked again into the faces of his companions for signs of weakness, and also to let the men at the back see the drawing. If every wall of the Temple heard that last sentence that Judas said, they would surely have collapsed sobbing for the number of times such words had been uttered over the centuries past, and for those in the future. If every brick was a bone, not one could bear to lay on top of another for writhing in agony at the self indulgence caused by people deceiving themselves into thinking they were acting in the name of religion.

The faces glowed in the light from the torches they carried, reflecting the zeal of their leader.

"I cannot promise you how this mission will turn out. We may sup from the cup of riches and glory; but if it is a poisoned chalice, we will drink from that also. If it is cursed and dangerous, we will embrace it. Now is our time. Restore the glory of Israel!"

There were muffled shouts of agreement from the men as they all rose and moved swiftly to the door that looked encrusted with age and lack of use. Although it had been part of the original Temple site, it had hardly ever been used in the last twenty years since Herod's restoration work had changed the layout. However, one of the sympathisers of the group knew about it and had alerted them to the possibilities. Scouting runs had revealed it still opened and they knew that beyond it would be a corridor leading to the main treasury with only two totally unprepared Temple guards, lacking the skill of Roman soldiers, between them and vast wealth. It was better guarded at night, or non-festival days, but nobody would expect a raid on this important day, with so many worshippers around. Nobody that is except Jehua, the once leader of King Herod's Bodyguard, now head of the Temple guards and an agent of the Roman Secret Police.

Ever since his days as Herod's right hand assassin the years had not diminished his talent for survival and instinct for trouble. He was nearly forty years old now, and although still very fit, got others to do the fighting needed. He wanted to acquire all the money he could for his old age and if it meant playing one side off against the other, so be it. Something said casually by one of his subordinates a week ago, about the rumoured robbery, had triggered a line of enquiry and then an outrageous thought, and plan, in his mind. Which was why, instead of only two guards at the treasury door, there were also Jehua and a mixture of Levite guards and Roman soldiers waiting out of sight in another corridor. Jehua had planned his operation carefully and made the whole issue top secret. His orders were explicit. No one was to move until the raiders had entered the room and begun to plunder the valuable hoard.

He had additionally arranged, with the consent of the Roman authorities, that one or two would be allowed to escape sometime during capture, so they would lead them to the rest of what the Romans considered a terrorist sect. Well, that is what he told them. In reality his reason was far more personal. The Prefect had warned him that such an action had inherent dangers of failure, and Jehua would be responsible if it was not a success. This did not bother Jehua, who had survived under a more malicious tyrant than this Roman Procurator. They had promised him a bonus in anticipation of the Zealots' capture, but Jehua's ambitions were greater than that.

To fully obtain all he desired, he had enlisted the help of Matthew, his remaining solitary friend from the day of the Bethlehem massacre, and whom he knew he could trust. Their plan was simple. In the disorder following the arrest of the "Brethren", Matthew would sneak into the room and gather as much gold coin as he could carry, to divide up later with Jehua. The deficit would be blamed on the escaping robbers who, though they might claim innocence, would not be believed by anybody.

Matthew would not attract attention, being one of Jehua's loyal guards and would be able to come and go as he liked. Jehua would make sure no one else got in Matthew's mode of operation, and if all went well, might even be able to lift some of the treasure himself. They could even return later to get more, to be blamed on the hapless insurrectionists. It was the perfect crime because all the officials would never seek for any other culprits than the ones arrested. It was a golden opportunity to get a piece of financial security. A proper reward for every devious activity they had ever carried out for successive employers.

Both men had never really been the same since the Bethlehem incident. The guilt that all the participants felt and shared had demonstrated itself in varying behaviour. Some had left soldiering and taken up less gladiatorial pursuits, but the majority had reacted like Jehua and Matthew. They felt remorse, but also felt they were too far down the road of the lost, that whatever they did now could not be worse than the memory of that single morning. There was no further shame to be endured. At least it was a private shame, for Herod had kept his word to suppress details of the act being recorded for history by applying less than subtle pressure on the scribes.

Judas and his men prised open the ancient door with some effort. The creaking made some of the men anxious and jittery.

"Do not worry. There will be nobody around this part to hear it," reassured the leader.

He moved his head through the gap made by the opening, and after a quick glance went through. The others followed. Stealthily they crept along the passage with only the shadows from their torches to eerily keep them company. They came to a T-junction with another path.

"Careful," said Judas, "we are near the chamber. It is just along there, to the right."

The group made the turn and came to another door. This one had been used many times and they knew it would open easily.

"This is the difficult bit," he whispered. " Beyond this door are the two guards. We must get to them and disable them before they can blow their alarms. Give me the robes, Simon."

His colleague untied the thin rope fastening a cloth bag and withdrew some white linen garments worn by priests. The two men put these on over their normal clothes, and practised concealing and withdrawing their daggers from within the folds of the sleeves. Simon started to take off his sandals.

"No need to do that. This is not holy ground yet. It will look funny if we are barefoot. Remember, we have come from the Priests' Court to get more bowls for the sacrifices if they ask."

"But isn't it the wrong direction? We should be approaching from that way," said Simon showing his concern. "It is a little different from how they described it."

"Look, it doesn't matter. We only need to get close enough to overpower them. By the time they start asking questions it will be too late. Anyway, they aren't going to say too much with our sicari held against their throats. You only need to be ready with an excuse for your presence if the guards call out before we reach them, or something unexpected happens. But it won't, will it? Man of Kerioth, you worry too much"

Simon nodded and smiled at the reference made to his birthplace. Kerioth was a town near Hebron, but Judas had used the Hebrew instead of the Aramaic, to remind him no doubt of the purpose of their mission. In the more familiar Aramaic version, "Man of Kerioth" was rendered as "Iscariot". Simon and Judas were close friends. That was especially made evident by the fact that Simon had named his son after Judas, and hoped that he too would grow up to be a Zealot leader. However, it would be almost twenty years before that Judas would make his mark in history.

The two of them paused, gathering their breath, and courage. Judas turned and spoke softly to the rest of the men.

"Follow us after the count of fifty. We should be ready by then. It is a short walk behind this door to the next, with the guards outside it. If we are not done with them, your appearance might create a necessary diversion. We will kill them if we have to. You never know, they might join us when they see what we get, and hear why we are doing it!"

The smiles helped relieve the tension felt by most of them. The door opened almost without effort, and the two leaders walked towards the next entrance with the paradoxical lofty attitude and fake humility of most priests of that time. Their heads were bowed, and their hands gripping the daggers were clasped behind their backs.

Ahead of them were two guards as expected. As was customary, they held javelins in their left hands, resting the ends on the ground. This was the traditional and uniform way of standing on duty, so the right hands were free to draw their swords in an emergency. They were leaning on the door lintels discussing the recent outcome of the gladiator games in Caesarea.

This was the coastal town seventy miles to the northwest with a magnificent harbour, which Herod the Great had rebuilt with Roman money to honour the Emperor Augustus for his help in establishing him on the throne of Israel. Caesarea boasted a fine amphitheatre, and the games held there were modelled on those in Rome.

The guards were in earnest conversation about the games, unaware of the greater game that was being played out around them. Jehua had decided to leave the guards in place. He had talked it over with Matthew and his cold, calculating reasoning forced agreement that the guards must stay to ensure the terrorists did not suspect anything was wrong. If the two men were killed, then it was a necessary expenditure. For this purpose Jehua had clandestinely reorganised the rota so two of the more slovenly men were on duty and would offer less resistance. If they were killed it might even help his endeavour.

In the clamour for quick justice afterwards, there would be less likelihood of the robbers receiving a proper trial, and difficult questions being asked or unresolved. The quicker a resolution to everything the better, leaving Jehua more time to enjoy his profit. He had also made certain that the Roman soldiers under his temporary disposal, as well as the Levite guards, did not discuss the plans with anyone else or each other. They knew pieces of the official plan, but only he and Matthew knew the complete arrangements. He had also arranged for someone to watch the entrance to the priest's tunnel and send a messenger by another route to warn him when the would-be thieves entered.

The two men on duty outside the Shekel Chamber ceased talking and straightened up automatically when they saw what they thought were two priests walking towards them. Judas and Simon kept their heads bowed slightly, and then when they were within six feet of the door, Judas raised his head slightly and said, "Peace be upon you."

The guards relaxed as anticipated, but as the two Zealots pretended to pass by, they swiftly pulled on the arms of each guard holding the javelins and swung round behind them, at the same time curling their right forearms around the necks of the guards and placing their daggers against their throats.

"Now, you can choose to die as an enemy of the true Israel, or you can cooperate by keeping silent while we do God's work," grunted Judas between gritted teeth.

"What do you want of us?" asked the bewildered Levite.

"Nothing but your silence and no resistance. If you give those freely, you will not have to give your lives. It is your choice. Drop your javelins and then, very carefully," Judas emphasised this by pressing his dagger strongly into his captive's throat, "take out your swords from their sheaths with your left hands and drop them on the ground."

Judas thought he had planned this operation thoroughly, but he had not been concerned with, or in the tension of the moment, noticed one little detail. He also did not know the true character of the man he was attacking. It was a trifling point really, but upon such things often turn the fates of men.

One of the guards, Andrew, was left-handed and being allowed to use his left hand gave him an unexpected advantage. What he now had to consider in an instant was whether to use that advantage or not.

He knew that his superiors did not consider him the brightest guard in the company, and he was usually the recipient of criticism more than praise. In fact he had been reprimanded only yesterday for another what they termed "slovenly" offence, and had his duty changed to this one. The warnings had stung him and further injured his inherent lack of self-confidence so that it bled away more profusely.

Yet here was a chance to change their perception of him, to earn a little praise, maybe even glory. The temptation was enough, even though the thought made him feel sick to his stomach. Fear of executing the deed was cancelled by fear of the unknown fate these strangers could inflict. There were only two attackers. If he could wound, or kill this one, he and his colleague could surely capture the other. He did not even calculate what might happen to them both if it went wrong. As far as he knew, these men might kill them anyway. You could not always trust the words of people these days, and especially people who would dare to impersonate priests and invade God's own Temple. The decision was made, and with it changed the lives of not only the decision maker, but also many others on this Temple Mount.

Andrew slowly drew out his sword as commanded. However, instead of letting it fall to the ground, he gripped the handle firmly, turned it so the sword point faced his assailant behind him, and thrust quickly backwards and across as he also twisted in Simon's grip. The blade slid into Simon's right side, into his liver, who gasped in astonishment and sudden pain. Andrew pulled out the weapon and sprung free. As he turned to his left he chopped at the arm of Judas at his friend's throat. It was inaccurate and made a superficial glancing cut across Judas' forearm, but it was enough to surprise Judas and make him loosen his grip round the guard's neck.

Andrew's partner also twisted free and pushed Judas against the wall. He drew his sword and held it towards the Zealot's chest.

At that moment the rest of Judas' men came along the passage, having finished their count of fifty. Andrew's colleague saw the men coming, backed away from Judas, grabbed his own horn and blew three piercing notes to sound an alarm. Judas, always quick to sum up a situation, knew that escape was now the best option. He realised the blasts would bring other guards and the feared Roman soldiers. There would be no time to plunder the treasury, so it was pointless to remain. The only treasure he wanted for certain now was his life. He shouted to his men.

"Turn back, it is no good. You are too late now, the other guards will come soon." There was already a hint of blame transference in his tone for the failure of the mission with the remark about lateness, as though it had been their fault things had gone wrong.

"But we don't know that they heard," said Simon shrewdly. "Shouldn't we wait and see if they come. Let's not panic. We can take these two."

"Doesn't look as though they are that easy," said another looking at the blood dripping from Simon's wound.

"Oh, that's not too bad. I'll live I expect. Do not worry about that," lied Simon.

"None of us will live if we stay around here too long," said someone else. "What are we going to do? Those horns can be heard a long way."

For a moment there was a standoff between the rival parties. The guards and the raiders looking nervously at the other. Just as Judas thought it might be worth entering the chamber anyway, Jehua's men burst through a side door in the tunnel towards his right, having been alerted by the sound of the horn.

When he had heard that horn, Jehua knew his plan had failed. He had known that there was a possibility of the chamber guards being able to raise the alarm, but thought it unlikely given the type they were. He looked over at Matthew and slowly shook his head signifying the plan was aborted. The only thing left for Jehua now was to act out the part of the hero in thwarting the raid. He was adept at turning most situations to his advantage, which was why he had lived so long under brutal leaders. He had given the order for his

97

men to proceed, and with it both his and the robber Judas' hopes of riches evaporated.

"Well, that answers that question!" exclaimed Judas as Jehua's men came towards them. "Get out as best you can."

He was not the best of leaders under pressure, and had overlooked the fact that his own band of men was almost equal in number to their adversaries. If, that word of a thousand unrealised possibilities, he had kept his men together; they might have been able to resist the impending arrest and withdrawn without further bloodletting.

It was too late. Judas' men were inexperienced in this sort of thing and in the resulting panic split into smaller groups and tried to run back down the tunnel from which they had come. Others went the opposite way heading under the very heart of the Temple complex. Judas tugged at Simon's sleeve and moved towards the latter way, hoping there would be another doorway or tunnel that would lead into the mass of people above. It would be difficult for the Romans or Temple guards to distinguish them from the worshippers there.

Simon knew he could not evade capture. The injury he had already received limited his movement, and his clothes were stained with the blood that still poured from his wound. He called out to Judas, "Leave me and live for another day. You can avenge me later. You cannot if you fall too. Look after my family for me, and make sure my son is used for the good of Israel."

Judas nodded and stared at the man who was willing to remain behind and probably die to save him. The damp, musty air was pierced by more horn blasts. The Romans would be here soon. His own men would be no match for those skilled artists of death. The number of blasts was the code for the location of any trouble. It would be picked up and passed on by all guards who heard it. Which way would they come?

"Go…now, please. Do it for me. I am lost."

The guards pressed on him within seconds. Simon tried to fight them. His brave action bought valuable time for his comrades, as in the restricted room in the tunnel, the skirmish blocked the other guards from following Judas and the men with him.

Judas took a quick look back and saw his friend starting to collapse from more blows. He then turned and followed some of the others. As he ran he had already decided to take a different route from them if possible. It would mean less chance of being detected. If he could just get to the crowds above.

Many thoughts passed through his mind as he ran. The failed mission meant that he would be a hunted man. If he could get his family, and Simon's, as he owed him that, away from the Jerusalem area, he would have to change his name. There was no doubt that those captured here would reveal the others' identity under torture. The Romans were renowned experts on that particular pleasure. Torture, and then death, was the standard way of dealing with anything, or anybody that opposed the steely rule of the Emperor.

Any sect or group that thought they could overturn the status quo was soon extinguished. Even if it was only propaganda by one sect or another, the Romans soon got to the truth. For truth was something they desired above many things. There were even stories of Roman officers being turned towards the Hebrew faith by the example and words, of not only Judeans met in everyday life, but also tortured captives met in everyday death.

Judas was now about seventy yards ahead of his pursuers, who were currently out of sight because of the bend in the passage. He could hear both the sounds of pursuit, and the scuffling of his friends in front who had started off before him. He had an advantage over them. He had seen the rough plans of the tunnels around this area, and how they linked into the main courts and building, on an old manuscript presented to him when he was plotting this raid.

Now a new plan was formulating. He would make his approach to the store rooms above where he might be able to hide for a while, take time to think, and possibly take some other clothing, so if the guards had passed on his description it would not match. They would post sentries on the exits from the whole of the Temple Mount. He knew there should be a connecting passage near where he was now. While his soon to be ex-followers charged on ahead, he saw the door he wanted and slipped smoothly and unseen into another corridor.

CHAPTER TEN.

A Mysterious Death.

While the scenes below had been playing out, Joseph and Mark were continuing their fruitless search above for Jesus. They had scanned the Court of the Gentiles and the perimeter colonnades where the teachers sat and made discourse, but the presence of so many people hindered their efficiency. They were making their path back to the Court of the Women, struggling against a tide of curious pilgrims as it ebbed and flowed with ripples of currents caused by individuals deciding to go in one direction, and then another. All in their quest to satisfy inquisitiveness at what was causing the soldiers and guards to assemble.

"This is no good at all," said Joseph, pushing aside a man who pressed on him too hard, while Mark kept close behind him and travelled in his wake. "I think Jesus might have already gone to where his mother arranged to meet him, even though it is not yet time. We must try and get to the ritual baths, but how I do not know with this chaos around us."

The carpenter stopped and stood on tiptoe, turning his body slowly like an old grindstone so he could try and see a favourable exit. Then over in a corner, he noticed a small door in the wall, which formed the rear part of the Women's Court. Three Roman soldiers went through it, revealing it was unlocked. It was the entrance to one of the storerooms. Mark mimicked his gaze.

"I have an idea, Mark. Stay very close and follow me over there."

He pointed to the corner. The man sliced his way through the crowd using those burly shoulders as effectively as he did when he cut through timber. It was though anyone in his path was eased aside like shavings planed off a plank of soft wood. The boy pursued him in the manner of a cygnet swimming in the still water behind the swan. They reached the door. Joseph gave a cautious look round before opening the door fully and signalling Mark through behind him.

They stepped into a large square room with little decoration. Unlike elsewhere in this building the plain stone walls stated functionality had won the battle over glory. It was much quieter in here.

"Where did the soldiers go, Joseph?"

"Through that door to the passageway behind, I would imagine. Or they might have gone on through to the main Court. The point is we need to go down the passageway. I know there are tunnels to the baths because a friend told me at a Carpenter's Guild meeting once. He had done some work shoring the timbers. We might get lost as I do not know the way, but it must be a lot quicker than working our way through that panicking herd out there."

Joseph moved over to the door and paused. He turned to Mark to issue another instruction when suddenly the door was pushed open, and the force, coupled with the surprise, knocked him backwards.

Equally surprised was Judas The Tanner, who had tried to bolt through the door to hide from the Roman soldiers he had seen further down the corridor, and fortunately for him going in the opposite direction. He stood in the opening, panting, with his sword drawn and stared down at Joseph who had been knocked to the floor.

However, his gaze only rested momentarily on the prostrate carpenter because next to him, glinting from the glow of one of the wall lamps, was something Judas instantly recognised as an essential for his pending flight from Judea.

It was a gold bowl, and from the look of it, something that he thought could be sold for enough money to feed him and his family for months. The resultant push had dislodged the item from Joseph's cloth bag, and it lay glittering, drawing all eyes to it. The bowl was exquisite, and Mark noticed the intricate carving round the rim and the unusual patterns that decorated the short, stubby stem, and which certainly did not originate from modern Israel.

For only seconds, the two men and the boy seemed to be frozen by indecision.

Judas was the first to react and stepped towards Joseph with the point of his sword aimed at his heart. As he moved over the bowl he stooped down and picked it up with his left hand.

"This will be very useful where I am going."

101

"If you take that, you may go to somewhere you do not want to go," said Joseph slowly and mysteriously.

"What does that mean?" challenged the robber.

"Only that the object you now hold will blight your life if you do evil," came the even reply, without hint of exaggeration.

"A fine try, old master, but you will have to think of something better to frighten me into not taking it. I have no time for riddles or superstitious rubbish."

Mark was strangely unafraid and also angry that this man should take the bowl from Joseph and his family. He had watched silently but then could not contain an outburst.

"What do you want with us? We have done you no harm. He is a good man, don't hurt him."

"What I want is some clothing, and if I have to hurt you, believe me, I will. Tell your son to keep quiet."

"He is not my son, but there is no need for you to use violence. I will gladly give what you want. You are obviously in desperate need. From whom are you escaping, the Romans?"

Joseph seemed completely calm and like Mark, also without fear.

"What is it to you?"

Judas thrust the sword threateningly at the man still on the ground. "Take off your robe, and be careful or…"

As he said this he altered his stance and held the blade against Mark's throat.

"Leave the young man alone. I have told you, I will give you whatever you want. But I tell you once more that to steal that particular gold bowl will do you more harm than good. I have other money. Take that instead."

"Take that as well, you mean. Let's see it. Now be very careful," he added while pressing the sword closer to Mark's throat.

Joseph rose slowly from the floor and reached under his outer robe to the belt around his tunic. He loosened a small leather purse and poured its contents into his left hand. There were three gold coins, some silver denarii, Tyrian temple shekels, and a few bronze as.

"Not a fortune is it?" sneered Judas. "You really expect me to take that as a substitute for this bowl. You Galileans are too simple and trusting. I'll have the money as well, and don't start with the curse of the bowl dialogue again. There's no reason why I shouldn't have both now is there? Especially with you being so eager to help me as you said."

Judas was mocking Joseph's Galilean tradition. He could discern where he was from because of his accent and clothing.

"Take it gladly, but I beg you, for the third and final time, let the bowl go. If you knew to whom it belonged you would not dare steal it."

"Galilean, I warned you…"

Then Judas stopped, his curiosity aroused in spite of himself.

"Who does it belong to? A very rich man? The Emperor? If so, I would give my soul to liberate it from that accursed pig tyrant."

Joseph realised he had made a mistake in mentioning ownership. He had rashly used a ploy to appeal to this man's better nature and now he could not divulge further details. He was stuck, but he had been truthful about the warning.

"If I told you who owned it, it would mean nothing to you, and you would probably not believe me anyway. But do believe me when I tell you that you cannot possess that bowl unless it is so ordained."

The carpenter shrugged his massive shoulders and stared impassively at his opponent.

"I weary of your insane babblings. Give me the robe and the money, and then the boy can use that cord around your waist to tie you up. I need to get out of here without you following and making a fuss. Although I suppose it might be easier and quicker to slice a leg off."

Judas had meant this as a deterrent to ensure cooperation from Mark, but it tragically rebounded on him. Stung into action by the thought of injury to his new friend, he twisted through Judas' grip and pushed him away from Joseph. His strength was all the more from the adrenalin pulsing through him because of his righteous anger. He did not have any plan of action in mind, but knew he could not passively watch this thief take all Joseph's possessions and maim either of them.

"No!" he shouted. "Run Joseph! Get out of the room."

Mark's brave action took both adults by surprise. Joseph had no intention of leaving the young man at the mercy of the rogue who was trying to rob them. Nor had he any intention of allowing the precious bowl given to his eldest son to be stolen. Just as Joseph was looking around for something to defend himself with, and about to tell Mark to get out of the way, Judas raised his weapon terrifyingly above his head.

The Zealot looked down at Mark with a grim snarl on his face. There was only a fraction of a moment before that sharp metal would implement its owner's brutal intent. Only a moment before the blade would carve through this wretched boy trying to foil Judas' plans. Joseph saw the image and could almost feel the consequences. He saw everything as if it was in slow motion, like a fly before the fall of the swat. Despite this he also received the realisation that he would be too late to intervene. His own power would not be enough.

Yet even as the sword began its descent, help arrived from the most unexpected source. Judas seemed to freeze. His arm stayed where it was and he emitted a strange choking sound. An odd looking brown mist seemed to come from the gold bowl, and swirled around his face. As it gathered momentum it looked like Judas was covered by a whirlwind. His whole body was now encompassed by this personal silent cyclone, which was drawing all the breath out of him.

He dropped both the sword and the bowl to vainly try and remove the grip of what felt to him to be an invisible python coiled about him. This action caused the swirling air to cease, but he still appeared transfixed.

Mark stood open mouthed in astonishment. "What is happening to him? What's doing it?" he stuttered.

"No time for explanations now, maybe later. But I counsel you, it would not be wise to speak of this to anyone."

Joseph quickly picked up the two items freed, and placed the bowl back in the bag. In his haste he failed to notice that the stitching on the cloth underneath was coming apart, and this had also been instrumental in the gold getting free when he fell.

With the sword hilt in his right hand, he put his left arm protectively across Mark's chest and gently pushed him back to keep him out of the way. While he was doing this, another person burst into the room.

In the doorway stood a young Roman soldier, trying to take in the scene. His training prompted him to address the armed man first. He pointed his spear at Joseph and barked out an order.

"Drop that sword and back away towards the wall."

"No, you don't understand. We aren't the robbers, he is!" shouted Mark pointing at Judas, who was still recovering from his trauma.

"How do you know about any robbery?" asked the Roman astutely.

"What? He just tried to rob us. He was going to steal Joseph's robe and…" He hesitated as his companion nudged him. "His money. Yes, his money."

"You don't seem too certain of that."

"My young friend is still shocked at what happened," interjected Joseph, "You will forgive him? He tells the truth. Look we are honest people with nothing but a desire to return to our families in the Court of the Women. Here, take the sword. It is not mine anyway, but that man's."

Joseph turned the weapon and held it by the point. He proffered the hilt to the soldier in an act of submission and continued his explanation.

"We came in here to look for my eldest son who was missing. We heard the horns blowing and knew there must be trouble, without knowing its nature. We still do not know. This man charged through that door and knocked me to the ground and then held me captive at sword point. He said he wanted my robe and my money. I assume he needed to change his apparel to make an escape from you. What has he done?"

"Never you mind. You Judeans could all be in this together for all I know."

The soldier took the sword extended towards him, and tucked it through the belt on his waist.

"If that were true, would I give you the sword when the three of us together could probably overpower you?"

The Roman seemed swayed by the logic, and then turned and asked, "What happened to him? He looks like he has seen the shades of Hades."

"He had the blade pressed to Mark's throat, but Mark bravely pushed him away. Then the man started choking and you came in. He still can't seem to talk."

The soldier nodded, indicating his acceptance of Joseph's story. When that man spoke, people believed him. The aura around him exuded trust.

"I'll look for my colleagues. They should have been behind me. Wait there and do not move while I open this door."

With a puzzled glance at Judas, who still gave the impression of being dazed, he pushed the door ajar and listened for sounds of others to assist him. Hearing nothing, he turned a bit more and gave a quick glance down the passageway.

Judas had recovered more than he made out. He feigned a dazed attitude to buy himself more time to wait for an opportunity to escape. This was it. With amazing quickness he drew his dagger from underneath his clothes. The inexperienced young soldier had assumed that the only weapon was the one on view. Such mistakes cost lives normally. But Mark had also seen the swift movement, and as Judas stated to lunge towards the soldier's back, he shouted a warning.

"Look out, the dagger!"

The Roman turned sharply with his spear. The point pierced Judas straight through the heart as he came forward. He had run on to the tip and invited his own demise by trying to stab the soldier, who now let go of the lance and drew his short sword. A horrible shriek of pain came out of Judas' mouth and his visage was contorted as he grimaced and struggled again for breath like he had done a little while earlier. He dropped down to the floor, clutching the spear embedded in his chest, without the strength to extract it. While kneeling he looked up at Mark and shook his head.

"Traitor," he gasped. "You love Roman dogs more than your own race? May the mark of Cain be on you for this."

All the emotions Mark had experienced in the last two days came to the surface, and joined with the normal angst that early teenagers feel. He exploded into anger. The same anger that had given him the courage to act when they had been threatened.

"You were going to kill him. If I had done nothing, and you succeeded, I would have been a party to that death too. You have nobody to blame but yourself. You would have injured us before if you could, so don't throw 'traitor' jibes at me. Even Romans are human beings. If anyone has betrayed someone, it is you. This is

106

God's Temple, and look at how you acted. You should have tried wise living instead of foolish dying, you…you stupid man."

The man on the ground gave a groan and relaxed. He was dead. Mark was shaking and confused by mixed sentiments. Although Judas had tried to harm him, he did not want to see him die like this, and he knew nothing about the aborted robbery below. His anger was directed at Judas because he had put him in this position.

Joseph came over to him and wrapped a big arm around his shoulder. "Easy, young son. You have done nothing to be ashamed of, no matter what is said."

He turned his gaze to the Roman. "You still believe we are in league with this man?"

"No. It is clear you told the truth. You may go if you wish, while I wait for my comrades. But one thing," he looked at Mark, "why did you shout? We are told that all Judeans hate us, and will do anything to help any rabble fighting against us. Surely it is true what he said?"

He glanced over to the corpse and then back to Mark.

"I acted out of instinct, I suppose. He was no friend to us, but apart from that I umm, do not hate all Romans. I have more in common with you than you might imagine."

The brash, impetuous young man of a few moments ago had given way to an embarrassed youth who now stared shyly at the ground.

"Well, I suppose I have to thank you for the warning. But for you, I might be lying there now instead of him. What are you called, and why do you have something in common with me?"

"My name is Mark, or Marcus if you like."

Then, noticing the slight pressure of Joseph's hand on his shoulder as a caveat, he added, "Forget what I said. It is too complicated and would take too long to explain."

He remembered that Joseph almost certainly knew about his paternity from Mary's relationship with his mother.

"I am Cornelius. Perhaps we shall meet again. I shall tell my friends of your action. It may help them to realise not to believe everything they hear about your tribe."

"And vice versa," smiled Mark.

"You know a little Latin. That is good."

"It is not as good as your Aramaic. Will you tell me now what that man was up to?"

"All I know is that some of us were put on standby to foil an attempt to steal the Temple gold and money. We have caught most of them. He was one of the last."

"What will happen to them?"

"Depends on who deals with them, your Sanhedrin or the Prefect. If it's us, they can look forward to the delights of crucifixion. At least he was spared that."

He indicated Judas.

The boy and the soldier stared at each other. The Roman was possibly only seven years older than Mark, who admired the uniform and felt again that it was his destiny to wear it also. He sensed that certainty burn inside him.

Then he nodded and started to follow Joseph who was beginning to draw away to the exit. No doubt he was impatient to continue the search for his son, or return to his family. In the excitement, Mark had forgotten all about their search. One thing that Mark was certain he would not forget was to ask Joseph about the gold bowl. He had to find out where it came from, and why it apparently had strange powers.

CHAPTER ELEVEN.

Joseph Of Arimathea.

They found Martha and Mary, and the children, still grouped by the wall where they had left them. Jesus was also there. He had tired of talking to the scribes about some words in the books of the prophets, and returned when he heard the commotion following the transgressions below. Mark followed Joseph's advice and kept quiet about all that had transpired since they left the women. There would be time enough tonight to talk over the events. Time enough to decide what needed to be said, and time to revise what did not.

The group walked back through the plazas with a different air than when they had entered, like a climax had been passed. Martha detected a change in her son, who seemed to be both excited and subdued. One moment bubbling exuberantly, and then strangely silent, apparently contemplative. She put it down to the effect of sacrificing for the first time. At least he seemed to have really taken to Joseph. Then she remembered that this was all temporal. A glimpse of what it must be like to live free, and spend time with friends whenever you wanted. Yet, true to her nature, she also knew there was no point in spoiling a good time by dwelling on visions of what might be.

They passed out of the Temple precincts and were about to start the journey through the crowds towards the elite Upper City where Mary was staying with an uncle. Joseph stopped for a moment and looked to the east across the Kidron valley. Dotted all around the slopes of the Mount of Olives were tents. Then he raised his arm and pointed.

"Look, that is where most of the contingent from Nazareth are staying for the Holy days, as do those from elsewhere in Galilee. The Mount of Olives is traditionally our site. Pilgrims from out of town tend to use the same sites to accommodate the overspill from the city, and people from different regions tend to stick together, mostly for safety on their journey."

"At least it makes it easy to find your family if you get lost," said Mark.

"You would think so, wouldn't you? But not so easy at night. To try and find one Nazarene on those slopes at Passover would be a difficult job, in the dark. You would need to know exactly where their camp was; otherwise it would be like looking for a needle, in a pile of needles!"

Joseph laughed loudly at his own joke.

Mark smiled but was thinking about the would be Temple robbers, and where the ones that escaped might be hiding now. He looked up at Joseph. How wise he seemed.

Joseph glanced at Mark and thought he had not understood what he meant, so he explained again. "You would need a friend to show you exactly where another Nazarene's camp was. See?"

"Yes I see, or, if that Nazarene was wanted by the authorities, they would need a traitor to the cause to guide them. It would be an important role if they wanted to arrest someone quietly, wouldn't it?"

It was now Joseph's turn to stare at his young friend, and think how wise he was for his age.

"Yes, that is a good point."

He shook his head, and stroked his beard. He remembered how Mark had questioned the unguarded money receptacles in the Temple, and had been proved right.

"I said so earlier today, and I say it again now. You and Jesus say the most extraordinary things, but they are not without substance. Martha, you have a bright son here, and perceptive too."

Joseph then turned and indicated the tents to Martha, and said that in other years he had stayed there, but though it was enjoyable, at his age he did prefer the unusual luxury of where they were staying now. He had added that no doubt in years to come, and at many future Passovers, his sons at some stage would sit out on that hillside full of olive trees, telling stories of their lives, praying, and reflecting on what roads they had to travel, and pondering choices they had to make.

Then he stopped for a moment, deep in thought, as if struck by a revelation of the future, as though he had spoken in prophecy. They all paused with him, staring out over the view that was the same now as it had been in the time of King David, the conqueror but not founder, of Jerusalem a thousand years earlier, and probably would be for centuries to come. Even Martha and Mark sensed that they had shared in a defining, mysterious moment of this family.

The jostling of the crowd broke their thoughts and they turned back to the west and moved away from the Temple walls. Snatches of conversation, drifting over from passersby, revealed that the afternoon's events were being quickly relayed, and no doubt embellished, by local gossip. Mark was bursting to talk to Joseph, or anybody, about all he had experienced today. There were so many questions unanswered. Where did that gold bowl come from; did it really have special powers? Why did Jesus have it? He could not believe those powers came from him, as although he did seem a bit different, his family seemed quite ordinary. And yet there was that peculiar omen at both their births referred to by his mother yesterday. Maybe one of them really was special, and that is why he had been saved this day from the sword of the potential thief.

Joseph looked completely at ease, as though nothing extraordinary had transpired. Had it all been an illusion, brought on by the awe of the Temple surroundings? Perhaps that was it. The robber had just suffered a self-induced choking fit, and Joseph's suggestion of a curse, although a bluff, had triggered a belief in his mind that something was attacking the man. That was unless this mild mannered carpenter was a lot more than he appeared. Mark had heard about magicians who could do wonderful things. Make sticks turn into snakes; turn a goat into a hen, or disappear in smoke. Was Joseph a sorcerer who could conjure demons to help him? The boy shivered at the prospect, yet could not really believe that any of his new friends were demonic. The people who were involved in those practices usually came from afar anyway.

Persia had men specially trained in the magic arts, and who could read the stars like a map to chart their lives, or so they said. Nobody was ever sure it was accurate his mother had told him, and the information was always vague and could relate to anything or anybody. Those astrologers never ran the risk of being specific. Their trade might suffer if things were too accurately forecast, and then never happened. They had a living to earn after all, and needed to enact whatever charades they used to maintain their worth to the monarch of the day.

Yet there were other more scientific men, who worshipped a strange god called Zarathustra, like The Persian they had met

111

yesterday in the market. Mark had heard one of Haaman's friends talk of these Magi whilst he was serving at one of the many dinner parties his master held, mostly for business purposes. They were like priests but also knew the ancient arts, those long forgotten practices that had been outlawed in Israel since when Moses led the people out of the Sinai wilderness. Despite this, legends abounded of magic acts being performed by clandestine cults who still survived, and prospered when the population's monotheistic faith was either not to the taste of the alleged intelligentsia, or academically unfashionable.

Mark recalled from his lessons, that the Book of the prophet Samuel recorded the infamous meeting between King Saul, the precursor of David, and the Witch of Endor. Even though the King had banned all use of mediums and fortune tellers in the land, he disguised himself and asked that woman to conjure the spirit of the dead prophet Samuel to help him know how to deal with the invading Philistine army. It is stated that she only did so at his specific order. The woman saw a spirit rising up from the earth, like an old man wearing a cloak, and had screamed when she realised that it really was Samuel. The prophet was none too pleased at the disturbance to his rest and had little comfort for Saul. He told him he would be joining him the next day after enjoying death at the hands of the Philistines.

All this came to pass, and seemed to be proof to Mark that often supernatural forces were at work, even if people in general were unaware of such happenings. That is why he preferred the Pharisaic view that there was resurrection after death, against that of the Sadducees who had no such belief. His teacher had employed a terrible pun to help him remember the difference by commenting about them, "That is why they are sad, you see!" and Mark had groaned, smiled politely, and wondered how many times that joke had been utilised over generations.

He had no problem in believing about resurrection. To him it simply mirrored an everyday concept. When you went to sleep at night, and woke in the morning, you had no idea of what had happened in between, or how much time had passed, unless you checked with somebody. Mark considered resurrection to be the same. You went to sleep, or died, and woke at some predetermined time when summoned by Yahweh. How long the interval had been in between was irrelevant when dealing with things immortal. But how long was immortal? Would a dragonfly, which only lived one day, consider a human life was immortal? These depths could not be plumbed by mortal reasoning. After all, what the pupae calls death, the moth calls life, so his rabbi had told him. The bulb "dies" in the soil, yet comes alive in the Spring transformed into something more wonderful.

Mark decided that it had not been an illusion, and that he had witnessed something incomprehensible in the Temple, but exactly what he did not yet know. He was also sure Joseph did know, and that knowledge would be extracted from him this evening at the Seder meal.

As they walked, James and Jesus spoke to Mark about the difference in city life to what they were used to back in their own village. The architectural transformation over the last century, mostly by Herod, was all the more astonishing to people from rural backwaters like Nazareth. The ancient marketplaces, great city gates, the swarms of visitors, all gave testimony to the history of the Chosen People's chosen city. The legacy of a pageant that had flowed from Abraham, through the great prophets, and Kings like David and Solomon; into the Holy City, and still coursed through the veins of the now kingless inhabitants as they spilled out of her Temple into the arterial narrow streets with clusters of houses; and into tents erected on the plains surrounding Jerusalem's tired walls, who could no longer contain the pressure caused by festival crowds. The first pangs of labour were there to be seen in her swollen insides. It would not be long before she gave birth to a new breed of Judean. One that would follow the Son as well as the Father. In so doing, she would finally lose her hold on her defences, and surrender herself to an invader that even now was pricking at her flesh. Her powerful heart, the Temple, would suffer an attack; break, and become a shell, and then a husk, until the winds of centuries blew it as flat as the mighty shadow it now cast.

Yet this was meant to be the Eternal City. How could a city live without its heart? It would be just a ghost. The answer was that a ghost would keep it alive, but one so Holy that nothing could ever destroy it again. For what has risen from the dead, cannot once more be killed. Some sixty years later, it would enable a man called John to write an apocalyptic description of a new Jerusalem in the future. This would complete the cycle of man, that began with Adam living in a garden, communing with animals and all nature, and would end with a new Adam living eternally in a golden city. The beautifully rural, transformed into the majestically urban.

Although they did not know it, the young men walking and talking so excitedly about the differences between rustic and urban life, were drawing a parallel with the words of the past and future prophets. But bearing in mind the company they were keeping, this was not really surprising.

There were a group of people ahead that were waving branches with green leaves. They were shouting "Save us now", or in the local dialect, "Hosanna". The cry did not seem to be directed at anybody in particular and hardly anybody took much notice, except for Mark and Jesus. Each stared at the group for different reasons. Mark because he was thinking about what had happened that afternoon, and Jesus out of compassion. It was customary at religious festivals for keen types to cut down branches (usually from other people's trees) or get palm fronds, and to shout quotes from the psalms of David. As always they anticipated their "Anointed One", translated as "Christ" in Greek, and "Messiah" in Hebrew, and as always they were disappointed. Mark considered it was particularly brave to make such a demonstration now in view of what the Romans might think, and the fact that they would certainly be edgy after the skirmish in the Temple.

Then another cry rose above the "Hosannas". A different, almost plaintiff appeal. It was a pomegranate seller. Immediately James beseeched his mother, and then his father, for a pomegranate. He knew that on special days, Holy Days, when they made the long journey, his parents would often buy the children a treat. His faith was not displaced. Joseph generously bought everyone with him one of the fruits. The next half-mile of their walk was mainly in silence, with only occasional sucking noises erupting from red coloured mouths coated with juice.

If they were fairly silent, there was one bystander who was not only silent but also motionless. In the hubbub of the noisy street he observed the passing party impassively and recalled two faces he had first observed on a majestic visit to a little town many years ago. The three adults he recognised immediately, but the children he did not, except for Mark. If Mark had turned his head to the side and slightly backwards he would have seen the Persian watching him. The same man he had encountered in the market place yesterday.

Then a smile passed across the wrinkled ingrained face, as though he had made a connection at last with a thought that had troubled him for some while. Yes, he seemed pleased at that revelation. The smile gave way to a gesture of satisfaction as he turned and slipped silently back through the crowd. Though if someone listened very carefully and closely they might have heard him mumbling to himself, "At last…At last it is clear."

Mark's friends followed the crooked spine of the road heading out of the tumult. They passed the High Priest's palace on the slope of the hill, and made their way gradually towards the affluent, residential part of town.

When they came to the destination house, Martha and Mark were surprised on two accounts. Firstly that it was so opulent, and secondly that they had never noticed it before, despite Haaman's house not being that far away.

Still, Martha reasoned that her excursions to the markets never provided any real opportunity for dallying in this rich neighbourhood, even if she had the desire to do so, which she hadn't.

As they walked through the courtyard it was evident that the owner was not only richer than Haaman, but also had better taste. It was what her friend Lazarus would call magnificent understatement. Standing in an archway was a well-dressed man in a clean white robe. Not only were his clothes spotless but so also were his hands and face. They fairly shone, and headlined the disclosure that this was not a man who had to suffer the indignities of manual labour any longer. This was indeed a wealthy man; and a studious man of great intellect and dignity. It was the man who Haaman tried to emulate…Joseph of Arimathea. (His name meant "heights", referring to an area ten miles northeast of Lydda).

"Ah welcome back. I see you have found some friends," he said as he approached Mary and Joseph.

His voice was mellow and smooth as befitted his reputation as an eloquent talker. Indeed, in some quarters he was regarded as a distinguished orator, and one who would someday grace the Sanhedrin with his abilities. At thirty he was only a few years older than his niece-in-law Mary, but quite a lot younger than her husband Joseph.

"Noble Joseph," said Mary in a mock ingratiation.

"My dearest niece?" he replied in similar vein and raising his eyebrows expectantly at what request would surely follow.

"This is Martha and her son Mark. They are old friends of ours. Well they are not old actually, but we became friends in Bethlehem. You remember?"

She nodded her head as if to enforce the memory on him and obtain agreement.

Joseph looked puzzled and then exclaimed recognition. "Ah yes. The girl you left behind and agonised over so much."

Mary looked embarrassed.

"Yes. Well, she and Mark have a few days free in Jerusalem but nowhere to stay. I said…"

"That is fine," interrupted Joseph, anticipating her words. "We have room, and it is nice to meet any friends of yours."

He smiled at Martha and Mark.

"Thank you sir," said Martha, "but I feel you should know that my son and I are slaves to Haaman. We are not on equal footing with Joseph and Mary and would not want to cause you any embarrassment."

Arimathea looked at her and smiled gently.

"Your concern and honesty do you credit, but how could I possibly be embarrassed by anyone Mary brings to my house. She is an excellent judge of character, but even without her gift, I can see for myself that I would be happy to know you and Mark."

"Thank you sir. Your reputation as a just and noble man is not exaggerated."

The host laughed. "And you, Martha, will get a reputation as a flatterer if you continue in that vein. However, if we are to be friends, and I believe we shall be, you must call me Joseph and not 'Sir'. Agreed?"

Martha smiled and nodded.

Joseph the carpenter took off his sandal, and placed his foot on the brace in the centre of a large stone foot basin resting on the ground near a doorway. As was the custom, a servant came and poured water over the foot, bathed it, and then the other. Mary declined an invitation to do likewise, saying that they had not walked that far. Martha and Mark stood back, feeling uncomfortable, because they were slaves themselves, and were not sure of the protocol. Arimathea smiled and signified that it was in order for them to avail themselves of the facility by gesturing towards the basin. Martha took her cue from Mary and declined, but Mark whipped off his sandal and put his foot down firmly on the stone bar in the middle. He had often had to do this for Haaman's guests, and this was his chance to taste the opposite experience.

"Now then", Arimathea continued, "it is time to get our meal prepared. I see you have the lamb Joseph. I made a special sacrifice earlier today so there will be plenty of meat for the whole household. We can give the rest to the beggars and our less fortunate brothers outside. My servants are at your disposal, and you, Martha, must tell me your story while we eat."

Martha looked in admiration at this man. He truly was a majestic person. She could imagine him being a king, such was his charisma, and she knew even on such short acquaintance that he could be trusted entirely. Honesty exuded from him, rather like his namesake who was now shepherding Mary and the children across the courtyard to their room. What was it about these people that made you want to be with them she wondered? Then she recognised the word that had been floating around the periphery of her mind. It was purity. There seemed to be a purity of their souls. The world with all its meanness, trickery, cynicism and selfishness had not adulterated them. They appeared as pure as the day of their birth. They were in the world but not of the world. How was that possible?

She knew for certain that Mary and Joseph had been through troubled times and she had heard stories of early misfortunes that had almost ruined the other Joseph. Yes despite all of that they seemed unaltered and at peace. It was also clearly reflected in the children, particularly Jesus who seemed so much in control despite his youth. She knew she would have to face telling the truth to these strangers, without embellishment. Normally this would have frightened her, but not today. After years of confiding in nobody, she now felt she was among friends at last. Some hope had come into her life.

Similarly, Mark was giving full vent to his imagination. He knew he was with people who were not only honest and kind, but also of some influence. He cherished a hope that Arimathea might buy him and his mother from Haaman, so he would be able to see Joseph the carpenter and his sons more often. Also, Mark thought that if that happened, he would stand more chance of being free, and even joining the Roman Army when he was of age. However, he was shrewd enough to not say any of this aloud, particularly the last bit.

For now he had some other issues to resolve. Why did Joseph the carpenter have a mysterious gold bowl?

CHAPTER TWELVE.

The Seder Meal, And More Revelations.

A few hours later they were all gathered around the low table, in an upper room, reclining on cushions on the floor or couches, as was the custom of the Romans, and which had been adopted by the Israelites. Joseph, as host, was lying on his side with his left arm propped under a cushion. In front of him was placed the Seder (or service) place on which the traditional symbolic foods were carefully laid out. There were three wafers of matzo (unleavened) bread wrapped in a napkin; the bitter herbs, the haroset or fruit pulp, the roasted lamb and hard-boiled egg. Additionally there were sweet vegetables and a dish of salt water for washing hands. Every participant had a wine cup.

Joseph was joined at the table by his three children; his wife having died a year ago. Justus and Anna watched while Joseph's youngest son, Josephes, began the "Four Questions".

"Why is this night of Passover different from all other nights of the year?"

His father began to recite the story of Israel's captivity in Egypt and the journey from slavery to freedom. In this way Joseph answered the questions, which also concerned queries about the unleavened bread, the bitter herbs, the dipping of vegetables, and even the cushions at the host's seat.

After the meal, while the servants were clearing away the remains and the children went off, Joseph turned to Martha and said, "You were going to tell me how you escaped from Bethlehem. I know most of your history before that from Mary."

"There is not much to tell really. When Mary left suddenly I did wonder what she meant the last time I spoke to her. All that talk about Bethlehem being a bad place for her family and mine, and the dreams she had, giving warnings. I still often wonder how you knew what would happen."

She turned her head to her friend, but Mary just smiled and made no comment. "Anyway I couldn't stop thinking about your advice to leave, but the thought of starting over yet again somewhere

119

else did not appeal to me. You never told me why it would be bad to stay, so I carried on as normal for a few days until an event which made me decide to try and follow you. I had been having trouble sleeping. The thought of your words would not leave me, like a light that couldn't be shut out."

Martha paused, and took a sip of wine.

"The seventh day after you left I was walking through the market with little Mark in a sling on my back. I was looking idly at some pottery when I saw *him* out of the corner of my eye, Zephas the Greek; trader in anything. I was not sure whether he had seen me or not, so I drew back behind a flap of a tent and listened. His unmistakably voice carried on the wind and I could hear his spiel. He was starting into his attract mode to gather customers around his makeshift stall. I decided that he had not seen me and started to move away. Unfortunately for me I caught the sling on a rope and it pulled part of the awning down. It wasn't much of a movement, but with Zephas looking around for customers it caught his attention. I froze when he called after me. He repeated my name three times and begged me to come and look at his wares. I used to talk to him a lot and get things for my father when we were back in Reena. He knew my history and me well. I could not think clearly for the fear that was rising from the pit of my stomach into my dry mouth. If he started talking about my family, my charade of being a widow would be exposed. He was always a loud mouth and would almost certainly start asking awkward questions about Mark and my alleged dead husband. I was so scared of being stoned as a traitor and harlot. You know how people are."

She looked round at the faces of her friends. There was no hint of judgemental expression found in any of them.

"Go on," said Arimathea softly.

"I walked on pretending that I had not heard him. I did fear he might follow me, but gambled that he would not want to leave his goods unattended. Providentially he decided that they, and a few potential customers, were more important than chasing after a girl he thought he knew."

She paused again.

"When I got back to my rented hut, you could hardly call it a house, I was very shaken and considered the consequences if Zephas came looking for me or making enquiries and putting doubts in peoples' minds. It was, still is, a very small town as you know, and I couldn't hide away forever. Anyway, I had my work to do. Washing clothes remember, Mary? Everybody usually wanted the garments returned the same day, unless, they were reasonably well off and had more than two tunics or robes. Even debtors were allowed their cloaks back for the night if they had pledged it for a debt. The law stipulates that; and people would often quote that requirement a great deal to put pressure on me to get everything done the same day. Life is never easy, is it?

Martha looked over at Mary.

"As I said before your words wouldn't leave my head and I thought that the revelation of my past by Zephas must have been what you meant. I made up my mind to leave early the next morning without telling anybody. So I finished the clothes I had to wash and returned them that night. An hour or two before dawn I put the few possessions I had in a sling with Mark and walked the north-east road out of Bethlehem that I thought you and Joseph had taken. I assumed you had gone towards Jerusalem, and I had visions of catching you eventually. I know now that you went south to Egypt. Silly really I suppose, but as it turned out it saved Mark's life, and probably mine. I can still picture Herod's bodyguard sweeping past us, as we hid by a rock. Their leather armour was as black as night, and as the deed they were about to undertake. I had no husband to support me and I just did not know what to do. Jerusalem seemed to be a good idea, as I didn't think I would ever find you. When I got there, it was difficult to find any work while looking after Mark. Washing clothes was mostly undertaken by big employers with slaves. Nobody knew me and I couldn't pay for someone to look after Mark while I worked, because the pay wasn't enough from an employer. So, I thought it best to become slaves so we could eat."

Martha stopped talking and shook her head. Mary rose and came over to her, placing an arm around her shoulders.

"What a tale you have to tell; and what a lot of incident has been packed into your short life," murmured Arimathea.

Then noticing one of his female servants standing idly at the back of the room, he said sharply, "If you have finished your work you may go to your quarters. Don't dawdle around here."

The servant turned away in embarrassment and left, but was secretly very pleased with herself. She would covertly try and catch further pieces of conversation. Knowing this information might be useful to her friend Jehua. Also, knowing that Martha worked for Haaman and Esherah could prove profitable when the time, and price, were right.

"Enough about me. Tell me Joseph, where did you and Mary go? At the Temple today, she said something about Egypt."

Martha smiled at the carpenter sitting quietly, apparently thinking deeply about something.

"Oh we went to Egypt. We stayed there for a few years. It was never our intention to stay forever. When Herod died, we returned to Galilee."

"Because you felt it was safe then?" asked Martha.

"Yes. We were led to do so."

Martha looked at Joseph and Mary; half expecting an explanation of that statement, but at the same time almost knowing none would be forthcoming. She was getting used to the way they sometimes talked in riddles. In any event, deep inside she knew what they meant, and who led and guided them in all things. These were special people and extraordinary things happened to them, and the people that knew them come to that.

"So what was Egypt like?"

"Well, there is more of everything down there. They regard themselves as more superior to us because of their culture, wealth, and philosophy. We weren't much impressed with their religion though, were we Mary?"

His wife shook her head in agreement.

"There is no love in the gods they worship. All the people think about is appeasing their idols to prevent some destruction or other falling upon them. Basic superstition really. As I am a builder and carpenter, I was asked to help refurbish the temple at Luxor. I declined, of course, as it would defile me to work on a pagan temple. However, I had to admire the sheer artistry and splendour of the building. All three of us used to look at the place in the evening, when torches combined with the sunset to make it so very attractive. We were tempted to explore it fully, but never did. I don't suppose Jesus remembers much about it now, although his little eyes did fix on it a lot. Those tall sculptured pillars and columns will last centuries. Yes, you had to admire the craftsmanship, if not the sentiment."

As Joseph said all this, it was evident that his mind was elsewhere. There was silence for a moment, and then, just as Martha was about to speak, Joseph made another sudden statement.

"Look, er Martha, you do realise that we had to leave Bethlehem when we did. I know you were upset at being alone again, but well we just had to go. We felt bad about it but somehow knew you would be alright."

"Yes I know. You explained at the time that you felt you were being called elsewhere. I was a little angry for a while, especially as you would not take me with you, but as it turned out Mary's warning about leaving the town was accurate, even if for a different reason. You knew didn't you, that the children would be attacked?"

Joseph and Mary looked at each other.

Mary replied, "Yes, we knew something bad was going to happen, but not exactly what form it would take. We couldn't say anything though, because I was told not to in a dream."

"And you trust your dreams?"

"Yes...when they are special ones."

"From God you mean?"

"Yes."

"Is that why your eldest son and I are special?" interjected Mark.

"Mark!" said Martha sharply.

"No it is good that he can speak now" said Joseph. "What do you mean Mark?"

"Only what mother told me yesterday. That we were born under a special star and Herod thought one of us was a rival to his throne. I wonder when it will happen, though. Neither of us, at the moment, look as though we are going to be kings, do we?"

"Who knows young man," laughed Joseph. "Yet I believe you are right. You have a sensible head on that young frame. I agree that our son is not going to be a king in the sense you mean, but as for you, it is still not too late to be anything you want to be."

"As a slave?"

"Slaves can be set free, Mark. Remember that," said the carpenter.

"But something is different about Jesus isn't it?" continued Mark. "He has gold, special gold. How did he get it?"

Mark had been longing to force this topic.

123

Joseph sighed and looked around the room. Martha looked perplexed, and Mary, the children and Arimathea were clearly curious. He knew he was going to have to divulge what happened in the Temple that afternoon, and that Mark would persist until his curiosity was sated.

"The reason Mark mentioned gold was because of an incident this afternoon. I will tell you all what happened but, and children note this especially, you must not talk of it outside these walls."

He considered asking the children to leave but the older ones would get offended and the younger ones would badger it out of their seniors, so to reveal all now and let them think they were part of a big adult secret was probably the best course. Besides, who would believe the tales of young children?

When he had finished the account, Martha gave Mark a hug, and James and Simon looked at him with awe for having been in a real fight where someone got killed. He shrugged off his mother's attentions and said, "Look, I am no hero, I just did what I thought was best at the time."

"But you chose wisely." said Joseph. "Life is all about making wise choices. It is why we were given free will by our creator. It is what differentiates us. I believe we are judged according to the choices we could make, not always by our resultant actions."

Seeing puzzled frowns around him he continued. "I do not mean that gives us a licence to sin. If we choose to hurt others the results can be destructive for everyone. When people make a wrong choice, usually out of selfishness, evil nearly always follows. But to make the wrong choice does not mean we shouldn't have the right to do so. Were that correct, we would be prisoners, God's prisoners, instead of his loved children. God wants us to choose the path of good, so we can get closer to him. That is a far better way than forcing us unwittingly to do what he wants. Every father knows the strife that is caused by ordering children to do something they don't want to do."

He smiled at his own giggling children, while Arimathea nodded in admiration at the wisdom of this man of humble origins now, but who could trace his family line back to King David. Perhaps some of the wisdom of David's son, Solomon, coursed through his veins.

"Just as a human father allows his children to grow and have freedom to choose, so does God. He believes in us. The pity is that not everyone believes in Him. Therefore, Mark, I repeat, you made a wise choice."

The boy shifted uncomfortably in embarrassment and then flashed another question at the man.

"With respect, Joseph, you still haven't explained why the gold is special and how it came into your possession."

Joseph laughed.

"I said this afternoon that you were as persistent as a mule. I was wrong. You have the tenacity of a hunting dog! Once you get your teeth into something you don't let go do you? I'll tell you soon, but for now I need to stretch my legs."

"Yes, let us go up to the roof. It is a clear night and we can watch the sunset finish."

As he said this Arimathea rose and went outside to give orders to his servants. The children were told to go to their room where they could play hopscotch if they wanted, but as Jesus and Mark were now technically adults, being twelve years old, they were allowed to accompany their parents to the roof.

The group made their way out of the upper room, which opened to a view across the inner courtyard below, and crossed to the small stone stairs which led to the roof. This was large and flat with a small balustrade around its edge as required by law to prevent anyone from falling off. The surface was covered with a form of cement that hardened in the sun. If this layer started to crack, then an emergency layer of grass was often laid to keep out rain.

Over in a corner were some small piles of linen and flax left to dry. In their season corn, figs and other fruits would be laid to dry. Joseph loved to come up to his roof as a retreat; where he could meditate and watch the Jerusalem skyline change colour at sunset, or even sunrise in the summer when he sometimes slept there for coolness. It was also a place where private conferences could be held. He suspected that Mary's husband had been concerned about servants listening, and had diplomatically switched the venue where he was going to talk about the gold.

There was a small breeze, but it was not cold. However, Mark shivered with anticipation at the prospect of finally finding out what the golden bowl's secret was.

CHAPTER THIRTEEN.

The Secret of The Gold.

In Joseph of Arimathea's garden were two almond trees and their pink blossoms sweetened the air. They always bloomed early and were sentinels for the changing season of Winter to Spring, which is why the Hebrew name for the tree is *shaked* meaning vigilant. The almond also reflected the enigma of humans. The nuts could be either bitter or sweet. The former made oil, but the latter was used for luxurious desserts. This one type of tree had two very different types of fruit. As Arimathea used to say to his children at the time of his wife's death, "Just like life, so bitter and so sweet."

The late evening sun gave up its struggle with a few clouds, and started to sink somewhere below the soft horizon of blue mountain ridges. As the summer drew nearer, so its fight to survive longer each day would be more successful. A dusky orange hue spread through the sky and small strato-cumulus clouds like small balls of cotton rippled outwards from the fading orb, adding their daubs of blue and grey and purple. Soon the first evening star would appear, but for now the reflected rays from the gold coverings of the Temple flashed in the distance.

Little wooden stools had been brought up from below, and the friends sat around in a circle with their goblets and the rest of the wine from the meal. Mark was anxious to push the conversation onto the origin of the gold again, but was constrained by his desire not to seem impolite. He had the feeling that he would have to prompt Joseph as the man did not appear to be over keen to pursue the topic. Although only knowing Joseph for a short time, he realised there might be a reason for that.

Some people on a neighbouring roof shouted across to Arimathea. This was the way news was exchanged. The neighbour's daughter was expecting a baby. He instructed Arimathea to pass it on to his other neighbours. Such good news quickly spread by shouting from one roof top to another. But other things, more secret things, would not be shouted from rooftops. These would be talked of more quietly, and if the participants felt very clandestine, they would gather only in upper rooms after dark.

Mary's husband was still thinking about the Zealot band and their families. There would be no shouting on their roofs this evening, only sobbing and whispers of mortality, while fear would taste even more bitter in their mouths than the herbs of their Passover meal.

Mary knew from Joseph's silence what he was thinking about. She had always admired his compassion, which had been so ably demonstrated when she had found out she was pregnant. Not many men would have taken so much trouble to protect her reputation, let alone believe she was still a virgin. She stood near him as he sat on a stool, and massaged his broad shoulders.

"What's this for?" he asked a little lazily, not wishing her to break her rhythm.

"For being so remarkable, yet not knowing it. You are thinking about the captured Zealot's families aren't you?"

"Yes I am. How well you know me. I wouldn't say I was remarkable. Just so very, very fortunate to have a wife like you."

"Well aren't we both a fortunate pair?" laughed Mary.

Joseph looked over to the others, who were busy with a game of "which hand is it in". He lowered his voice and said, "We are going to have to do something about Martha and Mark aren't we?"

"Yes I know, but how?" We cannot afford to redeem them. Perhaps if I asked my kinsman…"

Joseph shook his head before she finished.

"Let us not do that yet. He gives so much to us, it is not fair to place another burden upon him. I have an idea that Jesus may help."

Mary cupped Joseph's face and turned it towards her.

"You are not going to make him use his special gifts by talking to Haaman?"

"No nothing like that. As if I would. No, it is just that this afternoon I heard Mark make a little prayer in the Temple. He asked to be set free, and as he did so the gold bowl under my tunic came to mind. I think we should ask Jesus whether he will help, but we already know the answer to that don't we?"

"Yes. It's a good idea but surely the bowl is worth more than the cost of two slaves?"

127

"Umm, it is, but we can probably work something out with Haaman. Any difference can be made up in coin and given back to Jesus. We'll have a think about it and talk to him later."

Martha came over to them.

"I don't think Mark can contain himself any longer. He is almost bursting to hear about that gold bowl or vase, and I must confess, so am I."

The faint beams from the first star became visible and Arimathea brought shawls for the women to wrap around them, and lit a torch in its holder. Similar torches danced across the tops of other houses in the distance. Shadows competed with the fading twilight in making patterns on the roof surface, and six silhouettes deepened with the dark and drew their stools in a tighter circle.

Joseph looked straight at Mark.

"Enough already. You have been patient but I fear that the realisation of the story will not match your anticipation. You will remember Martha, that when we were in Bethlehem some visitors came to see us? Well, they brought some gifts for our baby son. They had come a long way."

Martha frowned as she searched her mind.

"Yes I remember now. There were five of them, but with their servants and baggage train they caused quite a stir in a little place like Bethlehem. You never talked about it to anyone though. Just kept saying they were visitors. Why so secret?"

"It had to be so. Even now I am not prepared to talk about why they came, only about what they brought."

"If that's what you desire, so be it. However, I did hear talk that their visit was what sparked Herod off on that killing spree."

"The children? Yes, it probably was. This is very difficult to explain Martha."

Joseph ran his hand over his furrowed forehead, as though seeking inspiration.

"There are some things that Mary and I cannot speak about. We cannot even say why that is so, but you must have come to some conclusions yourself in view of certain events. If you have, I beg you not to pass on such comments to anybody, and none of you must ask us questions about Bethlehem, Egypt or why the gifts were given to Jesus. I know that will be especially hard for you Mark, with your inquisitive nature. Yet I also know that you are a trustworthy young man and will comply with my wishes. My good friend Arimathea here does know something of our past, and he has had to trust us that when it is possible, all things will be revealed. That time is not yet."

"It is all to do with this "king" thing isn't it?" Mark had to ask at least one question. "If I'm not going to be a king, it *must* be Jesus," he said.

Martha looked disapprovingly at her son for doing the very thing he had been told not to do. Joseph smiled and held up his hand so she did not admonish him.

"Has it occurred to you Mark," he continued, "that neither of you will be King as you call it. That the rumours started in Herod's Palace at the advent of the visitors might have been the misinterpretation of ancient writings and signs in the sky?"

"Hmm, alright, but if that is true why the secrecy about Jesus?"

"Mark!" shouted Martha. "Don't keep on so. Do you not fear God?"

They all looked at her. Jesus, who had been sitting quietly listening to all the debate about himself suddenly raised his head and looked at the woman. He told her not to worry, and also invited Mark to be at peace. He commended Martha for her insight in realising that Joseph and Mary were carrying out God's instructions. Then he gave them both such a loving look, that both felt unable to say anything more. He lowered his head and idly started to draw patterns with his finger in the fabric of his tunic.

Joseph felt he could continue with his story. There was no tension in the group, only attention in their faces.

"Those visitors from Persia. They were very wise in many things, but misguided in my opinion, about religion. They worship one God, Zoroaster, or Zarathustra as some call him. Just a shame it is not the right one."

The scales fell from Martha's eyes. She remembered where she had seen the Persian she had met in the market place. Her expression was picked up by Mary.

"What is wrong Martha?"

"Nothing. I think I saw one of your visitors yesterday, in the market. In fact, I am sure I did. He spoke most mysteriously and I could not remember where I had seen him before. Now I do."

"Strange," said Joseph. "I wonder why he is here?"

"Perhaps he has come to visit us, or give me a gift this time." laughed Mark.

Joseph and his namesake exchanged glances.

"He was here to sell merchandise, and was part of a big caravan," said Martha. They had brought a lot of Arabian frankincense. He did say he was originally from Persepolis. Said something about hoping I found freedom, which I thought was extraordinary considering he did not know my position."

This time Mary and Joseph exchanged glances.

"It does not surprise me," said the carpenter. "He and his kind know secrets which amaze ordinary folk. That is why they are called Magi. They determine things about the world, science, even the stars. People who try to emulate their powers call themselves magicians, but they are not of the same calibre. The Magi do not amass knowledge for profit, only pleasure. It is said that some of these Zarathustrans have ancient manuscripts copied from the Great Library in Alexandria. Secrets from ages past, learned when man was not so wrapped up in material things, have been passed down through their generations. They tell no-one outside their own mystic order."

Joseph sipped his wine.

"Anyway, they came in their silks, smelling of exotic spices and brightening dreary Bethlehem for a while. They said they had been following an 'event'. Yes that's what they called it, an event in the sky. We all thought it was a star."

Martha nodded.

"Their charts had shown them that this was no ordinary star. We all know that when a hairy-tailed star comes, it is often a precursor of something bad. I must admit I do not believe all that superstitions stuff, but sometimes deaths of rulers, or of political people do occur after a comet has passed. Why? Who knows? What is a comet anyway? We know so much, and so little. We need eyes that can enlarge these objects; bring them nearer so we can see what they are made of. The heavens are a mystery, but thank God for the stars. Without them we could not travel by night. Certainly not at sea."

"Yes, Joseph. I often look up at the stars wondering what they are. My mother thought they were angels," giggled Martha.

The wine was having an effect. She was not used to such strong wine. This was real wine, for savouring, not swilling down when thirsty during the day.

"They are not angels, Martha. That I do know. But as in everything, if you look at the world through the eyes of faith, you see faith in action. If you do not have the eyes of faith, you never see it in action. You never see the miraculous or the divine, only the coincidental and mundane. I am comfortable with mystery. To have faith is to do this."

He sighed.

"But I digress. Any intellectual discussion of faith is immediately redundant. It is what you cannot prove, the unseen, the unknown, the taking a chance; it is…well almost, a gift. Which brings me back to the issue at hand. One of the gifts of the Magi was the gold bowl. The others were frankincense and myrrh. They were symbolic. Frankincense indicated priest-ship, and myrrh humanity, the embalmment in death. The gold symbolised kingship, which is probably where all this king stuff started once Herod heard about it. He was mistaken; so were the Magi. Kingship as you understand it is not involved, but that is another topic… and one not for discussion."

He grinned at Mark, and then continued.

"So they had noted this event in the heavens, checked their charts, made their calculations, and decided that Bethlehem was the place in which a child would be born at a special time. They presented their gifts, and then left as mysteriously as they came. Clearly the journey had not been to their liking, for we heard they took a different direction to return."

"And that is it?" asked Mark.

"Yes that is all. We kept the gifts for Jesus until he was old enough to decide what he wanted to do with them. Mind you, there were times in Egypt when we were very tempted to sell them to raise money. But we didn't."

"But the special powers?" said Mark.

"Oh yes. Well, there is not much I can add to what you already know. The Magi indicated that the gold bowl would protect itself until its destiny was fulfilled. We were not told what that was, only that until that time it would blight the lives of people with evil intent, and help those who used it for good. Rather like it had a purpose;

131

and something, or someone, wanted to make sure it would be used eventually for exactly what it was meant to be."

Joseph stopped, as though in reflection. He looked over at Mary who was nodding, almost imperceptibly, to show she knew what he was thinking. In the silence they heard the tinkling of a leper's bell in the street below.

"He is late, poor soul," said Martha. "He should have made his way to the colony before now."

Her remark was a comment on the fact that lepers were not allowed in the town at night, but had to stay in their colony just outside the city walls.

The conversation dwindled, and the group left the roof for their beds. Mary and Joseph, however, lingered a little longer, deep in discussion with their eldest son. They had a plan.

CHAPTER FOURTEEN.

Temptation and Negotiation.

The next day was bright and clear, as predicted by the previous night's sunset. Martha and Mary spent the day talking and relaxing. It was a pleasant change for them, to be waited on by Arimathea's servants, instead of the hard toil of daily chores. The next two days passed just as pleasantly except Joseph kept disappearing from time to time on undisclosed errands. On this, the third day since the Passover meal, Joseph the carpenter went on yet another errand and secretly arranged to meet Haaman that night.

When night fell, so did the weather. Rain lashed down on Joseph as he made his way to Haaman's house, after leaving the evening meal early. He was a bit perplexed by the sudden change in the weather. The cloth bag containing the gold bowl was looped around his neck, and he had still not noticed the tear in the stitching caused during the fight in the Temple yesterday. The rain noticed it though, and began to loosen the fibres of the cloth. So carefully, so gently were the contents being exposed by the rain, as though acting as an agent. But on whose authority was this work being done? Was it a good or a bad intervention?

None of these things troubled Joseph, who was rehearsing his bargaining with Haaman in his mind. It would need careful speech not to appear too anxious to purchase Martha and Mark's freedom.

Neither did any of these things trouble Lazarus, the beggar, as he made his way back from a reasonable day's work at the Damascus Gate, near the north-east of the city close to the Temple. Both had their heads down and as they walked towards each other around the corner of a dwelling they collided. After the murmured apologies Joseph walked on, but Lazarus stood for a second and noticed a gleam from something in the mud. Stray light from the house bounced off it, even in the darkened environment. It was as though the object would not be immersed in the grip of blackness, but emitted a silent plea, "Here I am, take me". The beggar knelt down and picked it up and gasped. It was a gold bowl unlike any he had seen before.

With a rapidity of thought belying his disabilities, Lazarus calculated where it had come from and the options open to him. He watched the disappearing back of Joseph. This gold object would give him food and clothing more than he had ever known. The temptation was overwhelming, he must keep it. Yet even as his hand felt the smoothness of the metal and its embossed designs, his joy was tempered by another feeling in the pit of his stomach. He might be poor, but he was not a thief. He realised that the man he had bumped into must have dropped it. It was surprisingly light, so it was no wonder it had fallen unnoticed and been received silently by the mud.

He started to walk after Joseph who was striding along in front, hunched against the weather and wrapped in thought. Then hope rose again in Lazarus. Perhaps when he asked the man in front if he had lost anything, the answer would be negative. That would be a wonderful positive for himself. If he was unaware of the owner, he could not return it. He increased his speed and as he did so, his withered arm began to itch. This was strange but did happen from time to time when he got excited. Lazarus brought his right hand across and used the bowl to scratch the itch. In that brief moment he lost sight of the man he was tracking. He started to run, although in his heart he felt like slowing down so that if he lost his quarry, he would have an excuse to keep the gold object.

Trusting to instinct he ran along a small street to the right. It proved to be a correct choice, but also a disappointing one. For Joseph had stopped and was examining the tear in his cloth bag. The beggar knew his tenuous ownership of the gold was over.

"Have you lost something?" said Lazarus as he approached.

"Yes, how did you know?"

Joseph looked very flustered and concerned.

"By your manner. What is it you've lost?"

Lazarus kept the bowl under his sodden robe.

"Something immeasurably valuable to me and my family…a bowl."

Lazarus felt a tingle, but this time not in his arm. He could see the anxiety and sorrow in this man's face and it warmed him to think that his simple action in returning the lost item would be so joyful to this stranger.

"What was it made of……gold?"

134

Lazarus laughed as he made his enquiry. He was asking questions which he didn't really want answered.

"Yes, it was actually," replied Joseph looking him in the eye.

"Well it's a good job for you I picked it up then isn't it?"

As he said this he displayed the bowl in front of him.

Joseph clasped both hands over it and repeated his thanks over and over.

"Look, I do not know how to reward you. I do not have much money with me, and despite what you may think regarding the bowl, I am not a rich man. In fact I am on my way to give this gold to someone else."

Lazarus looked bemused, and had not felt like this for as long as he could remember. He felt satisfied, and warm despite the cold rain. It was more than that though. He felt good about himself. His self respect had returned, and so had the sensation in his bad arm.

So it was not really surprising when he found himself saying, "I do not want your money, though the Lord knows I could do with some. Thank you for making me feel worth something. It is a very long time since someone did that for me. Yet, I suppose there is one person who makes me feel I am a proper man."

He paused, smiling to himself.

"Who is that?" prompted Joseph.

"Oh just a young woman I meet sometimes. Nothing romantic you understand. In fact she is not much better off materially than me, but she treats me as more than just a beggar."

"You're a beggar? I did not know. Not that it would make any difference."

Lazarus looked at Joseph and believed him.

"What is her name, this woman?"

"Martha. She is one of Haaman the metal trader's slaves."

Joseph smiled.

"A slave, yet she treats you so well? Obviously she is rich in spirit. Well, perhaps she will not always be a slave" he said knowingly, resisting the urge to reveal his errand to the beggar. "What is your name? I must know the name of such an honest man."

"Lazarus"

"Well Lazarus, I have a feeling that things will start improving for you soon; and for your friend Martha. My thanks again. I must go."

Having said that Joseph turned and walked hurriedly away, giving Lazarus no time to seek explanation of this comment. The rain soaked beggar stood watching him, puzzling over what this stranger meant. He had not even learnt the man's name. Then he turned and as he began to walk in the opposite direction, the sensation in his left arm grew stronger. It grew so much that he had to stop and grasp it with his right hand. He could not believe the sensation. More than this, he looked in amazement as first one then all his fingers gradually uncurled from the limp, useless state that they occupied normally. He rubbed them and realised he could flex them himself, like he could with his good hand. His withered arm was starting to come to life. After a few minutes the restoration of his hand and arm was complete. He could not understand what had happened. Was this some magic of the stranger? He could not believe that was so.

As he thought over the events that had transpired, he realized that the process had started when he picked up the gold bowl, and made the decision to return it. He remembered rubbing it on his arm to scratch the itch. This might be God's reward for his honest action, or the gold was enchanted; or both. If he saw that stranger again he would enquire. But for now, he did not care.

He leapt up and punched the air with his now healthy left arm. It felt so strange using it. As he ran back along the road to the tent he shared with other beggars, thoughts flashed through his mind. This meant he could work. What would he do? Would it pay more than begging? Most of all, what would Martha say?

Joseph, meanwhile had found Haaman's house again and knocked on the outer gate. The same servant as before showed him into an empty room and offered him a cloth to dry his face and head. The servant left to find his master who was engaged in a fierce conversation with Esherah. Their son Pheras had learned about the money given to Martha by Haaman to purchase a lamb. Mark had told Lois, whom he liked, and she inadvertently had let it slip to her brother. He hated Mark and would use any excuse to get him and Martha into trouble, so he told his mother. Esherah was now confronting her husband about the payment.

"You really expect me to believe that you gave her the money in a moment of weakness? In a fit of generosity? I always knew you had feelings for her and now it is confirmed. You tell me that money

136

for housekeeping is a bit short at the moment, but throw it away on that common girl, hoping to entice her into bed no doubt. Well, was she worth it? You might just as well have picked up a whore in the street!"

There was no subtlety in her words. This time sheer jealousy had given way to angry comment.

Haaman's eyes blazed. His chin lifted imperiously. His words were charged with lightning.

"Silence! You presume too much, woman. Have a care with your tongue, or I will have it bridled so you make your jealous jibes no more. I grow tired of your relentless insinuations, and you trying to change me into something you want, or criticising the way I do things. If you wanted me to be different, to be like you desire, you should have married yourself! I am my own man, and you have not done too badly out of it, have you?"

Esherah hesitated. She had to be careful she did not cut off a finger to spite a hand. Especially a hand that provided relative luxury. Her old fear of poverty revisited her mind. It was an unwelcome and infrequent guest these days, but an old acquaintance, nevertheless, that just would not sever ties. She was spared any humiliation by her failing to respond to her husband, through the servant's announcement of Joseph's presence.

Still glaring fiercely, but inwardly pleased to see he had scored a point against his wife, Haaman walked out of the room to meet his visitor. He had not had time to talk to this man earlier that day, but had promised to talk with him now because of the mention of "something to his advantage".

"Peace be with you, Haaman. How gracious of you to see me."

Joseph made a slight bow from the waist as the Syrian entered the room.

Haaman nodded and waved his hand impatiently.

"Yes, yes. What can I do for you? Or, more importantly, what can you do for me?"

A slight grin extinguished the fiery expression of before.

Joseph was not deceived by the delayed attempt at politeness.

"If this is not a convenient time for you, I can return tomorrow."

He did not want to negotiate in a hostile atmosphere. The freedom of two people was at risk here.

"No it's fine. I…I just had something in my household to sort out. You know how these things are."

Joseph thought it wiser to make no comment, but he smiled, waiting for his host to relax.

"You do a good deed," Haaman continued, "and people criticise your motives. Huh! What a world! What… a…world," he said more slowly to enhance the point. "I'm sorry. I did not mean to be off hand with you, er Joseph. I am normally far more polite to my guests."

"So I have heard".

Haaman lifted his head slightly, anticipating a compliment. He was not disappointed. "Your hospitality is famed all over Jerusalem."

"Really? Er, forgive me, I know your name but nothing about you. How have you heard about me?"

The Syrian was hooked.

"Through my wife's cousin, also called Joseph. He comes from Arimathea. You know of him no doubt?"

"Yes indeed".

Haaman began to think quickly. If this man before him, seemingly of humble origins, knew Arimathea the number one businessman in Jerusalem, maybe even Judea, then there might certainly be business opportunities here. If he treated this Joseph kindly, the other one might become more friendly. If the two of them could form some sort of partnership, they could control nearly all of the metal trading in the country. Up to now, Arimathea had never seemed to have time for him. All those "ifs" could be made certainties, considered Haaman.

"I am flattered," he said with mock modesty. "If so eminent a man as Joseph of Arimathea has noticed my small entertainments, it is reward in itself. Although, it is a pity that he has never attended in person. So many things compete for his time, it appears."

Joseph smiled to himself, and thought that this foreigner had a lot to learn about devout Hebrews. Arimathea in fact considered Haaman might be rich, but morally bankrupt, and would not readily associate with his type, especially as he was a gentile. The carpenter himself was risking public scorn in entering a gentile's home, but it was a necessary risk.

"Sit down please".

138

Haaman beckoned to a large cushion on the floor, and stooped to recline on a couch. "Would you like something to eat or drink?"

Joseph shook his head. "A while later, perhaps."

He wondered if Haaman was being clever. It was the custom of the time that once you had shared a person's food, under their roof, you could no longer be enemies, but were bound together in that quaint Eastern way of the era.

"So then?" Haaman looked enquiringly at Joseph. "I can see from your robe you come from Nazareth. Don't tell me, you are a carpenter, even though you do not wear the symbol of wood in your ear."

He laughed.

"Everyone knows Nazareth is full of carpenters."

"Well, yes I am actually. We do not wear the wooden chip on Holy days though, and this is still the week of Passover."

"Yes of course. Are you offering to make me something? The lid on that chest over there needs altering. It has come out of alignment."

Seeing the frown on Joseph's brow, he swiftly changed verbal direction.

"I am jesting. Tell me plainly, what do you want?"

"I have something that will interest a discerning person like you."

Joseph withdrew the gold bowl, and rubbed it on his cloak to remove a small piece of mud.

The light from the torches on the wall flickered around the exquisite object. It had two small handles either side of the shallow bowl, which rested on a short thick stem, with a wider circular piece of gold for the base. Embossed in a circle around the middle were grapes on a vine, just like the huge design in the Temple sanctuary. The gold was without imperfection, and soft. It could almost be described as a goblet if the handles had not been attached. The base had strange words inscribed, in a language neither Haaman or Joseph could understand. It also had the seal of Solomon, the two overlapping triangles forming a star, cut into the bottom; although this looked as though it had been added later.

The Syrian desired it immediately, and even though he fought to keep that desire under control, he was unable to conceal the fact.

His dilated pupils and the excitement in his face betrayed the nonchalant manner he tried to adopt.

"Hmm, that is a nice piece of metal work. I cannot deny that. Not the best I've seen in gold, of course," he lied, "but good nevertheless."

Joseph reached over and placed it in the hand proffered to him. Haaman examined the object carefully. The man who wanted to own so many things knew he had to own this.

"It looks very ancient. Is it?"

"Yes."

Haaman paused, seemingly looking at every detail of the object, but in reality thinking how he could begin negotiations without appearing too keen. There was also the not inconsequential problem of how he could raise the money for this wonderful item. Contrary to the impression he gave, but as some people were coming to suspect, his finances were stretched to the limit at the moment. He was beginning to regret expending the money on buying those two slaves a few days ago. He needed to lower this carpenter's expectations a little.

"This writing around the bottom, what does it mean?"

"I do not know."

"How old is it exactly?"

"Again, I do not know."

"It is yours, I suppose? Not been stolen from some ancient temple? It has an aura of deity, something I cannot determine; almost supernatural even."

Joseph bristled slightly.

"It has not been stolen from anywhere as far as I am aware. Its history is something of a mystery, but it is mine to sell. I can only give you provenance from the time it came into my possession. It was a gift."

"Indeed? You must have wealthy friends. But, of course, you know Joseph of Arimathea. Did he give it to you?"

"No."

Joseph kept his answers brief so that it would not encourage Haaman into talking about the gold and its origin, but would force him to make an offer. In any event he was not concerned about the façade Haaman was attempting to mask his true intent. He greatly wanted it, and Joseph knew it.

140

Haaman wondered whether he might have been too rude. He thought he had better soften his approach. No point in alienating this man too much, especially a friend of Arimathea. This gold was going to be his, and Joseph was clearly too shrewd a man to be flustered out of its true worth. But could he afford to buy it?

"Forgive me, Joseph. I am so used to dealing with rogues in my work, that a suspicious mind is second nature to me. I mean no insult." He paused. "How much do you want for it?"

"Well, I should now ask you how much you are prepared to offer. However, to save all that pretence that passes for haggling, let me be frank with you. I will only sell this bowl to you on condition that you release two of your slaves. The balance of value can be negotiated after that. If you are not amenable to that, there is no point in our discussing the matter further. What do you say?"

"That rather depends on which two slaves you require, does it not?"

"Martha and her son Mark are the ones."

"Now why did I know it would be those two? I have only just bought them a few days ago, and now you expect me to let them go? I will have to think about that."

Haaman began twisting his beard in his fingers. The habit that irritated his wife so much.

Joseph stood up and shook his head in exasperation so his long beard swayed from side to side.

"Look, do not go through your best haggling routine with me. I have already made my feelings known about that, haven't I? If you are not prepared to sell them to me, just say as much and I will leave. Mind you, if that is your choice, you are not the businessman I have heard you were."

He spoke with confidence and guile that came from the prompting of an inner spirit within him, and with the certainty of the justness of his mission.

Haaman quietly enjoyed the thought that he had a reputation as an astute businessman. It might have been only flattery, but his vanity soon persuaded him it was true. He considered his position. This was truly an amazing piece of luck. Perhaps that god of Martha's was rewarding him for being generous to her, for providing the lamb to sacrifice? He did not know. What he did know was that Joseph had provided him with a solution to several problems. If the bowl became his, he could sell the gold for a good profit if the balance in money was not too much; recoup the money expended on the slaves, and keep Esherah off his back with her allegations of adultery. Years of experience in the trade told him it was an extremely valuable item.

The down side of it all was that he would lose Martha, but Esherah's nagging about her was becoming a thorn in his flesh that would need extracting soon anyway. Alternatively, he could remove Esherah, but he had no stomach for that. In any event she was a good hostess, his business friends liked her, and there were no real grounds for disposing of her. She was still an asset. That is how he evaluated everything, into whether it was an asset or liability. Assets could become liabilities if care was not taken, but at the moment the balance sheet showed Esherah to be in credit. The decision was made.

"I agree. I will sell the slaves to you. They are worth eighty silver drachmas, I have the receipt if you doubt me. If we add another, say, hundred drachmas, that would be a good price in total for the gold. Agreed?"

Joseph smiled and shook his head slowly. "Just because I do not live in the city does not mean I am simple, my friend. The gold content of the bowl alone is worth more than that. Look at the craftsmanship. This is a unique piece of work, and it is reputed to have certain qualities."

"What qualities?"

Haaman's head raised slightly, and his face adopted a more questioning look.

"Well, for what it is worth, it is alleged that this gold will enhance the life of a good person, and blight the life of someone who is, er, not good. I make no claim myself, you understand, but that is what is said by the previous owner."

Joseph wanted to play down this aspect, as he felt it could unnecessarily confuse things. At the same time, he considered he had a duty to mention it.

"Who was the previous owner?"

"Oh, just some Persian. I do not know his name."

The carpenter was simultaneously evasive and factual. There was a silence.

Haaman stopped twisting his beard, and began nervously to turn the rings on each finger, one after the other. What should he do? This was not going to be as easy as he had thought. That comment about the bowl having certain powers was probably just a sales pitch, but it was interesting nevertheless. It made him desire the object even more.

"You make a fair point about the gold content."

He moved his neck and head together backwards and forwards, signifying agreement to that point. The black braids of his hair swung in time, with that hypnotic effect that Martha had noted before. Haaman wondered just how far he would have to go. Every increase eroded profit on the resale. If in fact he did sell it on. It was a very attractive item and would be a great showpiece. His friends would be so envious, and consider him such a man of substance. The thought both excited and tormented him, but... money for luxuries was short at the moment. Surely he could find a way, and give a good reason to Esherah. Getting rid of Martha would probably be enough.

"Hum, how much extra, as well as the slaves, do you want then, Joseph?"

"I want what is fair. I ask for no more."

"I suppose I could go to a hundred and fifty drachmas on top. Beyond that I will hardly make a profit if I sell it."

Joseph shook his head.

"Then do not sell it," said Joseph flatly. "Keep it as a display of your magnificence." Another silence followed.

"One hundred and seventy drachmas on top, and that is really as far as I can go. Do you want the slaves or not?"

Haaman thought he had wrestled back the initiative, but Joseph now played his master stroke.

"Are you aware of the ancient Hebrew custom of Jubilee?"

The metal trader looked puzzled.

"When all land reverts to its original owner after fifty years? Is this relevant?"

"That is for you to decide. Although it is little known, the custom, actually a law in this country, extends to ownership of slaves so that no Judean can be forced to be a slave after seven years. It is known as the 'Sabbath Year'. After seven years they have to be set free, if they so wish. It is different for non Hebrews, of course. How long have you had Martha?"

The Syrian's face turned paler as he felt the blood rush away.

"What trickery is this? I may have had her for a few years, but I have only owned her for three days."

"It makes no difference. The time runs from when she first became a slave of her current master. You may have rented her before, but you have, in effect, been her master for many years. The law construes both you and her previous owner to technically have been joint masters during this period."

Haaman started to bluster in panic. He fully realised the enormity of what Joseph was saying. He would appear a fool in the eyes of everybody when they knew he had paid top price for two slaves that would probably only be his for a few more years. He should have continued renting. No wonder Agothos had sold them. He must know about such things being in the trade, and sold them before they became almost worthless from an ownership point of view.

"Ah, you are bluffing. There is no such law."

Joseph stared so icily that Haaman felt foolish.

"Well, that is my interpretation. I suppose you could challenge it in the court, but lawyer's fees are expensive, and public debate is probably not what you want."

Haaman tried a different approach.

"Even if what you say is true, so what? Martha and Mark have no other means of support, even in a few years they will still want to stay as my slaves."

"I would not be too certain of that, my friend. If we cannot reach agreement, then I think you will find that Joseph of Arimathea may express an interest. I am sure Martha would welcome the chance to stay with my cousin-in-law. At the moment he is not in the picture, but you know what influence he has. And if he does not look after her, my wife and I certainly will. Look I am not trying to cheat you, all I want is to set Martha and her son free. At the same time I have a responsibility to get a fair price for the gold. Do we understand one another?"

Damn this Nazarene thought Haaman. For a carpenter he was one very shrewd businessman. Yet, there was something about the man he admired. He was an artisan, yes, but with such a nobility and honesty of spirit, he could not help but like him.

The mosaic on the floor caught Haaman's eye. It was a picture of Bacchus, the Roman god of wine and merriment, entertaining some friends. In his hand was a gold goblet. A vine was interleaved throughout the image. It symbolised prosperity. An idea came into Haaman's mind. This was an omen.

CHAPTER FIFTEEN.

Redemption.

The deal was done. Haaman considered he had retrieved himself
from an embarrassing situation regarding the tenure of Martha and
Mark; demonstrated his mastery over his wife's allegations, and
purchased a prized gold bowl for a ridiculously cheap outlay that
would enhance his reputation as a major businessman. True, he had
to pay more than he originally intended, but it was still a very good
price. He would keep it for as long as he wanted, and it would no
doubt prove good collateral for any future loans, but when the price
was right, he could sell it at an enormous profit. He was very pleased
with himself, and had spent most of that night reflecting on how
shrewd he was, and elaborating this fact to Esherah. The facts had
changed a little bit though. The introduction of the "Jubilee" aspect
was now the result of Haaman's careful research into the matter,
culminating in his quick grasp of what had to be done.

His wife on the other hand, considered that, once again, she had
been successful in manipulating her husband into doing what she
wanted. That wretched Martha and her son, with their insolent
attitude of non subservience, would soon be out of her life.

The next morning Joseph and Haaman met again at the main
city gate to conclude the transaction, and the papers of ownership for
the slaves were altered in favour of Joseph. It was customary for
business deals to be done at the gate, so that the many passers-by
could be called on as witnesses. Joseph took off his sandal and gave
it to Haaman to settle the issue in the manner of sellers of significant
property since ancient times.

With the completion of the manumission, Joseph now had to
give the news to Martha and Mark. Perhaps he should have
mentioned it to Martha before now, but he and Mary had agreed that
it would be cruel to enlarge hope when there was no certainty
Haaman would want the gold bowl. There was also the possibility
that Martha would not want the gold to be sold for her benefit. To
circumvent that they had set their minds on this course of action.

He knew how dearly Mark had longed for this moment, and was fairly certain Martha would be pleased too. From his discussion with his cousin-in-law yesterday, there would be no problem with the two ex-slaves staying with Arimathea, but if that was not to their taste, then they could come and stay with them in Nazareth until they were able to stand on their own feet. With his strong build, Mark would make an excellent carpenter, if he wanted to learn the trade.

The temporary loss of the gold the previous night had made Joseph just a little apprehensive about carrying large sums of money, so he clutched tightly the small leather pouch containing the coins representing the balance of the payment. His excitement to impart the news made his gait seem strange, as he speeded up then slowed in time with adrenalin bursts of energy.

After reaching the house, the smile on his face told Mary and Arimathea of his success. They had been waiting expectantly. Martha had sensed that something was afoot, but had met only evasive answers to her questions. They called her and Mark into the splendid main room, with its mosaics and wall paintings to match any of those in the royal palace, a quarter of a mile away. When Mary told her of her freedom, there were tears from the women, smiles from the men, and loud shouts from Mark. Later, he would remember his prayer in the Temple, but for now he was just too emotional to think about anything but the future.

Goblets of wine were handed around to celebrate and orders for a feast that night were given.

"Have you any friends you would like to invite, Martha?" Arimathea asked kindly.

"Not really. Everyone I count as a real friend is here now."

She paused contemplatively.

"No one at all then?" persisted her host intuitively.

"Well, I suppose there is someone who I see occasionally, but he is only a beggar and I wouldn't want to…"

"Then go and invite him, and anyone else we can accommodate. You should share this day with those you like. There are plenty of other days for being with those you do not," said Arimathea smiling.

"Thank you, Joseph. You are truly richer in spirit than you are in property. I owe you so much."

"It is not I to whom you are indebted, but these two."

147

He indicated Mary and Joseph.

"But you do know, don't you, that you and Mark are welcome to stay in my house until you choose otherwise?"

"It is not really us either you should thank. That gold belonged to Jesus. It was really him who redeemed you both," said Mary.

She nodded slowly, Martha raised her eyebrows, Arimathea stroked his beard thoughtfully, and Mark looked at Joseph in amazement. Deep in his heart he had always had faith that he would not remain a slave. He remembered the words Joseph had spoken on the roof two nights ago. *If you look at the world through the eyes of faith, you see faith in action. If you do not have the eyes of faith, you never see it in action. You never see the miraculous or the divine, only the coincidental and mundane".*

Mark thought how true that was and once again hoped that one day he would have such wisdom.

"You are right," said Martha. "I must go and thank Jesus. Where is he?"

"He has gone to the Temple again with James, and one of Joseph's servants to keep an eye on them. If our eldest ever goes missing, you can be sure that he will probably be there. Calls it his 'Father's House' if you like."

"That is a bit strange. What do you think of that, Joseph?"

"I do not mind."

He looked at Mary quickly, as if to reassure her he was not going to say anything controversial.

"On the basis that God is the father of us all, I suppose the Temple is His house, and Jesus is certainly a child of His."

Joseph laughed.

"Well, that's what I think he means. Who knows with Jesus? He says many strange things. Some are quite innovative though."

Martha smiled.

"Well, one day Mark or I will find a way to pay him back."

She then excused herself, saying that she had to try and find her friend Lazarus, and go to Haaman's house to gather a couple of small items she and Mark had left there. Moreover, she wanted to say goodbye to her former owner. He had treated her reasonably, and she was cognisant that had he not given her the money for the lamb, she might never have met up with Mary again at that precise moment.

148

She was intrigued to see his reaction, and that of his aloof wife, now that Martha was no longer his slave. She also knew, as women always do, that he was attracted to her physically and was surprised that he had let her go. It must be some bowl, she thought in a rare moment of vanity, to persuade him to release me. Perhaps she might get a look at it.

As she left the house, she considered how dramatically her life had changed in only a few days. This seemed to have been a pattern for her as long as she could remember. Periods of stability, then sudden upheavals would occur. It had happened with her parents' death; her meeting with Mark's father; her going to Bethlehem; the resultant escape from there, and finally her slavery and redemption. This had made her stoic in nature and adaptable. She felt like she was starting life again. She could feel that hope in the air that Lazarus had mentioned often occurred at the Passover festival. She was, in a word, reborn.

Martha hoped Lazarus would come to the feast tonight, but also wondered how he would take the news of her freedom. He might be jealous of her good fortune. Sometimes people were like that; feeling aggrieved instead of glad for the recipient of any blessing. She had learned that you never knew everything about someone, no matter how long you had known them. Certain traits of people were indiscernible, like footsteps in a mist.

She passed the Xystus, a big stadium enlarged by Herod the Great to emulate the games and gladiatorial combat held by the Romans. The original arena had been built by a corrupt High Priest called Joshua, who later changed his name to Jason, the Greek equivalent. He had tried to impose Greek attitudes and customs on young Judeans. The flagitious Herod had developed the site but had a softer approach to the Hellenistic culture. Nevertheless, it was still largely considered a heathen establishment, and its proximity to the Temple annoyed the more orthodox Hebrews.

It was decorated with all manner of gold, silver and gems. There were also trophies commemorating victories of the first Roman Emperor, Augustus. As she stopped to look up at some workmen carrying out repairs, she felt a tap on her shoulder. Martha jumped, and turned around to see a familiar turbaned head and bearded, mahogany face. It was the Persian.

"A thousand apologies for surprising you. It seems either I or my camel have a proclivity for making you jump," he said in his clipped tone.

"Oh, it's you. I am glad we have met again as I have a few questions to ask you."

"Really? How providential, because I also wish to speak with you. However, I cannot talk now. I have something to explain to you, or your son more accurately, and I choose not to do it now. Tomorrow will be the optimum time. Now you are free there is something which can pass into his possession."

"You know we have been redeemed? How do you know that? It has only happened this morning. What do you want to give Mark? There are even more questions now than I had before."

"I know many things about your life. But I repeat, I cannot discuss this at the moment. My presence here is only to ask you to meet me tomorrow, at the Damascus Gate at the northern end of the city. Be there at noon, as my caravan is leaving soon after, and we will not wait long. We wish to leave before the great exodus begins the next day. Come alone. Can you do that?"

Martha nodded, a little bewildered, and started to say something else, but the Persian turned quickly and disappeared in the crowd just as abruptly as he had arrived. She wandered on towards the Temple where she suspected Lazarus would be plying his "trade", but her concentration was on other matters.

She wondered why the Persian was so mysterious. Even Joseph and Mary did not know his name. Although a little apprehensive at meeting him tomorrow, she knew instinctively that it could only benefit her and Mark to meet this man.

She was thinking so hard about this that she failed to notice Lazarus approaching her. Martha assumed that he would be in the normal haunts of his group of beggars, for she was unaware of his new condition.

"Martha!"

For the second time that day she was startled. Lazarus excitedly started to tell her his news before she had a chance to mention hers. When he had finished waving his arm around, to demonstrate the truth of his words, she gave him a hug.

"Look, I can hug you back, with two arms. I still cannot get used to having the extra arm."

"You mean you have three now?" giggled Martha.

"You know what I mean. This opens up a new life for me. Everyone is amazed and treating me differently. It's like I have been reborn, raised from the dead. You cannot imagine what that is like."

"Oh, but I can, Lazarus."

Her remark did not truly register on her friend because of his jubilation. This was his moment, or so he thought. He continued his exposition on his past and present way of life.

"Before I was healed, my mind as well as my arm seemed to have wasted away. I could have pursued some form of employment, I suppose, if I had really tried. Instead, I just felt sorry for myself, and used my disability as an excuse for everything. It was as though I was trapped behind an open door. Thinking it to be locked was an abnormality of my mind, not my body. It left me frustrated, and apparently incapable to escape from the prison of my worries. I failed to see that adversity could be a breeding ground for success, not just failure."

"You *are* energised, aren't you?"

"Yes! I feel as though I can now get on with my life. I can forget about things that have served their purpose and move on."

"And have I served your purpose?" said Martha playfully.

"Oh no! Martha how could you think such a thing. I may be healed, but at the moment I am still a beggar. Even though you are a slave, I am no better than you. I will not stop being your friend."

"I should think not. For anyway, I am not a slave. I am as free as you are."

She laughed at his puzzlement, and then proceeded to reveal what had transpired.

When she had finished, they both stood looking at each other, not knowing what to say. Eventually the embarrassing silence was broken by Martha asking Lazarus to come to the banquet. After being reassured that his rags would not matter, he agreed, mostly because he wanted to see her again.

"But it is still true that I have nothing to wear. I will be as conspicuous as a scarecrow in a melon field, and have about as much to say, to the likes of Joseph of Arimathea."

"He is not like that. He treats everybody the same, regardless of their apparent status. Look how he has taken me in and Mark. He's told us we can stay as long as it takes for me to establish myself

151

again, and Mark to learn a craft. Now, stop all this nonsense and I'll see you tonight before sunset, round about the twelfth hour. Remember to let the past stay in the past. Don't try to keep dragging it back into the present. You're not a beggar anymore. You are a man, the same as any other."

They both smiled and hugged, and then stopped, both becoming self conscious because they were in a busy street and people were beginning to take notice.

"You know where Joseph's house is, don't you? I'll see you there. I have a task to perform. More like a debt to repay to myself. One which should prove quite enjoyable."

After saying this, Martha continued in her original direction to Haaman's house. She had to push her way through crowds that lingered, and would carry on lingering for the remaining days of the festival. While doing this, everything felt a bit unreal. She could take as much time as she liked without being fearful of a scolding from Esherah when she got back. It was dreamlike, but a chance bit of conversation outside the weaver's shop brought her back to reality.

A group of poorly dressed men were gathered there and were chatting about crucifixion. Considering the extra soldiers about, their complaints were not too quiet or discreet. Plainly their feelings were running high about the impending execution of a friend of theirs. Then one of them said something which made Martha stop and feel suddenly very cold. A terrible sickly sensation moved in her stomach.

CHAPTER SIXTEEN.

Martha Settles A Debt To Herself.

"**A**nd what makes it worse," said a scrawny man, with foul smelling clothes soiled from his work, "is the fact that the Temple guards say one of our own people betrayed Judas to the Romans."

There were cries of disgust and incomprehension from the others. Martha pretended to be idly interested in some cloth so she could listen further.

"I do not believe that. How much was he paid?"

"I am no liar! I was told by Bartholomew, you all know him. He works near my tannery. He is as reliable as the sunrise."

There were consenting mutters and nods from the others.

"It was not a question of payment. Apparently he gave the Roman a warning that Judas was hiding in the room, and the Roman stabbed him without any provocation at all."

"Sons of Beliah! Poor Judas. Are you sure?"

"It's what I am told."

The scrawny man opened his palms upwards and grimaced his blamelessness.

"Seems a bit strange to me," said a more discerning member of the group. "You know how these guards love to exaggerate. They are so jealous of the real soldiers, cursed though they are, that they will make up any gossip to put the soldiers in a bad light."

"Well, I speak what I am told. No more, no less. Oh, and another thing. I forgot to mention it was a boy that did it. He was with a Galilean. You can always tell them. Bartholomew heard that this man had also been seen with Joseph of Arimathea the day before. Makes you think eh?"

"Be careful Benjamin," said the more discerning one. "Arimathea is a powerful man and will not take kindly to you spreading rumours that he is a Roman sympathiser."

"Did I say that?"

"Not exactly, but you would have done if anyone had bitten on your implication."

He said this through a smile.

"I love you like a brother, but you know you are partial to more than just the facts of a story."

The men started to laugh. Someone else spouted up.

"Yes! Only the other day you said that you had to stop what you were telling us, because you had already told us more than you knew!"

There was more laughter.

"I did not!" Benjamin protested. "You have just made that up."

"He has learned from the master then!"quipped another.

"All right. All right. But I tell you this. The Brethren are talking of revenge for the death of Judas, and I would not want to be wearing that boy's sandals if they do. Some of the Sanhedrin have gone to Governor Rufus to see if he will release one of the captured Zealots, as is the custom at Passover. But you can be sure there will be trouble if the others go to the cross."

Martha had forgotten all pretence of stealth when she heard the reference to "revenge", and stood openly listening to the rest of their conversation with worry etched in her face. The men were suddenly aware of her presence.

"Is there something you want of us, woman?"

The rudeness of the enquiry warned her she should go. She shook her head and walked from the shop. This was a bad turn of events. She would have to discuss this with the two Josephs when she returned from Haaman's house, although she had already resolved that Mark should not be told about this yet. There was nothing he could do to change the situation, and therefore no point in giving him worry. In any event, perhaps the true version of what happened at the Temple would circulate, and forestall any action against Mark. She was sure that Joseph and her son had told the truth.

A little while later Martha arrived at Haaman's house. He was not there, but one of the other servants showed her to her old quarters, having first obtained permission from Esherah. Except for Pheras and his mother, the rest of the household were pleased at Martha's good fortune. She collected what she needed and came through the main room on her way out, still worried and anxious about Mark. As she did so, Esherah called out to her.

"What are you going to do now you have your freedom, if that's what you call it?"

Although there was a smile on the lips that spoke these words, Martha knew it was as artificial as the cosmetic colouring adorning the same visage. She also knew that this was going to be one more scene enacted in the power play her former mistress liked to adopt.

"Oh, I am not sure yet. Joseph, that's Joseph of Arimathea the merchant, has said that we can stay at his home as long as we like until we get settled again. You may have heard of him?"

Martha knew very well that Esherah knew who she meant, but if Esherah was going to play superiority games, she would find Martha a formidable adversary now she was not shackled by bondage.

Esherah sniffed, which was her habit when she did not know exactly what to say, but wanted to show disparagement.

"Yes, of course I know of him. My husband has had some dealings with him. They are in the same sort of business. I suppose you will be a useful addition to his servants, until you decide to do something different, of course."

"I am staying as a guest."

Martha looked the other woman straight in the eye. She saw the reaction which meant she had been unaware of her friendship with Joseph. Martha knew it was wrong, but she savoured the moment.

"Oh, that will be…" a pause registered the counter strike from Martha, "Er, that will be nice for you," said Esherah.

This was too much for her. She decided to regain the initiative.

"Well, I am glad you have somewhere to stay. Umm, before you go would you hand me my new robe. You know the one… with the exquisite purple dye. It is in the chest there."

She pointed to a large wooden box with elaborate carving.

"It is the new fashion, you know, and very expensive. I suppose you will be wanting to get a new wardrobe yourself now my husband will not be supplying your clothes any longer?"

Mark's mother saw immediately that this was an endeavour to establish a final act of dominance upon her. Esherah was trying to make it clear that there was still a gap between them in social status and class, or what she perceived as class.

There was a gap indeed, but it only served to emphasise how shallow and petty Esherah was compared to the good spirit in her ex-slave. This wife of a social climber had never come to terms with the fact that good breeding, class, intelligence, consideration, call it what you will, could never be bought. It was something inherent in you, developed by your background certainly, but it was more than a sudden influx of money could provide.

She looked at Esherah and shook her head.

"You just cannot stand it, can you?"

"What?"

"That I am free. You have no power over me now, yet you still think you are superior. You equate wealth with respect and self importance, but one day you might learn that riches do not make you better than anyone else. Money makes a person smug, and nothing more. I do not have to get your robe, or anything for you. But I will; solely to show you that you do not need domination over someone to have them do something for you."

She walked over to the chest and picked up the brilliant purple dress.

"It is certainly a lovely garment, but that is not why you appreciate it, is it? This is your talisman, your senator's rod; the centurion's plume, the High Priest's ephod; your very own badge of office. When you wear it, you think it makes a statement that 'I am somebody important, you will respect me'. I have to tell you that not everybody is deceived by such pretension."

"Hold your tongue, you insolent girl."

"Or what?" Martha laughed. "Look it in the face, stare it in the eyes. We are equals now. I have been redeemed by a friend's gold. That gold bowl displayed proudly over there. My price has been paid. Have you anyone who would do the same for you? You may be wealthy and rich in egotism, but you are poor in spirit. You cannot bear the fact that I see past your affectation, and know you for what you really are."

She held out the robe with her right hand, and shook it.

"This garment does not speak of quiet dignity. On you it shouts vulgarity. It screams it at the top of its fashionable voice. On you it declares, 'I want you all to know that I am not poor; because I am so afraid, so very afraid of being like you; you poor, poor people.'"

"It is nothing like that at all. I…I bought it for its good quality, and because it will last for ages."

"Oh, really? So, it will last you a long time? How long is that? Until it is no longer in fashion, and must be consigned to a concealed, lingering death of rot and mould in a chest again; not

156

hard wear? You pitiful woman. Your lies are so obvious. If good quality alone was the yardstick of your purchase, then why pay so much? No, it is the price that is important to you. If this robe was free you would not want it. Its only value to you is in its exclusivity. You think it makes you elite, above everyone who cannot afford it, and all through the purchasing power of your husband."

Martha paused for breath, while the recipient of her indignation was unable to conjure a retort. All she could manage was, "Have you finished?"

"No, I have not. It's all a pointless charade anyway. Yet I suppose we are all guilty of it—judging people by their appearance because we cannot see into their hearts and minds."

Then suddenly relenting, she continued, "Just like I am doing to you now."

Martha sighed.

"Oh, if we were forced to wear our thoughts as garments, how pretty or attractive would some of us look then? The real tragedy of you, is that all the expensive price shows is that your vanity is greater than your good sense."

"How dare you say such things to me. You, who have nothing to offer anyone."

Martha laughed a silly, affected laugh.

"Why are you making that silly laugh?"

Esherah frowned at her.

"Because I was always told it was impolite not to laugh at a joke," smiled Martha.

"You think *I* am a joke?"

"Well, you have said so, although I was merely remarking on your comment that I had nothing to offer anybody. I am sure your husband does not think that."

The final nerve end twanged loose in Esherah. Unable to control her rage at being insulted and outsmarted by someone she considered beneath her, she exploded, "Well laugh at this then!"

She picked up the nearest thing to hand and threw it at the younger woman. It was only a second afterwards she realised that it was the golden bowl. It missed its target, but crashed into the wall behind.

Martha stooped and picked it up. With a serenity that made Esherah seem foolish, she came over to her would be assailant and gave her the object.

"That is one way of bringing my price down, I suppose."

"What are you talking about?"

"The bowl is damaged. One of its handles has come off. Good day, Esherah. Enjoy your explanation to Haaman as to why his precious article is now worth less than he paid for it."

Martha walked away, leaving the agitated and sorrowful figure of the Syrian woman looking forlornly at the bowl in her hand.

CHAPTER SEVENTEEN.

Jehua Plots With Annas.

While Martha and Esherah had been exchanging invective, Jehua was considering whether some information just offered to him was worth placing before his masters. A servant girl had come to him with an interesting tale of fugitives from an old campaign of his, the culling at Bethlehem. The two of them, a woman and her son, were apparently staying as guests of the servant's master, Joseph of Arimathea. Their whole story had been overheard a few evenings ago.

Obviously the girl had no idea that Jehua had been in charge of that mission, because of the things she said. He was, nevertheless, very glad that her motives in divulging this information were pure and simple. Purely as her duty as a good citizen, and simply for the money. At first he had thought there might be a baser motive like blackmail, but he satisfied himself on that score and was sure she was unaware of his involvement. That was a relief. She was a pretty girl, and it would have been a shame to have her killed.

Charges of adultery, or immoral behaviour were easily brought, and the necessary witnesses just as easily bought. After a few stones had found their mark, her face would not have been so attractive.

Jehua was not averse to arranging such things for men who needed to remove a wife, or two. Nor did he shirk from helping to remove "obstacles" in the path of his business friends. But, it was always on his terms, and after the right consideration. The consideration meaning the right amount of money.

Since Herod had removed the power of the Sanhedrin to grant the death penalty, capital punishment always needed ratification now from the occupying Roman authority. Therefore, a silent slash across the throat with a sicari would be preferable to Jehua's clients, and bring the lasting silence required to their opponents. Robbers could be blamed for many things, and anyway, it saved the expense and publicity of court proceedings.

Had the girl tried to threaten Jehua with going to higher authority to reveal his ineptitude in carrying out King Herod's orders, it might not have mattered now anyway. Herod had been dead for some years, and the alleged threat to the kingdom from a new king, had never materialised. Unless, of course, this boy staying with Arimathea was going to make some claim to lead Israel.

That would be difficult. There was no king. Augustus had made Judea a Roman province, and installed a prefect, or governor, since Herod's son Archelaus had failed to rule properly. Annius Rufus was the current one, but he was subordinate to the governor of Syria, who ranked higher, and sometimes assumed charge in Judea.

Jehua's thoughts raced around many things. Possibilities for the present, and the impossibility of changing the past. He was reluctant to think about things that had happened long ago, as he could not change them. He was adept at blocking out most things, but that incident at Bethlehem had never really left his mind. He had always been intrigued by the persistent legend about a king being born in Bethlehem, and now this woman had resurrected that interest. If the boy she talked about had escaped being killed, perhaps he did have a charmed life. How could he, Jehua, use the situation for his own advantage if there really was a king in waiting?

Despite himself, he began to hear again in his head everything that had happened that morning. His eyes glazed, and once again he was there, back where his nightmares started. He heard himself give the command for his men to line up in formation, and the whole scene played in his mind as though it was actually happening again………

As the men closed in on the village Jehua thought the ride was taking far longer than it should. It couldn't have been more than three-quarters of a mile but it seemed like time was no longer operating. The horses' legs were visibly moving but the distance didn't seem to get any nearer. It was like a bad dream where you cannot seem to run from an attacker. Coupled with this, he could not dispel the awful feeling of doubt that clung to his mind, like a spider's web with too many fine strands to remove completely, no matter how hard he tried to flick them away.

Suddenly they were at the main entrance. There were no walls, and his squad swept towards the first batch of huts. A few early risers were outside and stopped to look incredulously at the onrushing soldiers. Clouds of dust were thrown up from the dirt road. The people thought that the soldiers must be going straight through the village and, because they were not enemy soldiers, were not alarmed. One act of brutality changed this in an instant.

A young woman was sitting by the road. Her husband had drunk too much wine the night before and was trying to sleep. So because he had complained about their son's crying she had taken the child outside. She was holding the baby and trying to feed him when Jehua reined in his stallion abruptly at her side. The black horse snorted as though to say, "You had better listen to this. My master is important."

"What do you call your child?" he asked her without dismounting and smiling broadly. His manner and bearing encouraged her to answer.

"Benjamin" she replied hesitantly.

"A good name for a fine boy. Place him on the ground by your side. I wish to look at him."

"Why?" the woman queried. Her instinct told her something was wrong but she couldn't fathom what. She could not discern why soldiers would be interested in her child.

"Just do it," smiled Jehua disarmingly again.

Years of experience as one of Herod's assassins had not been wasted. A younger man might have tried to threaten her and thereby wasted time. If adults as well as babies had been the subjects of his orders it would have been easier, and no need for any dialogue at all. But he didn't want her getting scared and have to chase her. He needed to lead by example as his three colleagues looked on, and the boy was clearly the right age.

The smile had its effect and she placed the small bundle of rags by her side. Well, that is what Jehua saw. He had to. He wanted to think of his target as an object, not a living human with thoughts and feelings, and a family. What the woman saw was her little son lift up his arms and stretch them out to her, annoyed at the separation. She obviously did not see Jehua raise his lance, or it come down through the air so swiftly with its point of destruction aimed at the little heart. There was hardly any cry from the child, but in one terrible moment the mother's shriek of anguish broke through the second's silence following the act.

Unfortunately for Jehua the force of the blow had pinned the baby to the ground and in a grotesque movement, as he tried to free his spear, the woman's son was lifted up in the air, impaled on the

161

wood. The vertical spear and the horizontal child formed a chilling silhouette against the sky, like a sword, or a cross. The mother stared in agony as other mothers had done, when their sons were crucified by the Romans, on another hill only six miles away.

The Captain shook off the small body from the lance as the woman screamed at him. She fell to the ground clutching at her son. Simultaneously there were screams from all around as the other soldiers had worked their way through the homes. The sudden noise made Jehua's horse rear up on his hind legs, and whinny.

"Come on, don't stand staring. Get on with it!"

Jehua ordered his three companions. He pushed the horse forward so it regained balance and rode on.

They moved to the next hovel, but as people stirred and came out there were attempts at resistance. There was no longer any facility for talking or selective killing. It was clear that the plan was not going to work as he desired. Panic had spread not just to the inhabitants, but to the soldiers also. This was not the sort of work they were trained for, and they resorted to kill and wound indiscriminately. They went through the village in about twenty minutes, from both ends. Fathers, mothers, anybody who got in their way when they saw a small child, felt a blade in their flesh. It was chaos and Jehua knew it. How he wished he'd handled it differently by rounding up all the children in the centre of the settlement on some pretext. Still, there might have been some in the fields or hidden, and they might still have had to have a house search.

Yes, he consoled himself with that thought. Jehua's instinct at the time had told him there would be no glorious record of this by the scribes, although his men had done a public service. Even though it may not have been officially written down, Jehua had known that this incident would be remembered for years afterwards and talked about around camp fires. He had been correct.

The images of the slaughter stopped for a moment. Jehua recalled that it had transpired that Herod had not wanted the Sanhedrin opposing him, so he had never mentioned it to them. He had his small inner circle of courtiers, advisors and flatterers that he had nurtured, and had discussed it with them. He was a great admirer of talented people and made sure that they joined his elite group and remained loyal to him.

Nicolaus of Damascus had been one such person. This man had been the official scribe who wrote about the life of the king. Jehua had to admire the way Herod had taken Nicolaus aside and promised him money for not writing about the killings that Jehua was about to undertake. It was to be a secret until they knew how the people would react. Herod told him they might not appreciate that he, the real king, was trying to save his people from possible civil war if this new king grew up and led a rebellion.

Herod had enough bad publicity at that time without wanting more. Also, any public riots would not have showed Rome that he could control his subjects, and the Emperor Augustus might have had him replaced. Forty years earlier the Roman Senate had placed Herod the Great on the Throne of Judah, but he was no more than a puppet king whose strings were pulled by Rome. So Herod had flattered Jehua and promised him a large bonus if he carried out his orders successfully. After he had said this, the diseased Herod had coughed up such a mixture of blood and phlegm that Jehua thought his reign was coming to an end right then, and he would be spared the mission. But the King recovered, and promised Jehua something else. He would make him Captain of not only his Royal Bodyguard, but also his Secret Police. He would be looked on as more than a legend, but a saviour for what he had done for the country. A saviour; Jehua had liked the thought of that.

Then the images played through his mind again. He was there once more, as he had been so many times in dreams and nightmares.

Back in Bethlehem Jehua turned to his second in command and ordered the men to regroup, as it became clear that their work was finished. Now he wanted to get as far away as possible from Bethlehem. He asked each squad leader to account for each killing and asked Matthew to total them.

"Seventeen, sir. More than we thought but no doubt there were casualties outside the age range given by Herod. There are quite a few wounded as well."

"Adults included?"

"Er, yes. I am afraid there were one or two killed as well as wounded. Better to be safe than sorry though, isn't it sir?"

"Hmm, I suppose so. Should keep the King happy although it might have been better if the men had applied a little less zeal in

163

getting it done. There were not meant to be any adults dispatched, only if unavoidable. It goes to prove what I've always thought".

"What's that sir?"

"That the smallest amount of stupidity cancels out the greatest wisdom," replied his commander.

"Move them out, Matthew."

It had not been until much later that Matthew had told him about the conversation he had heard about two children getting out of the village just before the mission. It had been a wailing, despairing comment from one of the women about how she wished she had left like Mary and Martha. At the time Jehua had not thought it significant, that it did not mean any children had escaped, but now it seemed to make some sense.

The soldiers rode out the same way they had arrived. They were two abreast but no one talked. There were no victory chants. No boasting of exploits as usual after a winning battle or skirmish. The silence was as heavy as the clouds that were now forming in the early morning sky. It started to rain. The men were glad. Some of them were basically still good men. God fearing men even, but also professional soldiers. If moisture crept into the corner of an eye nobody would notice.

The rain became heavier with a ferocious intensity. It suited the mood; as though heaven itself was trying to wash away the guilt covering that lonely patrol, and even wash the images out of their very minds. This thought was not lost on Jehua. The rain hammered into his leather breastplate, and lashed into his helmet and face; attacking both heart and mind in some mystic pincher movement. An unpleasant smell started to surround him. His armour smelt as leather does when it gets too wet, a mouldy bitter smell. He had smelt that before, but today it seemed to be stronger, like an invisible comment on the deed just done.

Then a feeling of desolation suddenly came over him as well, of utter loneliness. He squinted his eyes and looked around at the others just to make sure they were still there. He read the same feelings in all of them. Here they were, together in one place, but each riding alone towards their own private form of death. It was not just people that had died back there. The death of undisturbed sleep, of self-esteem, and of pride was a thing that would trouble many of these men for years afterwards.

But there was something else. There was death certainly. Yet here was also birth…of conscience…of repentance. This was a far more troubling introduction. These were new factors, and unwelcome in a soldier's armoury. Jehua knew neither he, nor his men, would ever forget these moments. These had been no ordinary killings today. For the first time he knew what innocence meant, and he shuddered. Not just at that thought, or because of the chill of the wet leather, but because of the realisation he had been a tool in implementing a plan far more devious than Herod had devised. The problem was, whose plan was it? Exactly whose agents had they been?

Jehua was no stranger to killing, so why did these killings trouble him so much? It was not just because some were children. No, there was something else. It was almost like the men that had carried out the mission were now under a curse, and had to find a way to redeem themselves before it could be lifted.

Jehua paced around the stone floor of his chamber, which was contained in the meeting house rooms, over the southern entrance to the Temple. It was natural for citizens to come to him concerning matters of security. Although in charge of the Temple police, he had wide ranging powers to act upon instructions from the Judean Council. No true native of Jerusalem would approach the Roman administration before going to their own Sanhedrin first, or their delegated officials. He thought hard. There must be a way for him to turn this news to his advantage.

Of course, he could simply ignore the matter, and tell Arimathea's servant that the information was inaccurate, and that there were no survivors of the "cleansing". Or he could say that it had been referred to the Sanhedrin, and they had decided to take no further action because the threat to the kingdom had been only in Herod's diseased mind, and was no longer relevant. Those were solutions, but they had no profit in them for him.

No, the best action was surely to present the Sanhedrin with a scenario that would make them ask him to rectify the matter, and earn him a little more towards his retirement fund. That fund which had been about to be swelled by the Temple robbery, before the plan had been cruelly thwarted. But how was that to be accomplished?

165

Jehua did have the occasional liaison with females, but it was purely to gratify his sexual urges, not to establish a relationship. A loving affiliation would never fit in with his type of lifestyle. He needed the freedom to go and come when he pleased, without feeling the necessity to make excuses or explanations to anyone. Sometimes his work required that.

Many women were attracted to him, but he did not fool himself it was because of his looks. Although he had a pleasant enough face and could turn on the charm when essential, he realised that his position and power attracted a certain kind of woman. It was especially useful in dealing with the lower class of female, like that servant girl. If he planned this well, he might not only make a profit, but acquire a new female conquest too. He was as ruthless as his ambitions required.

Jehua made up his mind. He stopped pacing around the room, and directed his steps outside. In ten minutes he was standing in the courtyard of Annas' house.

The High Priest lived a life of privilege, even though he was meant to be a servant of the Lord Most High and the people; the intermediary between them and Yahweh. Consequently his house reflected this paradox. It was a glorious building, even better than Arimathea's. Most of the apartments were on the first floor, but there were servants' quarters below and a porch at the front, in the courtyard. Here people would come and warm themselves at the large brazier against the chill night air in Springtime.

Cockerels could be seen strutting up and down the flagstones. They were silent; preserving their vocal energy until the dawn, when their cry drew attention to either the advent of the day, or the guilt of the night before. It was in this courtyard that twenty years later, a certain fisherman would find remorse.

In another couple of minutes Jehua was shown into the main room where the priest met his ordinary visitors. This was a little more basic than the rest of the apartments, as if to imply no Temple taxes were spent unnecessarily. Conversely, it was an acknowledgement that the rest of the palace was really too sumptuous for a servant of God. However, it was believed that nothing was too good for the Lord, and therefore nothing was too good for His High Priest.

Annas welcomed Jehua in his everyday robes, and not those that Mark had noted at the Passover sacrifice. Even so, his blue robe with long tassels and his ankle length tunic were of excellent quality, as was the white head-dress held in place by a striped thin band of cloth around his forehead. Normally this would have been accompanied by a leather band with a small black leather box positioned in the centre of the forehead, to hold folded slips of parchment containing four passages from the scriptures. These phylacteries were often worn on the wrist as well, but because this was a festival none were obliged to be worn.

The High Priest was an impressive figure, not allowed by law to have any disfigurement, and the customary long beard flowed to below his throat. One way of removing a High Priest from office was to chop off one or two of his fingers. Being so disfigured would disqualify him from holding the Holy Office, and the Romans knew this. It was what one governor had called "the fickle finger of fate", and would drop such a reference into any discussion where priests were reluctant to do his bidding, especially those who aspired to higher things.

Although not wearing the ceremonial gown, his clothes still outshone his visitor's rather drab black garments. His attire befitted someone who carried the highest authority of any of the Temple servants. He was leader of the people, and by law was head of the Sanhedrin, the assembly who made judgements in Judea's religious and legal disputes. This often included ex-High Priests, who were growing in number these days and were always an influential body.

Yet the supremacy of the office had been eroded by Herod the Great, so that it was no longer a job for life, but an appointment made by the Romans at frequent intervals from among some of the aristocratic families. Despite this, Annas still was a powerful and wealthy politician. He greeted Jehua with caution.

"Jehua, my son, whilst it is always good to enjoy your company, I wonder what serious affair of state has brought you. It usually I who ask to see you to resolve some problem or other. You are such an able exponent of your art, so rarely do you trouble me."

"Most holy Annas, you flatter me, but your perception is as sharp as ever. It is indeed an affair of state, but whether it is serious or not is what I would like you to decide."

"Intriguing! Sit down, please."

He waved at the cushions on the floor.

"Would you like some refreshment? A little wine to help your words flow smoothly?"

"Thank you. I have been agonising so long over this question that my mouth is dry."

"Really?"

Annas indicated to his servant to fetch the drink, and having placed two goblets on the small table, the servant was dismissed.

"So," said Annas as he handed one to his guest, "is it to do with that business in the Temple the other day? Most distressing to think that some of our own people could be so misguided as to try and rob God himself… to say nothing of the Romans,"

He laughed as he added the last comment.

"That was an excellent piece of anticipation, by the way."

"Thank you."

"Prefect Rufus has ordered the executions. They go to the cross the day after the festival finishes. He acknowledges our custom not to defile our Holy days by such things, and also to release one of the prisoners. Anyway the populace look forward to this festival, and a few crucifixions would certainly spoil the mood. There is enough trouble around without that, and even the Romans want an easy life, although you would not believe so with the stupid decisions they make sometimes."

"You mention trouble. Anything in particular, or just the usual empty talk of rebellion and fake leaders?"

Jehua's instinct for picking up on the slightest hint of something useful had never waned. If anything it had become honed as he grew older.

"Oh, you must have heard surely, a man with your contacts?"

Annas gently mocked him.

Jehua paused and pretended he was trying to remember, not wishing to reveal his ignorance.

His ploy worked for Annas continued, "You play the innocent so well, Jehua, no wonder they call you "The Fox". You know perfectly well that I am referring to that boy who saved the life of the soldier Cornelius. What a commotion that has caused among the followers of the Zealots. I am worried that all this talk of revenge will instigate a riot. But I expect you have the matter in hand, like always."

Playing for time, and making a mental note to reprimand his subordinates for not passing this information on to him, Jehua said, "It would help if I knew the name of the boy."

Like a lot of commanders Jehua did not want to be seen not in control of everything, and he thought his comment would either draw out further information, or deflect responsibility. He was astounded at the reply.

"What does his name matter? We all know he is staying at Joseph of Arimathea's place. There cannot be too many boys of his description staying there. Perhaps you should have a talk with Joseph. I must say that I am a bit surprised at his involvement. He is somebody we have considered will one day join our Sanhedrin."

Jehua saw his opportunity and immediately changed his tactic from what he had decided on the way to this house. He could find out further details later from his usual sources, but for now he would go with whatever came along.

"It's strange that you should mention this subject. As always our eminent leader is ahead of the pack. I came to ask your permission to send my guards to Arimathea's house to bring in the boy for questioning about this incident, and for his own safety, of course. I was undecided because I know how highly Joseph is regarded, and I did not wish to cause your Worthiness any embarrassment."

"How thoughtful and diplomatic of you, my son. But should we really become involved?"

"That is what has caused me agony of thinking. You see there may be more in this than shows at first glance. My instincts tell me that some other information I have may be relevant. I have a suspicion that this boy may be part of an alternative group who are preparing to lead their own rebellion."

"You mean they deliberately thwarted the raid on the Temple treasury to further their own ends? That could mean Arimathea is involved too. They would need his wealth to finance such a venture."

169

"Your Excellency is too quick for me. I had not thought of that, and I make no allegation as such. It might be expedient for our purposes just to interview the boy, and induce him to confess exactly who is controlling him, and what their plans are, if any."

"Yes, you are right. However, as I know the methods of how many confessions are extracted, be very careful with the application of *inducement*. I cannot afford to have wealthy citizens like Arimathea, and Prefect Rufus on my back if the boy dies. As you know, Rufus is reviewing my tenancy in this office in a few weeks, and the last thing I can afford now is a scandal, or a riot. My opponents will make capital of anything to get their man into this palace."

Jehua knew this very well indeed, as it was his motive in coming to Annas in the first place.

"I will do my best, but you know how stretched my resources are at festival times, with Jerusalem packed to its limits, even unto the Mount of Olives. This will need discretion, and sometimes discretion is expensive."

The High Priest took a large mouthful of wine, and swallowed it in one gulp. He and his Captain knew each other extremely well. They both needed each other, and each knew the other's needs. For Annas it was power, and Jehua it was money. There was an unspoken understanding between them, although they acted out the pretence of being unaware of the other one's intentions.

The captain recognised this was one of those moments, and pressed on with his plaint. "There is something you might care to know about this boy."

He paused, taking his turn to sip his wine, choosing his words warily to sound out his superior.

"You may remember that about twelve years ago a group of children were killed at Bethlehem, before you were High Priest. There were many stories about that, and I do not wish to explore them now."

"Yes I remember only too well," interrupted Annas. "I had a massive job in keeping the parents happy, under orders from the king, of course. It was alleged that brigands were trying to stir up trouble, or some outlaws or other. To be frank, I never really subscribed to that theory. There was talk that the king's own bodyguard were involved. Did you hear about that, Jehua? I suppose

170

you must have done. You were in charge of his men at the time were you not?"

Annas was just as crafty as himself, thought Jehua. Unless Annas genuinely did not know of his involvement. Herod had kept the whole thing very secret, and whilst it was not in the soldiers' interest to confess the truth, wine and guilt are a formidable enticement to loose talk. Jehua decided Annas was just fishing for details and reacted coolly. He was never one to panic.

"Yes, I was, and yes I did hear of such gossip," he said dismissively. "A terrible tragedy. But the reason I mention this is because some people started telling stories about a baby that escaped from the massacre. I must be honest and say that I only came upon this information recently, and the whole tale is very strange. Apparently, the baby and his mother are slaves, or were slaves, there is some confusion about that, and guess where they are staying now?"

"You mean...Joseph's house?"

"Again, you are so quick, Excellency."

"Alright, you can ease off the flattery...but not too much!"

Annas laughed at his joke, yet inwardly pleased at the recognition of his intellect.

Jehua smiled.

"Yes. Clearly this must be the same boy connected with the Temple raid."

"Yes, but what..."

"What is the significance of his escape from Bethlehem?" Jehua interrupted. "Ah, that is interesting indeed. It seems that there was some legend that the boy who escaped from the massacre would become King of Israel. Now once again my sources are a bit sketchy on this, and my informant who overheard the conversation in Joseph's house, could only hear so much. At one point it seems she was seen listening, and had to commence again a little later. No matter, the essential point is that if this boy, or his helpers, believe him to be a king in waiting, you can see why they would not want a rival group getting in power before them. I realise it sounds a little mad, but what other explanation can there be for a Judean saving the life of a Roman at the expense of a fellow countryman?"

Annas considered Jehua's words for a while.

171

Then he said, "You must be correct, as crazy as it seems. This gives credence to the rumour of revenge against the boy by the followers of the dead man, Judas. Oh sweet David, what a mess this could make if open fighting breaks out. I fear what the Romans will do. They will probably execute hundreds to make an example to deter others, and may even abolish our freedom to worship our God as we like."

"Indeed. Whilst that would mean merely more work for me and the guards, your Holiness might have to secure other employment. That would be terrible in view of our good relationship. However, I have a plan that might help."

"What sort of plan?"

Jehua made no comment, but just raised his eyebrows to signify it was a question he would not answer directly without something from Annas.

Hope lightened the High Priest's face, and then concern darkened it again.

"It will be discreet?"

"As far as I am able. But as I said earlier, discretion costs money. Mouths are only silenced by silver, gold or death, in ascending order. There will be expenses."

Annas sighed. "How much do you…er, will it require?"

"Difficult to estimate. Shall we say seven hundred and fifty denarii?"

"What! That is almost two year's wages for a labourer."

"I am no labourer, your Holiness, and the people I send are skilled at their um, work."

Jehua looked slightly aggrieved. Annas noticed that and softened a degree. He needed this man's skill and cunning, and raw power to get things done quickly and silently. If he did not pay him, others certainly would, and it was always best to keep men like Jehua on your side.

"Will that include your customary *bonus*?

The captain laughed aloud at the game they were playing. "Yes."

"On that basis you may proceed. I will give you half now and the rest after you report back to me. I want no killing unless absolutely necessary. Is that clear, or will it spoil your 'plan'?"

Jehua shook his head.

"Killing would be a last resort. It should be possible to accomplish what you want without too much violence; only a little intimidation maybe."

A short discussion ensued as Jehua outlined his course of action. He did not give too many details as usual, which Annas considered safer for himself. Sometimes it was better to be able to swear on oath that he did not know about certain things, without actually breaking the oath. He was Yahweh's High Priest, after all.

"What about the boy's mother? Will you take her too?"

"I do not consider it will be necessary. Best not to inflame too many people. She was not involved at the Temple by all accounts, and anyway, whoever heard of a woman leading a rebellion, or having a position of influence in a Zealot group?"

Jehua chuckled at the absurdity of it, and on his reflection of the importance of women in their society.

"Yes. I suppose you would only need her if the boy is not there."

The money was exchanged and Jehua went back to his chamber. He decided he would make arrangements for his guards to visit Joseph's house the next day, after he had called upon the leaders of the residue of the Zealots. It would be easy to find them from his contacts. He wanted to see whether he could convince them to leave matters to him, and gain any knowledge they may have about this boy which might become useful.

The matter would have to be finished quickly, for once people started to leave Jerusalem as the festival wound down, it would be almost impossible to find anyone in the seething mass that made its way along the roads to other cities, towns and villages in every direction of the known world. Jehua disliked crowds any time as they impeded his work, but to ask someone if they had seen travellers at Passover time was likely to elicit a rude response. If the boy got out of the city he would have little chance of finding him.

As he contemplated his action, he bit into a dried fig. Tearing a piece of the fruit with his teeth, he muttered darkly to himself. "You may have escaped me once, young man, whoever you are, but this time I will have you, and whatever secrets you may possess."

CHAPTER EIGHTEEN.

The Persian Makes An Offer.

When Martha returned to Arimathea's house, she drew the two Josephs aside and told them quietly about what she had heard at the weaver's shop. Neither of them displayed any alarm and did their best to reassure her that it was all idle boasting and nothing would come of it. Nevertheless, they all agreed not to tell Mark, and that he should not be left on his own for a few days. Someone would always be near to keep a watch on him.

Martha also mentioned the disagreement with Esherah, and the breaking of the bowl. Arimathea was particularly interested in that, and resolved to pay a call on Haaman. He had been thinking that it was not right that Mary, even though only his second cousin, should be deprived of something so valuable, when he was so wealthy and could have paid for the redemption himself. Family ties were important to this man, and he was humbled by the sacrifice made by her, Joseph, and their son, to free two people they hardly knew. He resolved to get the bowl from Haaman. Bearing in mind it was now broken, it might be at a cheaper price.

Arimathea knew an excellent goldsmith, Ben Huram-Abi, and if the broken piece could not be restored, he could always reshape it into a goblet. In fact, for reasons he could not fathom, when he had seen the bowl before, the thought traversed his mind that it was more like a shallow goblet, or cup, and should be used as such, rather than a bowl. It was the presence of the small handles that made it a bowl, and now it seemed one of those had been removed, removing the other one would present no problem for Ben Huram-Abi. He was descended from the famous Huram-Abi of many centuries ago, sent by the king of Tyre to Solomon, to help build the first Temple. That man was skilled in crafting gold and all metals, and endowed with understanding. It was said that he knew how to make all kinds of engravings, and to execute any design which may be assigned to him. Ben Huram-Abi had almost the same skill as his celebrated ancestor.

But all that was for another day. At the moment he had to issue instructions for the feast tonight and busied himself with that.

The evening came, and everyone enjoyed themselves, particularly Lazarus and Martha. Mark had never seen his mother like this before, and realised that it might not be long before there would be a new father figure in his life. Lately, he seemed to be acquiring them by the day.

His mother told him about her meeting again with the Magus, and how she had arranged to see him the next day at noon at the Damascus Gate. They both pondered what it was he wanted to give them. Mark could not remove the thought from his mind, and was still thinking about it as he fell asleep.

The next morning dawned expectantly. This was the last day of the festival, and the climate was beginning to get even warmer. Mary and Joseph started to make preparations for their journey back to Nazareth the day after this; Jehua instigated his plans to capture Mark; Arimathea paid a call on Haaman; and Annius Rufus gave the command for the crucifixion on the morrow of five of the band that had failed to rob the Temple. Martha borrowed a robe from one of Arimathea's chests to meet the Persian, and the eternal hand on the loom of the ancient tapestry of life began to draw in the threads.

Martha found the Damascus Gate busy with travellers. The creaking of wheels from over laden wagons added to the general hubbub. Many people were starting their return journeys a day early. The city walls stretched out either side of the small entrance, which was only just large enough for two carts to go through side by side. During the day, at busy times like these, the strong wooden doors on each wall were permanently open. It would be an impossible job to keep opening and closing them.

The hot sun was behind Martha's head as she looked out through the gate at the dirt track road which wound northwards into the distance, through hills, and on towards other cities and cultures. Tomorrow Mary and Joseph would take their family along that road with hundreds of others, maybe thousands. In large families it was often difficult to make sure everyone was together, and though there was safety in travelling in numbers, it caused its own problems for mothers trying to round up all the younger children and keep them together. The older children were often trusted to look after themselves to stay with whatever party of pilgrims they were with.

Martha smiled to herself, and knew that, as always, at least one child was bound to go missing. That was one worry she would not have.

Then, despite bathed in the sunshine, she shivered, as though struck with sudden premonition. An eerie feeling swept over her, as if a giant shadow had been cast. She had entered Jerusalem at the southern end so many years ago. Was she to leave it by this northern entrance? Joseph had told her that she and Mark were welcome to go and stay with him and Mary, but she could not make up her mind. She had Lazarus to consider now as well. Though it wasn't just that which had caused her to shudder. It was something else, but what?

Unable to define the cause she turned and saw the approach of a caravan. The camels were laden to maximum, and some even had riders swaying side to side as they rocked in time to the lumbering pace of the beasts. The camel men swished their sticks, and made strange sounds to urge their charges. Even though Martha knew they were foreigners, she was certain the sounds were no earthly language, just noises made up to command animals. This was a big camel train and she knew it was the Persian's.

Then she looked at the sky. There were no clouds. She half expected to see some massive bird of prey flapping away, so sure was she that a shadow had passed over her. There was nothing.

She turned back to the caravan and was relieved to see the familiar dark, wrinkled countenance smiling at her.

"Peace to you, my dear child. I hope you have not been waiting too long. Let us go over here for a moment. It will be a little while before my party navigate all the animals and baggage through the gate. They will not leave without me, anyway. Hah!"

He laughed at the ridiculous idea.

Looking into her eyes in that manner he adopted so often, he asked, "So, what have you decided?"

He seemed to look at her innermost mind.

"What do you mean?"

Martha was startled. Could he read thoughts? Did he actually know that she had been thinking about whether to stay in Jerusalem or go to Nazareth?

"Why do people always say that when they know perfectly well what I mean? I saw you thinking, before you saw me, and your face pulled the shape of someone worried or trying to decide what to do. It is a logical assumption, isn't it? No Magi's trick, you know. Hah!"

176

He beamed again.

Martha relaxed and said, "Well, yes you are right. I was wondering what to do. This freedom business brings new responsibilities, doesn't it? I think I know what I would like to do, but I have other people to consider."

"Yes, I know very well. More than you may imagine. But have you considered that your son may not want to be part of your plans?"

"Oh, yes I have."

Martha was startled again. This man was so direct, and his finger always on the needle. "He has been talking about joining… well, doing all sorts of things"

Martha was reluctant to speak of the Roman army for fear of what questions and disgust that might provoke.

The Persian smiled.

"You do not have to be so coy with me, Martha. I told you previously that I know many things about you and Mark It is only natural for him to see himself as someone important, as a soldier perhaps? But if that is to be, there are many things I need to teach him."

"You? Why? And another thing, how do you know so much about us, and what is it that you want to give him?"

"Ah, I am afraid I am guilty of a little subterfuge. I wanted to talk to you alone so we could discuss him coming with me to learn things that he could not learn elsewhere. I recognize this is a shock to you, and that you do not know me, but you also know, deep within you, that you trust me, don't you? It is an offer that will benefit him greatly as he grows, and I have something else to give him, but the time has not yet come for that."

Martha now knew what that shadow meant that she felt earlier. It was that she would not be leaving this town with her son. She could not explain it, but knew it to be true.

The Magus continued.

"I owe you some explanation, but we do not have the time now. All I can reveal at this moment is that your son has been an interest of mine since the first time you saw me and my associates back in Bethlehem. We came to that little village, driven by an event in the heavens. We expected one baby to be born under that cosmic happening, not two. It was only afterwards that we learned from Mary that your child had been born too, although not actually in

Bethlehem. Mary's child is to be a very special person. Just how special none of us know. Yet the proximity of your son's birth interested me greatly, and my research has revealed that Mark also has a special destiny."

Martha started to ask something, but the Persian cut her short.

"Do not ask what it is. I am not the fount of all knowledge, but I have learned to trust my instincts, and you should do likewise. Only certain things are revealed to me at one time. Others come later. That is why I came to Jerusalem this Passover. I knew, as surely as I followed that star years ago, that I would find you both. Do you believe me?"

Martha nodded, uncertainly.

"Do you trust me?"

After a pause, the young woman looked into the eyes of this mysterious man. How could she not trust someone of whom Mary and Joseph had spoken so trustingly? She nodded again, still thinking about what had been said to her, and trying to understand it.

"If you knew you would find us, why have you taken so long to tell me about it? Why wait until the festival is almost over?"

The Persian stroked his long greyish beard and breathed deeply, considering how much he should declare.

"All I can say is that I was led bit by bit. In fact it was not until I happened to see you and your friends coming out of the Temple the day after I first spoke to you, that a lot of things came to have meaning. It is the same now. I have had my friend and bodyguard watch over Mark. You met him the other day…Hiro."

"Oh, the giant! Yes, he said he had a master. He was mysterious, like you."

"Ah! There are reasons why we had to be *mysterious* as you call it. There are other forces at work. It is true, I could have come to you earlier, but only now will you both be amenable to what I suggest. You will find in life that certain events must come to pass before the really important things happen. You know that Mark is in danger, don't you?"

Martha was alarmed.

"You mean from the Zealots? How did you hear about that? Is it being spoken of that openly in the streets and taverns?"

This time it was his turn to nod.

178

"And not only from them. I have many people who gather information for me, apart from Hiro. Any household with servants, and thinking itself able to hide secrets, is either ingenuous or stupid. There are others who are becoming interested in Mark. An old adversary called Jehua is making enquiries. Enough talk! In anticipation of our conversation I have instructed my people to wait for me on the outskirts of the city once they have passed through the gate. They can rest from the noon heat while we go and talk to the young man himself. You trust Mary and Joseph. Let us have their counsel on this. The time is very near. I feel it. Look how there are now extra guards on the Gate. They are Temple police, not Romans."

Martha saw it was true, and her face creased with anxiety.

"Do not worry. Everything has a purpose. Come, we must go."

He took her arm and started to propel her through the crowd, when a shout stopped both of them immediately.

CHAPTER NINETEEN.

Jehua Sees The Light.

While Martha had been preparing to meet the Persian, Jehua had finished his enquiries and was making his way to Joseph of Arimathea's home, with seven of his best men. He had wanted more with him but with the policing of the Temple still a priority, and extra guards for the exits out of Jerusalem, this was as many he could spare. In any event, he did not consider it would be too arduous an assignment to arrest the boy. Their arrival would be unexpected, and Arimathea's servants would offer scant resistance.

Jehua's party caused many comments as it threaded through the narrow streets. People knew that the Temple guards did not go anywhere in a group unless the Sanhedrin had considered something threatened the normal existence of the community. The usual Passover talk of messianic leaders abounded, and rumours were rife since the rebel activities days earlier. As this was still a holy day, and many were not engaged in their normal work, some men followed the guards at a discreet distance. Curiosity multiplied the followers, so that eventually a sizeable crowd travelled behind Jehua. As the crowd grew, so did the mob instinct that something must be worth looking at, and the followers became totally disproportionate to the event.

Jehua became aware of the presence behind him, and cursed himself that he had not anticipated this. Subtlety had never been one of his strong points, even though he had a keen brain. He wished he had chosen a night excursion now, or sent someone to check that the boy was in the house. He would lose face if all this fuss came to nothing because he was not there. But time was against him. Every hour of delay meant the greater risk of the boy learning what was in store, or simply moving on after the festival. If he tried ordering the crowd away they would probably not comply, and become all the more curious. There might be a skirmish or two, and that would displease Annas who still held the balance of the funds for this little escapade.

In the meantime Joseph of Arimathea had just arrived back at his house. His mission to recover the gold bowl from Haaman had proved even easier than he expected. Apparently Martha's former owner had become very distressed at the breakage of the object, and linking that to a virulent outbreak of his skin disease, believed the gold was cursed. Therefore, a generous offer from Joseph, and a chance to ingratiate with him, was far too good an opportunity to miss.

Mark and Joseph were standing in the main room looking at the bowl. Mary and her husband had taken their children for a farewell look around the city. Three servants were carrying out their chores in the courtyard and outer rooms.

"It is impressive isn't it, Joseph?" said Mark rhetorically. "Not that it is particularly beautiful, but there is something about it I cannot explain. Even with one of the handles missing."

They stared in silence for a few moments. Joseph tried placing the detached handle in position to judge how it looked, and then shook his head.

"No, I still believe it would be better to remove the remaining handle and make it a goblet. What do you think, Mark?"

The boy tilted his head to one side, as if that made imagining the image easier.

"Yes! I think you are right. With the short stem it would make an excellent drinking cup for special occasions. Somehow it seems like it should have always have been like that."

"You feel that too? So do I."

The man looked at his young friend, and felt a bond between them. Then his head lifted, as he strained to listen.

"There seems to be a lot more noise than usual outside. I wonder what is causing all that."

Joseph moved to a shutter and glanced out. He saw some of Jehua's men coming into the courtyard, and a large crowd of spectators outside of that.

"Now what brings the Temple police here?" he mused.

Joseph was a devout man, and had tried to carry out the ordinances of his faith since his youth. He quickly realised that the guards were not present at his home for any transgression of his own, and that it must have something to do with Mark and the rebels. Perhaps they had come to protect Mark against attack?

181

Still clutching the bowl he instructed Mark, "Stay here and keep out of sight while I go and see what this is all about."

In the courtyard Joseph's servants tried to do their duty and bar the way into the house. It was customary for Mehu, the head servant, to make visitors wait in the courtyard while he went and announced their arrival to his master. Jehua had no time for politeness and pushed his way past Mehu who followed him still asking him to state the purpose of his visit. Joseph saw the difficulty placed upon Mehu, and not wishing him to be embarrassed or sustain injury if the guards turned nasty, he came out and confronted Jehua. He spoke to him in a calm and dignified manner.

"Peace be with you Jehua, although your task seems anything but peaceful for you to charge into my home like this with armed men. It appears you have brought half of Jerusalem with you as well."

Joseph signified the crowd by glancing at it.

The captain stopped and met Joseph's iron gaze.

"I apologise for disturbing your peace, Joseph, but I am here on an important task of city security. You have a boy staying here?"

For a moment, Joseph thought he might have assumed incorrectly. Was this something to do with Mary's son and not Mark? He knew how Mary and Joseph had to flee to Egypt years ago to safeguard Jesus, and how they were always reluctant to talk about the details of his birth. If he did not handle this correctly he might endanger both boys staying with him. It seemed prudent not to reveal there was more than one boy here. Mark was also an escapee from the purging of Bethlehem. Was this still part of an ongoing policy to exterminate anyone born in that village at that time? He decided it would be futile to lie, and his best option was to play for time.

"Yes. How does that interest you? Are young boys once again considered a threat to the peace of Judea?"

Jehua felt the impact of those words as though Joseph had struck him. He looked at him with eyes that scanned every vestige of the merchant's face for a hint of whether he was referring to the massacre at Bethlehem. It was uncanny how references to that incident kept occurring lately. Perhaps Arimathea was involved with a rebel group after all? Was Jehua's involvement in the murder of the children not such a secret as he believed? Or was guilt, that thief of peace, probing at his paranoia?

In fact Joseph, like many others, had heard the rumours about Jehua's time with Herod, and was just using his oral skill to prompt the captain into revealing more about this visit now, by teasing him.

"I am not certain what you mean by 'again' but that is irrelevant. I wish to question your guest about the Temple raid at the beginning of the festival. He may have some information to help us."

"What with?"

"Our enquiries."

"But surely your *enquiries* are finished? Unless you are saying that innocent men are going to the cross tomorrow?"

"That is not what I am saying at all."

Joseph raised his voice.

"So you consider they are guilty then? You obviously have no sympathy with your fellow Judeans in their fight against Rome?"

Some of the crowd who had filtered into the courtyard to hear better, gasped. Jehua dare not let such an accusation go unchallenged. It would hinder him in his work, and tarnish his reputation as a neutral observer, and occasional enforcer. He could not be branded a Roman sympathizer, but he did not know how to answer Joseph without making an anti Rome comment which might get back to Prefect Rufus. Then he had a spark of inspiration.

"I make no comment about their guilt, or otherwise. As for having Roman sympathies, that is rather the province of the boy we have come to question. Was it not him who saved the life of the Roman soldier?"

At last Joseph knew for whom they had come, but was Mark in more danger from Jehua than the possibility of any Zealot revenge? His instinct told him all was not what it seemed. He would employ his stalling tactics again.

"Is it not good to save a life?"

"Yes, I suppose."

"Then you would have done the same?"

Jehua was becoming rattled. He was a fighting man and knew he would lose a battle of words with this eminent talker. He was also conscious of his men behind him, waiting to see what he would do, and could almost feel their smirks at his discomfort.

"Why are you trying to trick me? Let us get on with our work. Are you going to let us in or not?"

"You had not said you wanted to come in, and I am hardly in a position to prevent you. I still query why you need so many with you just to talk to a boy. However, I am sure he will not mind sparing you a few moments here."

"We are to take him with us. Please step aside."

Joseph now was sure that Jehua had a more sinister agenda.

"So you are here to arrest him? On what charge?"

"I never said he was under arrest. It is better for his own safety he comes with us."

"But he is safe here. If he is not under arrest, he does not have to go with you."

Jehua's patience snapped.

"Enough of these ridiculous questions. If you will not help us, stand aside while we do what we have to do."

He turned to his guards.

"Enter and seize the boy. He had better be here, for everyone's sake."

The captain glared at Joseph as he said this.

Mark had been crouched behind the door listening to the dialogue. He remembered what his mother had told him almost a week ago about Bethlehem, and how the authorities might still be looking for him. He also remembered that his mother might be in trouble for having an illegitimate son by a Roman. If Jehua was more a man of action than words, so too was his intended prisoner. Mark was not going to let them torture him into trapping his mother. He had heard stories about what soldiers did to captives. He reacted spontaneously.

Jumping up, he ran through the room to the back of the house and made for the stairs to the roof. Jehua entered the building just as Mark was disappearing, and saw him trying to escape. He ordered some of his men to follow the boy, and two others to go back through the courtyard to try and get around the rear of the house. The adrenalin surged through both the pursuers and their quarry as the excitement of the chase gripped them. Mark was unarmed and an easy target for shows of bravado from the guards. It was easier to be brave and carry out orders when there was no fear of retaliation.

Mark made it to the roof. He had realised immediately that he would not be able to get through the crowd amassed at the front of the courtyard. His plan was to drop down the side where a lean-to structure rested against the house wall and run to find his mother. He knew she would be at the Damascus Gate, and had to warn her about the danger he thought she was in. By running up the stairs he thought he would get the guards to follow him to the roof.

Meanwhile Joseph had sensed where Mark was going, and left the front door to cross the courtyard. He entered a rear passage by a side door and saw Mark drop down onto the ground from the lean-to. He shouted after the boy as he ran in the opposite direction, and ran towards him, still holding the gold bowl. There had been no time to put it down somewhere safe.

"Mark! Stop! There is no need to run."

"I must warn mother. I'll come back to you later."

As he said this, he halted and turned slightly to Joseph who had approached to within a few feet of him.

"I must go."

Just as Mark turned to resume his escape, a guard on the roof drew an arrow across his bow. His forearm muscles tensed with the strain of holding his aim.

"I'll slow him down a bit," he said to the man next to him. "The boy won't get too far with an arrow in his leg."

At the instant he was about to release the arrow, Joseph suddenly moved across the line of sight to try and get Mark. Simultaneously a dazzling light came from the bowl. It grew in concentration and power until everybody looking at the man and the boy were temporarily blinded. Only Joseph and Mark were unaffected as they were not looking in the direction of the light. Even Jehua, who had wondered where Joseph had gone, and had eventually followed him a few seconds later, was dazed by the strong reflection of what he thought were the sun's rays from the gold object held in Joseph's hand.

The arrow flew harmlessly past Joseph, who looked up to see where it had come from. He saw the archer staggering blindly, and noticed others rubbing their eyes with their hands. Mark ran on oblivious to all of this, but Joseph knew he could not follow him and risk being regarded as a fugitive also. Apart from that, his instinct told him that Mark would be alright. A sense of peace came over him, as though this was meant to happen.

He turned and came back to Jehua who was still confused and without sight. He put his hands on the captain's shoulders to steady him.

"Who is that?" asked Jehua.

"It is I, Joseph. What is the matter? Why can't you see?"

"It was that light from that object you carried in your hand. The sun reflected so brightly it has made my eyes become full of stars and red mist. Didn't you notice it?"

"No, I saw nothing like that," said Joseph puzzling over why the men on the roof had also been affected when they were at a different angle to the sun.

"Where are my men? Has the boy gone?"

"Some of your men are on the roof. I do not know where the others are. Probably still trying to force their way through the front courtyard to get here. Mark has run off, but he shouted he will return."

"What are my men still doing on the roof? They should be after him. Lazy sluggards."

"I believe they are in the same situation as you. Their eyes were affected too."

The frown on Jehua's face advertised his bewilderment.

"Say that again. What sort of item are you holding, and what in heaven is it made of to reflect so strongly?"

"It is a simple gold bowl that is all. In fact I had just returned from purchasing it from Haaman, the metal trader, when you arrived, which is why it was still in my hand."

Jehua shook his head.

"Must have been a freak of the light. Never heard of anything like it," he grunted. "Just hope it wears off soon," he added somewhat anxiously.

"I am sure it will. If you remember your scripture, it is not without precedent. Do you recall how the Lord told the Hebrew commander to get his men to polish their copper shields to dazzle the Midianites so their chariots went over the cliff?"

"Er, yes, now you say it, I do. Are you trying to tell me this was divine intervention here today?"

He snorted at the thought.

Joseph said nothing, but the comment rattled around his mind for a while.

"Here, let me lead you back into my house, until you have recovered."

Joseph took Jehua by the arm, and once more the pragmatic combatant was left puzzled by the actions of this extraordinary merchant.

Jehua let himself be led, muttering softly, "Twice this boy has crossed my path, and each time he has eluded me. I have never even seen his face properly. Perhaps it is not meant to be."

"That may be so. Come, I am sure your sight will return soon. Come and rest. Mark will not go far. He has nowhere else to go."

Mark kept running until he reached the Damascus Gate. He did not know that the pursuit had been temporarily halted, and assumed the guards were immediately behind him. At first he thought his mother had left as he could not see her in any of the crowds threading their way through the narrow entrance. There were so many women around wearing the same brown robe and headscarf as Martha, that differentiating between them was difficult. Then he noticed a man's blue turban and a woman's head disappearing up a side street. He shouted after them, and his mother recognised his voice, even above the clamour of the travellers, merchants and animal carts.

He went to them and outlined what had happened at Joseph's house. Martha and the Persian exchanged knowing glances. This was confirmation of their previous talk before Mark arrived, and now Martha knew there were at least two sets of people after her son. However, what touched her more deeply was the concern he showed for her, thinking her to be in danger, and not worrying much for his own safety. She explained that she felt the only real danger was to him and that it might be best that he went with the Persian for a little while until she knew where she and Lazarus were going to stay.

Mark felt pressured by the thought of imminent apprehension by Jehua's men, and could see that his mother's fear was for him. It was the Magus who decided the issue.

"Mark. Do you trust your mother?"

"Of course. That is a ridiculous question."

"Do you believe that her wisdom may be better than yours at this moment? Because if you do, then there really is no reason to doubt that her advice is sound. I also advocate that you come with me. I have many things to teach you, and also something to give you

187

which you will need when you are fully grown. Please do not press me further on this, because there is no time, and more explanation will only lead to more questions."

The remaining part of the child in Mark let his curiosity, and fear of capture, overcome his fear of leaving his mother. Martha saw the weakening of his resolve and felt she needed to affirm that she was not just trying to abandon him so she could lead a new life with Lazarus. She drew him close and hugged him. Tears started to seep onto her cheeks.

"If there was another way, you know I would take it, don't you? You can send messages to Joseph's house. That can be done can't it?"

She looked over at the Persian, who nodded.

"We can keep in touch until it is time for you to return. It will only be a little while. I will be perfectly safe with either of the two Josephs. You will be safe in Damascus. That's where the Persian is going"

She lifted the head of what seemed to be a much older young man than yesterday, and held his cheeks between her palms, so that it made his lips pout slightly. Then she smiled, controlling her emotion, and placed a long kiss on his forehead.

"Go. From what you have said the soldiers will be here soon, as they start to trace where you went."

The Persian took Mark's hand and gently moved him towards an approaching camel, some fifty yards from the Gate. The animal had two baskets strapped either side of it. He signalled to the rider to dismount. The man made a guttural sound and tapped the camel's front leg with a stick. It dropped onto its front legs and then lowered its back. The man alighted and the beast remained crouched.

"This is part of my caravan. Get into this empty basket. It might smell a bit of the frankincense we've sold, but it will hide you while we go past the guards over there. There is no one looking at us. I will stand in front of you."

Mark took a look at his mother, who urged him with a smile, and then he lifted one leg over the rim of the basket, and then the other. When he had checked that Mark had sat down, the Persian replaced the lid and sat astride the camel.

"I do not expect you are too comfortable there, but directly we are a fair way from the guards I will let you out. Do not speak until I tell you. The guards are not looking at travellers like my entourage. They have probably had instructions to look out for a mother and son."

At the Persian's command the camel raised its back legs and then the front, and stood up. The brightly coloured tassels around the edge of the apron covering its back swayed in time to the motion. He raised the stick to make the animal move, when Martha suddenly blurted out, "Wait! I do not know your real name. How can I contact you?"

The smiling face of the Magus turned to her, as though what she said had amused him.

"What name do you use for me now?"

"We just call you the Persian."

"Well that is the name by which you will find me. I abandoned my birth name long ago. Everyone knows me by different names but generally they call me 'The Persian'. Is that a problem for you?"

Martha shook her head. Everything that was happening seemed like a dream. She felt that far from being in control of her life now she was freed, the opposite was true.

"If we move from Damascus I will send you word. Do not fear for all will be well."

The stick resumed its journey onto the camel's flank and Martha believed what was said to her. After all, this was the same man who had given gold and other treasures to Mary's son. His motives must be good.

The man charged with her son's safety manoeuvred the creature into the queue of other animals and people. She saw the basket lid lift very briefly, and a small hand wave out. She automatically waved back, even though Mark could not see her. Then she let the tears overwhelm her. She had the feeling it would be the last time she would see him as a boy, and that great black shadow seemed to cover her again from out of a cloudless sky.

CHAPTER TWENTY.

Revelations.

And so Mark came to leave the land of his birth, and the city of his childhood. With the change of habitat also came a slight change of name. The Magus advised him that it would be safer and perhaps more opportune for his future to adopt the Roman form of Mark, and to establish his Roman identity. Henceforth Mark, as was the custom, would assume his father's name; Marcus Favonius Facilis.

One evening, seven days journey and a hundred and ten miles from Jerusalem, the caravan was strung out against the skyline on large sandy mounds in a sort of desert wilderness. They had travelled north through Samaria into Galilee. There they turned east to follow the northern shores of The Sea of Galilee, through Capernaum, and across the smallest part of the river Jordan. They were now in Syria, about forty miles from Damascus, and with another two and a half days journey to reach it. Once there the Persian had promised Marcus he could send word to his mother by courier.

The caravan was making about sixteen miles a day, and could only travel as fast as the slowest walker. It was not possible to provide everyone with a beast to ride. Even if they had, it would only have pushed up the daily average by another five miles or so, and was therefore considered not economic by the owners of the goods and animals. The human walkers had a different view of that economy.

The command to halt and make camp was issued, and the long, undulating line of camels and mules, silhouetted against the evening sky, changed to a closer circular formation, and sank down to the sand.

A crescent moon hung in the air like the tip of an abandoned fingernail, pointing the way to the first constellations blinking blearily from a darkening cobalt canvass. Such a tempting silhouette was often the target for bandits, but the Romans had recently cleared out most of the usual larger groups in this area, and a caravan of this size would provide a stern test for a small band of robbers. Even

Marcus, as he would now be called, knew that thieves are naturally lazy, often cowardly, and prefer easier victims.

Many merchants would travel long distances in a large group, and split up later as towns were reached along the way. This was the practice of The Persian and his friends, who always travelled with a retinue comprising many servants and hired hands who would be good in a fight. Sometimes the danger might come from the people actually hired to protect the group. The more cunning brigands found it easier to infiltrate a caravan by this method, thereby eliminating the protection and making it easier to steal the goods. For this reason the Persian used a trusted servant as a bodyguard, and general recruiter of strong men.

This man was Hiro, who himself had immense strength and was also renowned as a wrestler. He had been in the Persian's employ for some years, and there was a deep bond of friendship between them. Marcus was also entrusted to his care, for it would mean his physical education would be developed as well as his mind. Hiro was an enigmatic man, in his late twenties, but looking older because of the tough corporeal life he had led, and the amazing body-art he wore. His origins were a mystery, although it was believed that he had told some of his secrets to his master. If he had, they went no further, for the Magus himself was a man celebrated for knowing secrets and keeping them. It was for this reason that Hiro's race or tribe were not known generally, and with his six foot five inch muscular frame being quite a good few inches taller than the average height in that era; nobody would dare pursue the topic with him if he did not want to discuss it.

Marcus had noted the first time he saw him that Hiro looked like he was of deepest Asian descent far beyond Armenia and the Caucasus Mountains, but his four strands of braided hair and body art were more Babylonian. Marcus wanted to ask Hiro what all the coloured circles and swirls on his skin meant, but thought he would get to know him a bit first. He had seen Hiro's many earrings shake when he laughed, and at the moment he did not want to see them shake when the giant was annoyed.

Over the last few days Marcus had become familiar with the evening routine of making camp at twilight and eating around a large fire with the Persian's friends. After the meal his new mentor would draw him away from the fire to a darker area and teach him the constellations. It was the intention for Marcus to learn a new set of stars each night, and the stories and legends of the people immortalised in the heavens.

This evening, after the camels and mules had all been attended to, the meal eaten and the watchmen appointed, Hiro joined Marcus in listening to the Persian expound expertly on his favourite subject. The wise man from another culture seemed to have the world's knowledge at his finger tips, and had a habit of seeing things from a different angle than most people. Hiro had heard these talks often, but he found there was always a little more information gleaned each time. Different questions would be raised.

"Persian, isn't it amazing how all those stars revolve around us each night," asked Marcus laying on his back so he could see the whole expanse of the sky without getting an ache in his neck.

"Ah, now that is a debatable point. You probably are not aware, in keeping with many others I might add, that around four hundred years ago Aristarchus the Greek published a work saying that the Earth, as well as the sphere of fixed stars, orbits the sun."

"What? The stars and our Earth revolve around the sun. That is crazy because you can see the sun actually move across the sky."

"Have you not learned by now that all things may not be what they seem. If everything revolves around the Earth, why then does the North Star always remain constant?"

Marcus shook his head, unable to grasp the problem.

The Persian continued. "Aristarchus was a brilliant astronomer, but his work is ignored, because it does not fit into our way of thinking. People never want to look beyond their first impressions. They accept the easiest explanation because they are not bothered about anything apart from their own small, personal world, and it saves time and effort. However, the curious ones, the open minded thinkers, realize that what we can see is not always what we know, and what we can know is not always what we can see."

Marcus looked perplexed.

"Is this a riddle?"

"If you think that is a riddle," laughed the old man, "consider this. What shape is our world?"

"Well, it's a flat circle. Everyone knows that."

"Are you sure? How do you know that?"

"Because our teachers and best researchers in all disciplines have made it known."

"And you trust their judgement, quite so. But do they know all things? The depth of their knowledge is their limit. Have you not noticed how when some new discovery is made, their knowledge increases and adapts? The conclusions once set in stone are then moulded like potter's clay into a new belief, and it becomes the new fact, or wisdom. Consequently, can you ever be sure of what you are being told where science is concerned? We are all a product of our age. From generation to generation we determine new knowledge which we think is fact, until some other discovery is made that alters it. What concerns me is that too many make science their religion, trusting in the judgement of man, and yet ridicule people like you and I, who believe in things we cannot see, and are open to what might lie beyond this world. We believe there is a God, some believe there is not. Both have beliefs that are not provable in a scientific sense. It's all a question about where you place your faith."

He shook his head and stroked his beard.

Marcus looked puzzled again.

"Yes, I think I follow what you say, but what has that to do with the world being flat?"

"Aha! It has everything. If it is flat, then where do the clouds appear from and disappear to? Why do the oceans stay the same distance away on the horizon? Why cannot we see past the horizon into what must be an abyss beyond?"

"I don't know. I have never thought about it."

"Then think, Marcus, think. Always think and never stop challenging what you are told. Unless, of course, it is something that you can feel in your heart, and just know is true. Trust your instincts, Marcus, for these inner voices tell us things we cannot possible discern by any other means. Often, instinct can be your best counsel. Think on these things."

The boy sat up and thought for a while. Then he said, "I will do so."

A few moments later, after some consideration and thought, he spoke again. "Well, is the world flat or not?"

Both the Persian and Hiro burst into laughter.

"My little Marcus you are priceless. You expect to solve the conundrums of this age after only a few minutes thought. I do not

193

know the answer either, but I do have my doubts. So did Anaximander of Miletus. Over six hundred years ago he believed the Earth was curved. I have a feeling he was right. Maybe one day someone will go on the longest voyage ever known to find out."

Marcus laid back down and looked at the glorious panorama above them.

"Which is the star that shone so brightly at my birth, and why doesn't it shine so well now?" he asked.

"That is an excellent question, young man. It is also one I am not sure I can answer. You see there are different types of stars. Some remain fixed in relation to others, like those you see now, and there are those that do not. The latter we call 'wanderers', or planets. There are even some who appear for only a short time before seeming to disappear for years, and then return. We call these hairy-tailed stars comets. Finally there are those which shoot across the sky for only a few seconds, and we call them…"

"Shooting stars!" exclaimed Marcus.

"Exactly. However, I, nor my fellow stargazers, could understand the nature of the star to which you refer. Two of the 'wanderers', which the Romans call Saturn and Jupiter were very close together at the time, and looked almost as though they were one single bright light. Such a joining in this way has been known by the ancients, and does sometimes signify a royal birth, or great leader. Yet that was not the only thing. There seemed to be a comet as well, but like no other in our records. It moved in a mysterious way. We did not know what it really was. All three things combined to make an unusual event, a sort of three in one, and we could tell that it all pointed to Jerusalem being the focal point. It was this that persuaded us to undertake the long journey before we were really ready."

"Before you were ready?"

"Yes. We had made provisional arrangements to come to Jerusalem some months later on business, but an event like this was too good to miss. Our charts showed us that somewhere near Jerusalem would be the best place to view the event, and even the writings of Zoroaster confirmed that such a thing might happen to herald a king. However, when we arrived, the focal point was not Jerusalem, but Bethlehem. Strange how only a distance of about six miles made such a difference. The light was not so splendid just that

194

short distance away in Jerusalem. That is how we found Joseph and Mary. Well, that and Herod's so called experts. They gave us the clue to Bethlehem, through your ancient scriptures. It was then I became more interested in your religion. Over the following years it has become more attractive to me, except there are some practices with which I am not comfortable."

He grimaced.

"Circumcision for one, and the restriction on certain foods. Perhaps one day if those are relaxed I might even embrace your faith."

"Really?"

"Yes. I am disillusioned with the cult of Zoroaster. I began to wonder if my god, Zoroaster, was the same as your god Yahweh. But I know he is not. The more I learn of your God, the more I realise how you believe He has cared and interacted with your people through the ages. His commands are not just the arbitrary whims or rules of an obsessive deity. They are for the people's good, to prolong their lives. His patience seems to be amazing, and it needs to be. Not just for dealing with transgressions, but for His plans. His time is a vastly different dimension to ours. As your scripture states, to Him 'a million years can be like a day'; and one of His days can be a million years to us. The future is like a scroll we cannot read, but not to God."

"Sounds like you have adopted the Hebrew faith already to me," interrupted Marcus.

The Magus smiled.

"Apologies, I am digressing. Anyway, it is only now that I realise we had made an error about the royal aspect, and that was not what it meant at all."

"Is that why you brought the type of gifts you did?"

"You are a bright boy, my son."

"Well, not really," confessed Marcus. "I heard Joseph, Mary's husband talking about it at Arimathea's house."

"Your honesty is to your credit. Does Joseph talk much about such things?"

"Oh no! He had to be forced to say anything at all."

"I am not surprised."

"He seemed to take his lead from Mary about what should be told, and what should not."

195

"Quite so. She is unique among women, that one. Wise beyond her years, but humble in character. She is not educated in the classical sense, but knows many things."

"Yes. She knows too much to argue, or to judge people."

"Well said, Marcus. Already you have learned from her. Never underestimate the female. In another age you might find women on the same level as men."

"Really? How could that ever happen?"

The Magus laughed at the boy's incredulity.

"Freedom, my son, freedom. When the world's knowledge enables instruments or mechanisms to do the daily chores, and women have more time to think for themselves, and about what they are doing."

Hiro broke his silence with grunt. Then, in that almost cultured mellow voice that belied his more animal physique, "They will never replace men as the provider. They are not built physically to do it."

He inhaled and let his enormous chest enlarge as if to emphasise the remark.

"My dear Hiro, that is exactly my point. With increased knowledge will come inventions that enable us to live without the dependencies we have now. Imagine being able to store food for long periods so it does not have to be prepared and cooked every day. Imagine homes where a fresh water well could be pumped. Women always draw the water here, but in some countries it is not only women's work."

"Where?" queried Marcus, who was hearing things thought unspeakable in Jerusalem.

"Rome for one," said the Persian. "The wealthier homes have heated pools to bathe in, and water is pumped everywhere by the ingenuity of their engineers."

Marcus whistled in amazement. "I want to go there."

"Therefore, if man can do all this now, imagine what he might achieve in centuries to come," reflected the Persian.

Hiro spoke again.

"You mentioned freedom before. What you are saying then, is that man by his own ingenuity will free women to do as they like? What sort of a world would that be? I am thankful that I shall not live to see it."

196

He shook his head disbelievingly, and the four strands of braided hair on his otherwise shaved head, swayed in agreement. The strands were of equal length and arranged in the shape of a cross. Each pair of diagonals was dyed a different colour, yellow and black.

Marcus laughed, and Hiro pretended to cuff him around the ear. The Persian chuckled at his friend's apparent unhappiness.

"Anyway, you were talking about the gifts you brought. I have seen the gold bowl. Where did it come from, because it is very special isn't it?"

Marcus wanted to change the topic to something more interesting to him than women.

"Hmm."

The Persian thought for a while and then continued. "I suppose it will do no harm now to reveal its origin. You must have been taught by your rabbi about the sacred vessels used by Moses to worship the God of Abraham, long before Solomon built the first Temple. What do you know about them?"

Marcus smiled at the opportunity to demonstrate his own knowledge. It seemed recently that his guardian knew nearly everything, and that he himself knew very little.

"It is believed by the Samaritans that Moses buried the sacred Temple vessels on Mount Gerizim," he said as though recalling word for word what his rabbi had taught him. "This is the mount upon which Moses had to set the 'Blessing'. Nearby is Mount Ebal, where the 'Curse' was set. As you know both the Samaritans and we await a deliverer, the Messiah, *but* they believe that one day the sacred vessels will be unearthed, and that whoever does that will deliver us from our oppressors. I don't know where such a belief comes from, and my rabbi thinks it is all nonsense. Most true Judeans have no time for the hated Samaritans anyway, so that is not really surprising is it?"

Then in a flash of realisation he added, "You mean the bowl is one of those sacred objects?"

"Er, yes and no. It was discovered with some of those objects, but there is no evidence to say it was once used by Moses. It probably was, but the issue is open to argument, and to an extent irrelevant. It may have been used to hold the blood of sacrifices. We decided to offer it to the baby we thought was to be a new king of your people. Gold denotes kingship, and if the child was to be a Hebrew leader, then it was fitting to return it, especially with its history."

"How did you obtain it, and the other vessels?"

"Do not press me on that. I might tell you more another time. Suffice it to say that they were part of some of the treasures stolen during the destruction of Solomon's Temple by the Babylonian King Nebuchadnezzar many centuries ago. It was also at that time the Ark of the Covenant disappeared."

The Magus paused and had that distant look again, as though directing his eyes into the past.

"You see, Moses had indeed buried some sacred objects on Mount Gerizim in two separate places, but a long time later one of the places was pillaged and a few objects stolen. I suppose the others are still there somewhere. Some found their way to Babylon, and my home city of Persepolis, while some were returned back to the Temple, from whence they were subsequently stolen by Nebuchadnezzar's forces as I said before. Ultimately the bowl passed into the hands of a fellow Magus; one of our group that came to see Mary's son just after his birth."

"How many of you made that visit?"

"Well, we started out with seven Magi that being the sacred and indivisible number, together with all their attendants and hired hands, for safety reasons. You could not really travel safely with less. But we had such a hard time on the journey that a few gave up. It was though powers of another realm were working against us. But we were still a large enough group to make Herod sit upright on his throne. Oh my, how he sat up! He tried hard to be amiable and relaxed, but the stench of fear was on him, and anger seeped through the cracks of the affable mask he wore. Evil permeated the whole palace, and we sensed his presence long before we had been told he was resident. We left him a gift of some balm to soothe his sores, and some perfume. This seemed to please him, although he probably still stank even after he had used it."

"Why?"

"Well, his whole body was a putrid mess and you could see his disease, but I was really referring to something else. He thought he was clever by telling us he would like to worship the new king himself, and that we should return to him later. He did not deceive us. Did not your Solomon write, *'Dead flies make a perfumer's oil stink, so a little foolishness is weightier than wisdom and honour.'* We saw the magnitude of his foolishness. I also had a dream warning of Herod's intentions."

"Amazing. I never get any good dreams like that. Did each Magi bring a gift? Joseph only mentioned three gifts, but were there others?"

"No. We agreed on what should be presented before we began our journey. They were basically just symbols as we thought that any king would have enough material things. We were not to know it was not the usual form of royalty we would meet. The golden bowl was chosen by all of us, as though the idea was planted simultaneously in our separate minds. As you know, it is something very special. Did Joseph tell you what the other gifts represented?"

"Yes. He said that the frankincense indicated priest-ship, and the myrrh was to do with mortality, or death."

"You have an excellent memory, Marcus. I have many things to show and tell you, and I hope that you will remember them equally as well. What did he tell you about the powers of the gold? I am sure someone as insatiably curious as you must have asked about that."

The Persian chuckled.

Marcus looked towards Hiro and hesitated.

"Oh, do not worry about Hiro. We share many secrets and are bound to each other by such trust."

"I see, only Joseph said that I was not to talk to anybody else about it. He told us that it had the power to enhance the lives of good people, and blight those of the wicked. He also said that the bowl had a purpose, and it would protect itself until its destiny was fulfilled."

This time the Persian looked amazed.

"Really? He said that? I do not recall ever telling him such a thing, although we did know it had power. It seems Joseph has found out certain things for himself."

"Or it has been revealed to him," added the youth.

Again the man looked at Marcus in surprise. He paused, deep in thought. Then he continued in his trance, cross legged, head bowed down, and neither Hiro nor Marcus wanted to interrupt him. Eventually he raised his head and spoke.

"There are many more facets to this business than I knew, and more to your Hebrew religion than contained in the scrolls of the prophets. By providing you with answers, you have instilled in me as many questions as there are stars above us. I must consider this further. It is time for my bed. May a peaceful night be yours."

With this abrupt ending to their discourse, the Magus rose and left for his tent. Marcus turned to Hiro.

"Have I upset him in some way?"

"No. When he is on a line of thought he concentrates only on that, and has no time for irrelevancies. He is a great thinker. One of the greatest of our age, I believe. If you stay close to him and pay attention, you will advance in wisdom far beyond what is available to most of us."

"Is that why you do not say much, but just listen?"

Seeing the frown on the giant's face he made a supplementary remark.

"Oh, I am sorry. I did not wish to be rude, but you are very quiet, and I noticed this since I joined the caravan."

Hiro relaxed and smiled.

"It is true I am not a talker like some people. Sometimes I wish I had that gift. It is easy to be friendly with such persons because they become attractive by their speech."

"Doesn't that depend on what they say? Moreover, a good listener is of equal value, and you are an excellent listener, Hiro."

The man beamed at the compliment.

"You and I are going to be good friends, young man. Many speak of my physical strength and see no further. You have made me recognise I have another quality. Thank you. In any event, Persian told me long ago that it is better to keep quiet and let people think you are a fool, than to open your mouth and remove all doubt. You see? I told you he is wise!"

He shook with laughter and his earrings jangled again. Marcus laughed too, more cautiously. He could sense the power of the man even in laughter. He did not want to ever test the power of his anger.

CHAPTER TWENTY-ONE.

Endings and Beginnings.

A few days later they had reached Damascus and Marcus duly sent word to his mother. His new guardian identified a reputable courier, and paid for the message to be delivered to Joseph of Arimathea's house. Marcus was made aware of the possibility that the message may never arrive, but there was very little choice unless you had your own servants or slaves to send on such errands.

Even so, he felt better now he had done what he could to tell her he was safe from harm. Whereas he would have once been appalled at the thought of separation from her for so long a time, with the natural insensitivity and selfishness of youth, he was now swiftly adapting to life with this erudite and interesting man, and all it had to offer. Her worry was not his. He was learning far more than he could have achieved in Jerusalem, especially since his rabbi's teaching had ended, as was usual at his age. Anyway, he knew it would not be long before his mother married Lazarus judging from the things she said, so that made him feel less guilty about leaving her.

Hiro taught him some special wrestling tricks each day, and he was ready to absorb new cultures, new learning, in fact anything new that was exciting and different. His slavery was over. This was the beginning of his new life of freedom.

It was also childhood's end and the beginning of responsibilities. He knew he was being taught those each day, but Marcus was also aware that he was being groomed for a certain destiny. Although he now had a great fondness for The Persian and his mysterious ways, there were times when Marcus thought the man was more in love with the mystery of things, than actually revealing what those things meant.

For all that, Marcus knew he was in the presence of greatness. What was even more amazing was that it seemed like his own destiny had been linked with this magus since before he was born.

There were still too many unanswered questions for the curious Marcus, but The Persian said that each year he would find out more answers. It was not good to learn all knowledge before you knew how to deal with that knowledge. That is what The Persian had said, and though Marcus suspected it was true, he dearly wished it was not. He was one of those that desired patience, but immediately!

One evening, a month later, Marcus was looking at the stars, and a similar fingernail moon that he had seen in the desert was pointing the way to a brilliant star that he had not noticed other nights. It was a wanderer, a planet, The Persian told him. It would be visible for a while and then disappear again.

The young man thought about the star that had been present at his birth, and wondered if he would ever such a sight, or see Joseph and Mary's eldest son again. In a way he could not understand, just pure instinct, he knew that somehow his life was linked to his.

Many people had spoken of how special Jesus was going to be, and if that was true, then Marcus knew Jesus had many adventures to come. Marcus hoped he would also be a part of them, and had said so to his new guardian. The Persian had looked thoughtful, and then told him to be careful for what he wished.

"A torch lights the darkness in the forest, my friend," he said, "but it also shows the wild beasts around you."

When Marcus said he did not understand, the wise man had just shrugged and said that it meant what it meant.

Out of the confines of Jerusalem, he was already starting to convince himself that he felt more Roman than before. He looked up at the planet again, and thought that for a while he would also be a wanderer. That excited him. He looked forward to seeing new places, new people, and eventually joining the Roman Army. He was not sure how he would do it, but he just knew that he would. It was his dream.

Even more exciting was that The Persian had told him he had not seen the last of the gold bowl that Joseph of Arimathea had now turned into a chalice. Forsaking his normal reticence, The Persian had informed Marcus that he had learnt in a vision that wherever the cup went, Marcus would follow it, for that was part of his destiny.

It was no wonder that Marcus felt exhilarated, for as Hiro pointed out, where the Magus was concerned, dreams came true. And that night Marcus did have a dream. He saw the gold chalice, locked away in an upper room in Jerusalem, in a house owned by Joseph of Arimathea. He saw the years pass by and then a group of men sitting in that room having an evening meal. A man broke some unleavened bread. It was a Passover meal. Then he took the gold cup filled with wine and said some words and handed it to each of the men. The cup glowed brighter and brighter. Its light was so strong that four rays seemed to emanate from it. They formed a cross.

Louis

25575515R00114

Printed in Great Britain
by Amazon